From Newsprint to Footprints

Elaine L. Orr

From Newsprint to Footprints

is the first of the
River's Edge Cozy Mysteries.
Iowa Nice Meets Murder

All Rights Reserved

Cover by Angel Nichols

Look For The:
Jolie Gentil Cozy Series
River's Edge Mystery Series
Logland Mystery Series

Copyright 2020
Lifelong Dreams Publishing
ISBN: 978-1-948070-47-8
4th edition
Previously published, in 2015, by Annie Acorn
Publishing, LLC

www.elaineorr.com
www.elaineorr.blogspot.com
ISBN 13: 978-1-948070-49-2
Library of Congress Preassigned
Control Number 2020900101

Elaine L. Orr

CHAPTER ONE

"DAMN IT TO HELL, Perkins. I sent you to grab photos of a car accident, and half the ones you took are a bunch of crappy flowers."

I managed not to say what I thought. "Those hybrid anemones don't grow here without..."

"You're fired."

"Excuse me?"

"You heard me. Pack up."

With that, Hal Morris, irascible editor at the *South County News*, walked into his office and shut the door.

Silence can be really loud, sometimes.

A low voice behind me said, "Uh, Melanie."

I turned to face Sandi Malcolm, the only full-time staffer younger than my twenty-seven years.

"I'm sorry. I knew he was ticked, and I wanted to warn you. You just came in..." Her voice trailed off.

I let my eyes travel around the small news room and noted that everyone but Sandi seemed engrossed in their work. Or pretended to be. Our tabloid-style paper only publishes three days a week now, and half the desks are empty.

"It's my fault, Sandi. I meant to only load the accident scenes onto the system. I wasn't paying enough attention." Images of the deep blue anemones among a large patch of red and white peonies flitted through my brain. I had thought they would make a great photo for the paper's Fourth-of-July issue.

I registered that the typical newsroom sounds of fingers flying on keyboards and the whish of the copy machine had resumed.

Hal thinks subscriptions are down because the economy's been bad. It's because in terms of the news business, he's a dinosaur. If he would just let us do an electronic edition we could sell more advertising.

Us? It's not us anymore.

Pretty soon all the desks would be empty. Still, it was the only job I had. And now I didn't have it.

Sandi had the guilty look of someone who has a job when the person they're talking to doesn't. Freckles stood out more on her ashen skin. "You want me to help you pack your stuff?"

"It's not that much. I took a lot of gear home after Fred got canned."

Fred Simmons had written half the stories for our county paper. Besides being a good friend, he had also been the highest-paid staffer. When revenue took a nose dive, Hal wanted him gone. Fred's protesting his denial of unemployment benefits. I think he'll win.

If I tried to get unemployment, Hal would dispute it, and I probably wouldn't win. He's told me a bunch of times that I'm only to take photos of story material. I don't know why he cares. It's not like it's film.

Hal's door was still closed, so our oldest reporter, fifty-something Betty Castaway, and perpetual intern Ryan Nichols, offered murmured words of sympathy as they walked by my desk.

It only took five minutes to pack my stuff. I would have left it all, but I had a twenty dollar bill taped to the bottom of my desk drawer and a pen my parents gave me for college graduation inside it.

Each reporter had a small cubicle, but the walls were only four feet high, so no real privacy. We worked separately, most of the time, coming together to do our sections of the paper's layout on a large-screen monitor.

I looked around the expansive room in which all staff except Hal sat. We called it the bullpen, most of the time. If Hal was especially obnoxious, the part-time sports reporter called it Detention Central.

I would miss a few staff, especially Sandi, but even more I'd miss knowing what was going on around the county before the paper reached the streets.

After I filled the copy paper box, Sandi and Ryan walked me to the door. I told them I was fine. If it wasn't for money, I would be.

I have friends, and when I'm willing to get off my tailbone I can do a ten-minute mile. Only problem is, even though rent is cheap in rural Iowa, it's not free. I had four hundred twelve dollars in savings. I had paid this month's rent. I could get by for a month.

I THOUGHT my inquiries would generate at least a nibble within a week, but I had nothing by the end of the first week of May. I don't know who I thought I was kidding. Hal writes snotty stories when he's ticked at a local business. Mostly when they cut their advertising budget at the paper. No one wants to irritate him too much.

River's Edge is a community of 7,400, much of it spread along the Des Moines River about fifteen miles before it meanders into the Mississippi in Missouri.

In many ways, it's the best of small-town living. There are baseball diamonds for kids' sports, a huge town chorus that performs for free a few times a year, and an all-day Fourth of July celebration that starts with games in the morning and goes through fireworks at ten.

Idyllic as life along the usually tranquil river can be, there aren't many jobs unless you're into meat packing or working in tourist gift shops, which I'm not. You also don't want to live within a block of the river unless you're willing to risk being flooded out every fifteen years or so.

A couple of the guys at Mason's Diner have told me to look in Des Moines, but I don't want the crowds or the traffic. I also don't want to be away from the garden my landlord let me plant in back of the duplex I live in. Two weeks before the firing, I had put in enough vegetable seeds to feed twenty people all summer, and almost all the bulbs I planted last fall bloomed.

My brother and his wife live in Dubuque. They said I could stay with them for a couple of months. Trouble is, I like it here. It's mostly friendly, and now that I don't work at the *South County News*, people don't watch what they say to me.

It was warm in my two-bedroom apartment, and I debated turning on the air conditioning, an extravagance in the first week of May, especially given my budget.

Instead, I stared at the clipboard on my lap. I had several pieces of lined paper fastened to it, and the top one had a sixth version of a list of my skills. Except I didn't really want to write articles or teach English as a Second Language. I wanted to plant flowers. Weed gardens. Anything that put me outside in the dirt.

The phone rang.

"Melanie? It's Sandi."

"Why are you whispering?"

"Because Hal's door is open. Listen, we just got a classified from the guy who bought the Silverstone place on the edge of town. He's looking for someone to clear weeds and stuff, and then plant some bushes."

I sat up straighter. "Yeah? When will it be in?"

"Who cares? You could call him now and...gotta go." Sandi hung up.

I pictured the acreage that sat at the end of the blacktop. A barn for hay and horses sat not far behind the house, though I didn't think anyone had boarded horses there for years. I'd heard that the man who had bought the place was some sort of consultant who traveled a lot.

The property had been mowed regularly since Mr. Silverstone died. However, the bushes were unkempt and overgrown weeds and roses stood tall against the fence in the front of the two-story house.

If I could convince the man to hire me, I'd be busy all summer. What was his name? Sigmund? Seymour? Something with an S. *He won't have to change the initial on the mailbox by the street.*

I felt a slow grin spreading. Hal Morris would have to drive by that house on his way to Fairhaven, where he keeps a small power boat. I could hide behind tall bushes and throw mud balls at his car.

Very unprofessional, but I'd feel better.

I DIDN'T BOTHER changing out of my denim shorts and t-shirt that boasted a "Pella Tulip Festival" insignia. I didn't need to wear a suit to apply for a job as a gardener or landscaper, or whatever.

The place was about a mile from my house, but I decided to drive. It was one thing to show up in work clothes, another to smell as if I'd been working all day in the May sun.

The driveway had little gravel, and ruts had likely come from some heavy truck or tractor. Probably a moving van.

The end of the drive was wider, so more than one vehicle could park there. A late-model, four-door, green pick-up truck graced the spot closest to the side door. It looked as if it had just been through a car wash. *This man is not used to country living.*

I studied the broad porch as I got out of my truck. Someone had replaced a few boards on the steps leading to the porch, and the front door appeared to be new. Solid oak and expensive looking.

As a reporter I could be quite pushy. As a woman looking for a job in an area where she had no formal work experience, I felt suddenly nervous. I'd trailed my dad around our family's dairy farm a few miles from town, planted gardens, and mowed lawns since I was nine or ten. I had plenty of experience. I had to concentrate on selling myself.

Mr. Whoever-he-was answered the door within ten seconds.

I'm not sure what I expected. Someone older than forty-something. And maybe not so tall.

"Hi, I'm Melanie Perkins. I live here in town, and I wondered if you needed any work done on your property. On the lawn. Like landscaping."

Why are you babbling?

He stared at me for several seconds, and then fully opened the door and nodded. "Sylvester Seaton. Syl. And I need a lot of work done." He gestured that I should come into the foyer.

The house is a center-hall colonial that has had a couple of additions. At the far end of the main hall from the foyer is a large kitchen, with a formal dining room behind it. I knew this because when I was a child, the then-owner, whose name I'd long forgotten, put the house on the town's garden tour, and I'd gone with my mother.

I followed Sylvester, Syl, into the living room. It looked as if it had had a fresh coat of paint, but its wood floors needed to be refinished and someone appeared to be stripping paint from the wide mantle above a stone fireplace. Boxes were piled against one wall, and several Queen Ann chairs were grouped in front of the fireplace.

At his gesture, I sat in one, and he sat across from me.

I could tell from his expression that he wondered if my five-foot-four frame would let me dig out dead bushes and pull huge weeds from the several flower gardens that surrounded the house. What I lack in height I make up for with broad shoulders and sturdy legs. I'm not heavy, but no one would call me a pixie.

"Your timing is good. I stopped by the paper today to put in an ad for some yard work. Do you have experience?"

"About fifteen years, but not for pay. You could go by where I live here in town to see what I can do. You'd get a better idea if I showed you the before pictures I took." I grinned, hoping to hide my nervousness. "I get reduced rent for maintaining the property."

"Ah. Okay." He hesitated. "Tell me where you'd start."

"Anytime, really. I just..."

"Not when. Where. What would you do first?"

I should have been prepared for the question, and the lawn was so neglected I found it hard to quickly think of priorities.

I swallowed. "At the Keyser place, that's where I rent the top floor, I started with the growth around the house. It wasn't as overgrown as here, but I think you see progress faster when you make the area at the front of the house look better. Clear out growth, put down mulch."

He nodded slowly, still appraising. "You have your own tools?"

"I have tree pruning shears and any hand tools and shovels. Rakes, that kind of thing. If you want big stumps taken out, a couple guys in town have equipment for that. Cheaper than paying anyone to dig them out manually."

Syl's direct look unsettled me. He had dark brown eyes that didn't seem to blink, and as I held his gaze, I took in his styled brown hair with its distinct part on the left side of his head. It was not a haircut you'd get at a corner barber.

He stood. "Come on. Let's walk around outside."

I followed him off the front porch, and paused by my twelve-year-old, dented pickup. It looks more grey than black because I often drive on gravel roads. "Have to grab my hat."

He waited while I reached for it. The one I use most is black canvas with an Iowa Hawkeyes logo and has a brim all the way around. Maybe the sweat lines on the band would convince him that I worked outside a lot.

Syl looked amused for a moment, and then was straight-faced again. "Trying to keep the sun off your face?"

"Trying not to get skin cancer on my nose. We redheads burn easily."

"Ah. Of course." We had walked behind the house, and he pointed toward a dense clump of bushes by the back door. "I hear rustling in there, so maybe that's a good place to start."

"Rustling like ground squirrels or snakes?"

"Not real loud," he offered.

I pointed at the exterior of the stone fireplace. "Even before that, I'll take down all that ivy. Won't take long. Do you want me to burn…?"

"I kind of like the ivy look."

This must be the first house he's owned.

"It's pretty, but it eats into whatever it latches onto." I walked a few steps and pulled a trailing end back and snapped it. "See these tiny growths on the vine? Those are roots, and roots look for a place to expand. These dig right into even minute cracks in stone or brick. In a few years, moisture'll get in, and you'll be good friends with the stone mason."

The amused look again. "If someone had asked me if there was still a stone mason profession, I might have said no."

I shrugged. "His name's Stooper. He mostly makes markers for the cemeteries."

Stooper is in his mid-thirties. He inherited the business from his father, who died of cirrhosis of the liver in his early fifties. At the rate Stooper is going, he may get to the pearly gates about that age, too.

This brought a full stare. "What did you say you did before now, Ms. Perkins?"

"It's Melanie. I, uh, worked at the paper."

His expression didn't change. "Now I know why you appeared today."

"Your ad will still run," I said, quickly. "If you don't like what I do, you could hire someone else." I straightened my shoulders. "You'll like my work."

We continued toward the barn. "That's a pretty quick grapevine. Why don't you work there now?"

"I got fired. I did a lot of the photography, and Hal Morris thought I wasted time by taking extra photos."

"Usually newspapers like options."

"True. But mine were usually nature shots, flowers. Hal only runs those when there's a garden show or something."

The front barn door stood ajar, so Syl slid it a couple more feet on its track and walked in.

Lighting was dim because the back door was shut, but I could make out a couple shrouded pieces of equipment. Closest was in the shape of a small tractor or huge riding mower, and it looked as if there was a bin on wheels behind it. Other than a couple of decaying bales of hay and an old broom, nothing else sat on the hard dirt floor.

"Do those work?" I asked, nodding toward the two shrouds.

Syl pulled the piece of rotting canvas from the closest one. "I had a mechanic check out the tractor last week. I don't know what all he did with it, but the guy drove it around the barn after he finished. I thought it might be good for hauling out all the overgrowth."

I walked to the tractor and placed a hand on the housing. "Did you know this is an old John Deere L? These were made, oh, maybe around World War II. Somebody did a nice paint job."

"Guess I don't know much about tractors."

"Must have been kept indoors all the time." I stooped to look at the wheels. "Kind of old, but as long as I don't run over a sharp rock or piece of metal, these tires'll get you through this year."

He nodded. "Probably not expensive."

"Probably not, but Jody at the hardware store might have to special order. These haven't been sold for a while." I looked at him directly. "If you can afford it, you might ask him to order one for you now, so it's in stock. You'd probably have to pay him when it comes in."

He jerked his head toward the house. "I can afford it. Let's take a look at the front. The bushes and weeds aren't as dense as back here."

We walked without talking and stopped near the driveway.

"If you call the farm implement store, they'll have someone drop off a big load of mulch," I suggested.

He had a sort of can't-you-handle-it look.

"I can't do it the first time. You'll have to let those guys know I can order for you and tell them how much I can put on your account, say, on a weekly basis."

He stiffened. "I don't usually let others authorize expenditures."

He really is citified. "We're talking like one hundred dollars. Unless you want to have to call them if I find a patch of poison ivy and want to spray it."

When he looked skeptical, I added, "They've known me all my life. They'll tell you I won't cheat."

He flushed. "Sorry, I guess that's how I sounded. What's the name of the place?"

"Farm and More. And if the Welcome Wagon woman visited already, she left a magnet for your fridge with the phone number."

He had folded his arms across his chest when we were talking about the line of credit at Farm and More, and now he let his hands fall back to his sides and laughed. "I can't believe how everyone knows everything here."

I smiled. "You'll get used to it. It's kind of like a self-monitor to avoid getting drunk at the Oktoberfest tent."

After about five minutes more walking the large yard, I realized that Syl's frame of reference seemed to be an arid climate with grass that grew slowly. "You realize that if you have all of this land mowed regularly, your mowing bills will be equal to your utilities some months?"

"Seriously?"

We had stopped by my truck. "Sad to say, but yes. You might want to think about having an acre or two mowed weekly and the rest mowed monthly, or maybe twice a month if it's real rainy."

"Will do. You're hired." He nodded and tossed over his shoulder as he turned to walk toward his front porch. "Keep up the advice."

Syl Seaton didn't talk much, and I decided to accept his somewhat abrupt nature as direct rather than rude.

I drove my truck forward to where the driveway was wider, did a three-point turn, and steered toward the road. When I got there, I didn't go in the direction of the blacktop and town, but drove right onto gravel, headed to my late parents' property.

Our family far was only a mile or so from Syl's, and I put my window down to sniff the air. Unless you're near fields when they put down mushroom fertilizer, the air is perfect. Soybeans stood just more than a foot tall, and a field of sweet corn was about the same. I passed our old neighbor's field of feed corn, and it was already close to three feet tall.

County road 270 took me all the way to my family's mailbox. I turned off the truck and got out. The two-story, yellow frame home with its huge attic looked the same, but the barn needed paint.

I didn't want to walk onto the property. It's tied up in a lawsuit brought by Peter Frost, who owns the farm that abuts ours on the north and west. He maintained that my parents had promised to sell it to him for a ridiculous price per acre.

My brother and I knew there had been no such verbal contract. Not only was my father a smart farmer, he and my mother were shrewd about business matters. The case would wend through the court system, and our family lawyer had assured my brother and me that we would not be forced to sell the farm to Frost.

In the meantime, we paid to have the property around the house mowed and contracted with two other farmers to plant and harvest corn and soybeans. Our lawyer had suggested we put any profit, low after two dry seasons, into an escrow account.

I got back into my truck. I didn't so much want money from the farm's sale as much as I hated being swindled.

As I drove by Syl's place on the way back to town, I thought about the hourly rate we'd agreed on. I liked it. Syl had promised to call Farm and More and order the mulch to be delivered to the end of the driveway and let Jody know I could place orders on credit in the future – not bad.

No more Hal Morris and I would get to play in the dirt.

AFTER A SUPPER of cornbread and split pea soup that I'd put in the crock pot that morning, my favorite comfort meal, I called Sandi. "It's Melanie. I owe you."

"Oh, good! Everybody feels real bad about you being gone, especially Ryan. He gets sent out for most of the pictures now, and he never aims straight. Hal gives him an earful almost every day."

I grinned. "I take it he has Hal's boot prints on his posterior."

"Nah. Ryan's uncle owns the motel, remember? He buys ads before every holiday."

I had forgotten that. The ads occasionally raised eyebrows. My favorite was a Valentine's Day ad that read, Revisit your honeymoon suite. Rates by the hour.

"When I get my first paycheck, I'll take you to lunch." I had some money left in savings, but it was going fast.

Sandi said I'd do the same for her, but when I told her I'd spring for the huge Cobb salad at the diner – fresh ham and chicken and homemade cheese – she acquiesced. The conversation left me hungry, but I would soon have a paycheck that would let me get more than cornbread and beans.

I headed for the Hy-Vee store. No grocery chain would put a store in a town this size today, but the small brick store had been built more than forty years ago. It doesn't have everything the larger Hy-Vee stores carry, but at least it's a chain store with better prices than an independent grocery.

IN THE DAIRY AISLE Hal's voice reached me. "Melanie Perkins! You cost me a thirty-five dollar display ad!"

I whirled toward the rancor and dropped the carton of eggs in my hand. The lid opened and one rolled out, cracking when it hit the wheel on my shopping cart. *Nuts. Does he know Sandi called me?*

"You couldn't of waited one more day to knock on Syl Seaton's door?" Hal walked toward me, face red and fists clenched at his sides.

Good. Syl didn't tell him I had inside information. "Gee, Hal. If I hadn't lost my job I wouldn't have been pounding the pavement." The image of Syl's gravel driveway came to mind, and I almost giggled.

He exploded. "I shoulda fired you two years ago. Always correcting grammar in my editorials. Taking twice as long as anybody else to finish a story."

It didn't seem like the time for a lesson in verb tense or to remind him that, because I took more time, he rarely had to edit my stories. "Gee, Hal, chill out."

He stopped only three feet away from me, which is pretty close when someone is spewing spittle.

"Do you have any idea how hard it is to get people to buy an ad? I bought that guy coffee. I..."

"Mr. Morris!" The store manager had approached from behind me.

I turned to look at Calvin Jenkins. Usually he has a smile. Not now.

"You can be heard across the store. I have to ask you to tone it down."

Hal sputtered. His face reddening even more, as he turned to walk away. Then he spun back and threw the orange he had been holding. I almost caught it, and Calvin managed to duck.

I TALKED CALVIN OUT of calling the sheriff. I was surprised he wanted to. Hal has thrown much bigger things at people at the paper, but Calvin probably didn't know that.

I fumed as I drove. My apartment is on the north side of town on a block that once held beautiful Victorian homes. The remaining ones are past their glory days, and nearly all have been subdivided into apartments. I'm fortunate to live in one of the smaller houses, a Sears bungalow that's been converted to only two units. It feels more like a private residence than an apartment.

When I got home I wandered into my garden and inspected the nearly depleted strawberries and the lettuce that was almost ready to be picked. Instead of the calm I usually felt in my garden, anger began to bubble.

Who does he think he is? I was the best reporter he had. After Fred left. By the time I'd walked the length of four forty-foot rows, I felt boiling mad.

I told myself I couldn't do anything about Hal's temper, and I should be glad I found work. Maybe someday I would have a whole landscaping business. The side of my brain that has less impulse control reminded me that Hal badmouthed me all over town, and I'd feel better if I threw an orange at him.

I saw Mrs. Keyser looking out her kitchen window and waved, before walking toward the exterior steps leading to my apartment. I could go in the front door, but I wasn't in the mood to talk to my landlord. My stomach clenched, and the wine I'd had with the cornbread didn't taste too good as bile.

After I got into the apartment and had a minute to control my breathing, I dug the phone from my purse. Syl Seaton might not have told Hal someone had directed me to his house, but Hal could figure it out. I had to warn Sandi, so she could practice denying that she'd called me.

The call went to voice mail and Sandi's cheerful voice annoyed me, so my tone was terse. "Hey, Sandi. I ran into Hal at Hy-Vee tonight. Syl canceled the ad. I don't think Hal knows I heard about the job from any of you guys. I kind of made it sound as if I was out knocking on doors."

I paused for a second. "Hal threw an orange at me, and Calvin Jenkins told him to pipe down. Getting fired was the best thing that could have happened to me. I'm tired of putting up with that...douche bonnet." I'd planned to call Hal a lot worse, but you never know who's listening on the line these days.

I DIDN'T KNOW if Syl slept late, so I didn't want to show up Tuesday at the proverbial crack of dawn. Anything after six seems late to me. I went by Farm and More at seven-fifteen and learned that they'd delivered the mulch at six the night before. Probably trying to impress a new customer.

When I got to Syl's place at eight o'clock, his fancy truck wasn't in the driveway. I could've started earlier.

I planned to clear the area on each side of the front steps, put down mulch, and maybe transplant some day lilies that were in a huge patch by the barn. Their root system is fierce. It's rare even weeds crowd them out. I'd save the ivy for tomorrow.

It felt good to yank at the thick vegetation and then dig out some of the roots with the thin, steel weeder. After about fifteen minutes, I was reminded that I should be squatting rather than bending.

I stood to arch my back, and turned slowly to take in all the area in front of the house. We'd had a moist spring, so everything was green, especially the weeds along the white board fence by the street.

At one time there had been two large flower beds, one on each side of the front walk, not too far from the house. The beds were still raised above the level ground around them, but they were all weeds and vines, except for a forsythia bush in the middle of each patch. The bushes had already bloomed, so the yellow blossoms were gone. The bushes added height, but they were too tall.

Rather than squat down, I walked to my pick-up and opened the back. It took a few seconds of wrestling to remove the wheelbarrow. I put a short shovel in it and started for the huge mound of mulch. It was almost five feet tall and easily six feet wide. I couldn't see the depth from where I stood.

As I got closer, I saw footprints in the soft dirt and the mulch had been disturbed at the edges. Probably some cat had used it as a litter box last night. Ugh.

The second thrust into the mulch hit something hard. Not metallic, just solid. I squatted and used the tip of the shovel to gently move the mulch. If a dead animal was in there, I didn't intend to touch it.

Hal Morris's face was covered in bits of bark. He had a small tangerine in his mouth, and his eyes were shut. Permanently.

.

CHAPTER TWO

AFTER I THREW UP, I called the South County Sheriff's Office. River's Edge has no police force, but the Sheriff's Office is in town. I used their main number to keep from dialing 9- 1-1. If I did that, the call for deputies would go out fast and wide, and it'd be all over town in three minutes that Hal had been murdered. Plus, if I had started to blubber it'd be on tape.

I sat in my truck, leaning against the headrest. What did the tangerine in his mouth mean? Did someone know Hal had thrown an orange at me? It seemed like something you'd see on a gory cop show on TV, the serial killer leaving a gross calling card or stealing a kitchen knife to use in the next murder.

I thought for about the tenth time about calling the paper, but it didn't seem smart to irritate the sheriff when Hal had yelled at me last night in the store. I didn't think anyone would suspect me of murdering anyone, much less carting a body to Syl's place and burying it in the mulch. But still...

After another three or four minutes, the sound of a siren reached me. Car tires screeched as the patrol car turned into the drive, signaling that Deputy Aaron Granger drove it. He seems to think he's more important when he squeals into a crime scene. I've seen him do that a bunch of times, but this would probably be his first murder, too.

I got out of my truck, and the deputy pulled up next to me and leapt out of his car. "Where's the body, Melanie?"

I pointed. "You can just see his head at the bottom of the pile."

Hal has... Hal had dark hair, so it took Granger a few seconds to see it.

"Good God!" He walked slowly toward the pile, hand on his holstered gun until he stood within a couple of feet of Hal's head. Granger turned slowly. "You found him like this?"

"No, Granger. He was sitting on the porch, and I moved him."

He raised both hands to his shoulders and dropped them back to his sides, clearly frustrated. "I don't need your smart-ass side, Melanie. This is serious..."

A red Ford Fiesta, horn beeping, turned into the driveway. It belonged to the paper, and I did a mental groan.

Deputy Granger raised his arm, palm out.

The car stopped twenty yards from him, where Sandi and Ryan almost ejected themselves from it.

"Why the hell did you call them?" Granger asked, walking back toward me.

"I didn't. They listen to the scanner."

"Scanner didn't say it was Hal," he muttered.

I matched his quiet tone. "So they probably don't know."

Sandi was almost breathless as she got to where I now stood next to Granger. "Scanner said someone found a body here! I told you about the job." She hiccupped a sob. "We were so worried..."

Ryan let out a breath and put his hand on the camera, which was on the strap around his neck.

"No photos," Granger growled. "Get back to the edge of the property."

Sandi strode into my arms, and I hugged her. "Come on, I'll walk back with you."

"You stay here, Perkins," Granger said.

I let go of Sandi and gave her a gentle push toward her car. "I found...it."

"Ohmigod. I'm so sorry, Melanie."

Granger had pulled a phone from his shirt pocket, and he must have placed a call because I heard him say, "I'll need a crime scene unit, and you might want to call IDI." He turned his back and walked toward Hal so I couldn't hear more.

Sandi and Ryan paused in their walk to the car and looked at me. It's uncommon for the Sheriff's Office to ask for assistance from the Iowa Division of Investigation first thing. Their eyes telegraphed questions.

"It could be someone...prominent." I said this quietly, to be sure Granger couldn't hear me.

Ryan made a 'gimme' gesture with his fingers, but I shook my head. Everyone at the paper would be furious with me for holding back information, even if it was only for a few minutes. Partly it didn't seem right to say who rested in the mulch before the sheriff did, and partly I knew I couldn't because Sandi has the opposite of a poker face. Granger would know I told her.

"Melanie." Granger's tone was sharp. "I need to ask you to sit on the porch. You two, out on the road."

Another siren sounded in the distance as I turned to face Granger. "They'd take crime scene photos for you. You guys just have a point and shoot camera, don't you?"

"I don't need your friends padding around the crime scene." He pointed. "Porch."

Granger and I walked side by side. "I saw footprints, but I don't think my feet left the edge of the driveway."

Granger said nothing, so I asked, "How long has he been there?"

"No idea. That your wheelbarrow? Why are you here?"

"Syl, Mr. Seaton, hired me yesterday to do some yard work."

I sat in one of the canvas porch chairs, and Granger, who is fortyish and about six-one, towered over me. "What did you and Morris fight about last night in the store?"

"Nice grapevine." I couldn't quite keep the bitterness from my tone. "We didn't fight, it…"

"That's not what I heard."

"Then talk to the manager. Calvin Jenkins will tell you Hal did all the talking. Yelling, actually."

The ambulance slowed on the street and did a careful turn into the driveway.

"What's the ambulance for?" I asked. "He's dead."

"I'm aware of that." Granger walked down the steps.

I sat on the porch and watched him brief the paramedic from the fire department who had accompanied the ambulance driver. Martin was the paramedic, but I didn't recognize the woman who had been behind the wheel. Probably new.

I stayed seated while Granger and the other two looked at Hal. It would have been better for me if another sheriff's deputy had taken the call.

Aaron Granger was Peter Frost's nephew and probably believed his uncle's lies about my parents agreeing to sell Frost their farm for a rock-bottom price. The last couple times I'd seen Granger around town he'd either not acknowledged my hello or spoken in a clipped tone.

My mind working more normally, I went over the morning. The Farm and More clerk had said the mulch was delivered last night about dinner time, and I'd seen Hal later than that.

I couldn't tell how long Hal had been in the mulch heap. I recalled that the bottom of the pile was messed, but other than that, the mound didn't look disturbed. Surely whoever had put Hal there had dug a lot in the mulch.

Had Syl Seaton left because he killed Hal? If he didn't, how could he have slept through a murder? Where could he be? He didn't mention going out of town. Not that he needed to tell me his schedule.

I glanced toward the driveway entrance. Ryan and Sandi had backed up, but they hadn't gone onto the narrow road to park. The Fiesta would get hit by a tractor or the next patrol car at the scene.

Ryan had taken the camera off its strap and surreptitiously took photos of the ambulance, which pretty much blocked the mulch. He kept his eyes on Granger, making sure the deputy didn't spot the camera in action.

Sandi waved slightly, trying to get my attention without letting Granger see her. I squinted and finally realized she was mouthing, "Who is it?"

I stood and walked to the edge of the porch to peer toward the mulch mound. Granger and Martin squatted in front of it, and the ambulance driver shined a flashlight on the spot they were studying. I moved closer to the porch steps, took my phone from my pocket, and held it up. It vibrated with Sandi's call in two seconds.

She was breathless. "Who is it?"

"Listen, you need to turn around, and you can't do anything to indicate what I tell you."

"What do you mean?"

"Maybe I should tell Ryan."

Her tone grew impatient. "Come on Melanie, who told you about this job?"

Remind me to thank you later. I drew a breath. "Turn around."

She did.

"Sandi, it's Hal."

If she hadn't screamed so loudly, Granger wouldn't have figured she was talking to me.

I'D BEEN SITTING in the sheriff's private office for twenty minutes, and the shock of finding Hal was slowly seeping in. My heart beat faster, and I felt cold. Who would have had the nerve to commit a murder and then brazenly bury the body at Syl's place?

Sheriff Gallagher walked in, stopped, and stared at me. "You all right?"

"Not really. You're the first person to ask. Thanks."

He leaned his head out of his office. "Bob. Can you grab a decaf for me and a regular coffee and sugar for Melanie?"

I've been to too many of his press conferences if the sheriff knows how I take my coffee.

Sheriff Gallagher probably weighs close to three hundred pounds, and he's only about five-ten or eleven. Oddly, he doesn't look terribly fat. I see him on the high school track, walking not running, so he tries to stay in shape.

He sat across from me at the small conference table. "You need to see the doc or anything?"

I shook my head. "Guess I've only seen dead people in the funeral home."

His expression softened. "And you wouldn't even have had that chance with your parents."

I frowned. My parents' car had been rammed by a semi and pushed into another one on an icy highway north of town. I've always been glad I didn't get called to cover the accident and ensuing fire. The fire was so fierce it was a couple of hours before it was clear who had been in the car.

Bob, who's on desk duty because he broke his ankle chasing a burglar who could run faster, limped in with the cups of coffee. He set them down and tossed a packet of sugar at me. "Sorry you had to find him, Mel."

I nodded, not sure I trusted myself to talk. Bob left. I busied myself with the sugar packet for a moment and, finally, met the sheriff's eyes.

"I need you to take me through your morning, and I want to hear about last night at the Hy-Vee."

"Sure...hey, did Syl ever show up?"

Gallagher shook his head. "Not yet, but a neighbor had his mobile number. He was in Des Moines for a meeting. Told me he left not long after six this morning."

"Oh, good." I straightened my shoulders and started with the call from Sandi to tell me Syl had placed an ad. I made it clear Hal sought me out in Hy-Vee, outlined my stop at Farm and More before going to Syl's this morning, and mentioned the time the clerk said they'd delivered the mulch the evening before.

"Right," he said. "I stopped by Farm and More on my way in. Tell me everything you did at Mr. Seaton's, before you found the body. Found Hal."

I shivered and took a sip of coffee.

He didn't interrupt me until I started to describe sticking the spade into the pile of mulch. "Did you see anything besides footprints and the small disturbance at the front of the pile?"

"No, and that struck me as odd." My reporter instincts were back. "Nothing showed he was in there. How would anyone do that? Or do it quietly, anyway."

He hesitated. "We aren't sure. Mr. Seaton sleeps on the side of the house farthest from the end of the driveway, where the mulch was, and he took a sleeping pill."

"A sleeping pill? Why'd he need that? He doesn't do shift work."

Gallagher looked amused for a moment. "I didn't ask. In any event, the only light would've come from the porch light. It's a good-sized bulb, but it wasn't on."

"So someone would have had lots of time to, um, put him there." I wondered if Syl's truck had been parked at the end of his driveway. If so, the mulch mound could have been largely hidden from the street.

"Anything unusual at the paper the last few days? Nasty letters to the editor, or Hal seem especially angry with anyone?"

"I wouldn't know. Sandi would. We talk almost every day. The only thing I remember her saying was that Hal kept his door shut more than usual." I shrugged. "That's a good thing, less shouting."

"Now, Melanie, I have to ask this. You were at Mr. Seaton's yesterday, and you suggested getting the mulch delivered."

My mouth dropped open. "But I would never..."

"I've known you a long time, Melanie, and I'd be as surprised as anyone if you had anything to do with this. But he fired you and hollered at you, and you do like to do a lot of garden work and such."

I felt my cheeks redden. "Yes, but I didn't plant Hal."

He grunted and tapped his now-empty paper cup on the table. "Go over your evening yesterday, after you left the grocery store. Did you see or talk to anyone?"

"I waved hello to Mrs. Keyser. When I got to my apartment. I left Sandi a message, kind of warning her Hal was mad that I got the work with Syl. Mr. Seaton." If Sheriff Gallagher was being formal, maybe I should.

"Why would Sandi need a warning?"

"She, uh, called to tell me about the ad, the one Syl pulled because I stopped by his house before it ran." When Gallagher looked nonplussed, I added, "But I don't think Syl told Hal that anyone called me. Hal would probably have started out throwing oranges. Or gone looking for Sandi first."

Gallagher started to chuckle, but stopped himself. "Nothing funny, of course. But the thing that connects you to the murder is the tangerine in his mouth."

"Hal threw an orange at me."

"I believe an orange would have been too big for Hal's mouth."

My tone was bitter. "Nothing was too big for..." I clasped both hands over my mouth, then removed them as he stared at me. "I'm sorry."

"He was loud." He looked at the piece of paper on which he had taken very sparse notes. "Anything else, Melanie?"

"I can't think of anything."

Sheriff Gallagher stood. "Go on home. Take it easy today. You've had a big shock."

I stood. "Thanks."

"And call me if you think of anything else."

"Yes, sir."

I had reached the door when he said, "And don't talk a lot about this with your reporter friends."

I faced him. "Can you tell me what you told them?"

"Why?"

"They'll expect me to tell them something. I don't want to interfere with your stuff, so if I know what you told them, I won't tell them more."

He studied me a moment and then smiled slowly. "You're always a pistol. All we've really done is identify Hal, mention when the mulch was delivered, and say when you found him."

"That's more than I wish I knew."

CHAPTER THREE

IT WAS ALMOST NOON when I left the Sheriff's Office, and Fred Simmons was waiting in his car when I parked in front of my duplex. Since my truck had been in the Law Center parking lot, Fred likely saw it and figured I'd get home eventually.

He jumped out of his car and hugged me before I could push the button to lock my truck. "Melanie. Good God. Are you all right? What a horrible thing!"

Fred's black hair had its usual windswept look. On a model it would look cool, but for Fred it meant he'd forgotten where he put his comb. Which would be typical.

I disengaged and stood back, with Fred an arm's length away. "Did you think I was there when it happened?"

His expression began to look less panicked. "That's what I heard."

I gestured toward the exterior stairs. "Come on up. It's five o'clock somewhere, and I'm going to have a beer. You look like you need one."

Fred switched from concerned friend to reporter as we walked. "You know I freelance for the *Des Moines Register*, right? Anything you can tell me that they won't pick up elsewhere?"

We walked next to each other, and I half-turned my head to look at him. "I have to be really careful. Sheriff Gallagher asked me…"

Several sharp beeps announced the Fiesta. Sandi, Ryan, and Betty almost flew out. Even from ten yards away, I could see Betty had been crying. A glance at Fred said he didn't want to share anything I might tell him.

As the babbling trio got closer, Mrs. Keyser opened her front door and stuck her head out. "I told the girls at the beauty shop you didn't kill Hal. You wouldn't be walking around if you did." This sounded more like a question.

"No, Mrs. Keyser. I didn't." The others had stopped talking, likely not so much to be polite as to see what they could pick up. "I found Hal."

"In a pile of mud?" She didn't come all the way onto the porch. Mrs. Keyser has a weekly shampoo and set at Marvie Marvel's beauty salon. She apparently didn't want the light breeze to mess it up.

"No, ma'am. It was mulch." I started edging toward the exterior stairs, and my reporter buddies matched my progress. The image of a vaudeville act with people walking sideways, in sync, crossed my brain, and I started to giggle. Then I couldn't stop.

Sandi had just put one arm around my shoulder when the giggles turned to gulps, and I stood in the front yard bawling my eyes out.

The way they fawned over me, you'd have thought a lost puppy had appeared. Then Betty joined in. Ryan handed me a tissue from a wad in his pocket – he'd apparently been with Betty for a while – and, when

Sandi joined the chorus, it sounded like a gaggle of geese honking by the river.

After a few more seconds, I waved people back and pointed to the stairs.

"You can come through here," Mrs. Keyser said, still protecting her hair.

"We're good," Fred called to her.

I blew my nose and then reached into my pocket for the key to my apartment. Betty was still sobbing as I let them in, so Ryan guided her by the elbow.

My apartment had been created from an attic, with a couple of dormers added. Except for the bathroom, the walls follow the pattern of the roof. There's plenty of room to stand up if you stay near the middle of the rooms. Ryan would have to be careful to do that.

I opened the fridge and looked at the three beers. "Who wants water and who wants beer?"

Sandi said she was driving, and Betty said she'd already thrown up breakfast. Fred, Ryan and I popped the caps on the glass bottles. I gestured with my beer that we should leave my crowded kitchen to sit in the living room. Waiting for no one, I sat on the couch, leaned my head into it, and put my feet on the sturdy walnut coffee table.

"Melanie," Ryan said, "you want us to go?"

The giggles were back. "Yeah, I want you and Fred arrested for violating the open container law."

Ryan looked uncomfortable, and Fred took charge. "We aren't staying long, unless Melanie wants us to. But, uh, Mel, the *Register*'s deadline…"

That brought me back to reality. They might want to comfort me, but the story came first.

I sat up straighter and took another swig of the comfortingly cold beer. "Sheriff Gallagher made me promise not to tell you guys more than he did."

They issued a collective groan, with even Betty joining in.

"But I can tell you where to get some information. You'd want to dig yourselves anyway."

Four pens and small tablets emerged from pockets and purses, and they stared expectantly.

"Okay, let's see. You know when the mulch was delivered, right?"

"Don't you?" Ryan asked.

"Shut up, Ryan," Betty said, but in a fairly amiable tone.

I glanced from Ryan to Sandi. "And you already know there's only one place in town that delivers mulch in bulk rather than in bags."

"Dibs," Sandi said.

"I'll go with you. Different paper," Fred said.

"I'm not going to referee. I want some Tylenol and a nap." I could almost see Sandi's fingers edging toward her mobile phone, but they quieted. "And you'll of course want to ask Syl Seaton where..."

"Who?" Fred asked.

I'd forgotten that Fred stayed much of the time with a friend from college who lived near Des Moines.

"Bought Silverstone's place, so it was obviously his mulch," Betty said. Now that she was on a story, she had calmed down.

"Ah," Fred said.

"So, he wasn't there?" Sandi asked.

I blew an exasperated sigh. "I'm too ragged out to be interviewed. Just *listen*."

I figured that, by now, lots of people knew Syl had gone to Des Moines. I told them that and suggested they talk to neighbors if Syl still wasn't around. The only new information I gave them was my timeline of the morning. They could figure it out eventually, and I couldn't see how that would interfere with the sheriff's investigation.

"I have to ask, Mel," Fred said. "You didn't do this and have no idea who did?"

I shook my head. "You know as well as I do that no one liked Hal. But kill him? I can't think of anyone."

Betty looked up from her note pad. "I could think of some people, but they probably wouldn't know how to do it without getting caught."

I couldn't tell if she was serious or not, but if she could get leads with the thought, more power to her.

"Hal didn't really have family," Fred said, almost to himself.

"Someone will have seen him last night," Sandi said.

Betty looked as if she would cry again.

"Check the grocery store," I added.

"Why?" Ryan asked.

"You guys are reporters." I took a last pull on my beer.

Sandi looked disappointed. My phone message last night meant she knew I'd seen Hal in Hy-Vee. She had probably hoped to get there before the others.

My Comforting Committee stood as one, emitting various platitudes and, in Betty's case, an idea for using cucumber slices to reduce the swelling of my puffy eyes.

Fred stayed for a few extra seconds. "I'm really sorry you had to go through this. You know my mobile number, and I'm not just reminding you of that because I want leads."

He hugged me for several seconds, and I let myself be comforted. Fred and I had been buddies and competitors for five years. Neither of us would want some of the things we knew about each other's love lives to show up in the paper. Not that mine was all that interesting.

I pulled back and smiled. "Thanks, Fred. I promise I'll call if there's something you can do to help."

"Or even if you just can't sleep." He pulled the door shut on his way out.

I sat on the couch and leaned forward to put my forehead on my palms. My mind wouldn't, or couldn't, quit thinking about Hal. If only one person killed him, whoever put Hal in the mulch pile had to be pretty strong.

And who would be that angry with him? *Anyone who worked for him.*

"That's ridiculous," I said aloud.

Hal would top almost anyone's list of obnoxious bosses, but he had a couple of good points. If anyone close to you was really sick, he'd let you take off with no notice. We always got our birthdays off, and he gave us an ever-smaller Christmas bonus every year.

He also called us all idiots, questioned that we'd ever be any good as reporters, and threw things across the room. Doc Shelton had bought him some foam baseballs after a stapler hit Ryan and he needed three stitches. Hal wasn't aiming, and he had felt bad about it. It was his first stapler throw. A few months before that, he had broken two mobile phones aiming for staff.

I stretched out on the couch, lying on my side. A photograph of my parents sat on top of a shelf, so that I could look at them from the couch. "I miss you guys."

THE SHARP RAP on the door woke me. Late afternoon streamed through a window, meaning I'd slept for several hours. My sinuses were totally clogged, and I had a headache. "Coming."

I peered through the curtain on my door and saw Sheriff Gallagher. *This doesn't bode well.*

"Come in, Sheriff." I stood aside so he could walk into the living room.

He took in my swollen eyes and probably mascara-lined cheeks, but he didn't sit. "We need to talk a bit more, Melanie."

"Sure. Just give me one minute to splash some water on my face." And get rid of my beer, but I didn't say that out loud.

When I walked back down the very short hallway from the bathroom to the living room, he turned to face me. "Are you missing anything?"

My eyes strayed to my parents' photograph.

He followed my gaze. "Any *thing*," he said, sort of kindly.

"I don't suppose you could be a bit more specific."

"Can you walk outside?"

"Um, sure. Where are we going?"

"Right now to the shed at the far end of the yard, where Mrs. Keyser says you keep your gardening stuff."

I must have had a blank expression, because he said, "Just take a look," and turned to walk out the door and down the steps.

Something's not right. I followed him. We got to the bottom and turned left, and I saw the shed door was open. He must have already looked there. But why?

"Your lettuce looks better than my wife's."

The polite Midwesterner, trying to put me at ease.

We got to the shed, and I peered in. There's no electricity, but the sun let in enough light. "You going to tell me what I'm supposed to look for?"

"Is something missing?"

I studied the items lined against the wall. There were the steel rake and the plastic one for leaves, the fertilizer spreader, two bags of compost, the large bucket where I keep trowels and other small tools. I turned to face the sheriff. "Where's my hoe? I just bought that."

He sighed. "The hoe was in the mulch with Hal."

CHAPTER FOUR

I GAPED AT him. "It's... I would never... How the hell did it get there?"

Sheriff Gallagher looked at me in a way he never had before. Unless he's testifying about a case or cussing at his neighbor's cat when it pees on his patrol car tires, he's a genial guy. Not now.

He pulled a vinyl glove from his pocket and shut the shed door, then turned to face me. "IDI will send someone over for prints on the shed. When's the last time you used that hoe?"

"Last Sunday. I was loosening the dirt around the rhubarb in the back of the yard."

"You never had it at Mr. Seaton's?"

I shook my head.

"I have a hard time believing that you'd kill Hal. Knew he fired you, but he ticks off half the people in town. Trouble is, either you did it or someone is sure trying to make it look as if you did."

My mouth felt dry, and I swallowed. "Who would do that?"

"You'd be the most likely person to know your own enemies." He pointed in the general direction of the driveway, where his patrol car was parked, and we walked toward it. "You done any stories that really skewered anybody in town? Only one I can think of was about the pet store selling food from China and not telling folks there'd been problems with it in other towns."

"And he doesn't live here now," I murmured, remembering that the man left because customers stopped coming.

When we reached his car, he turned to face me. "You'll be interviewed tomorrow by the folks from IDI. Aaron Granger's going to work closely with them. You think hard on the last time you used that hoe. Maybe it'll help you figure out who's so angry with you."

He opened the car door and sort of slung himself behind the wheel. "If you decide to go out of town other than for a story close by, you tell me, hear?"

Granger, great. "I will. No plans to go away until Fourth of July."

He stared at me for a couple of seconds, then turned the ignition and backed out of the driveway.

I was watching his fading tail lights when Mrs. Keyser's front door opened. "What is all this about, Melanie? Why did the sheriff want me to let him in the shed?"

She wore what is euphemistically called a house dress and translates to a shapeless shift that hides an extra thirty or forty pounds. As usual, it was a brilliant print. Today's had huge purple flowers with dark pink for the stamens and carpels.

Mrs. Keyser wanted gossip to take to the beauty parlor, but I was in the mood to be obtuse. "I guess he didn't know we leave it unlocked." Before she could say anything else, I turned and walked the short distance to the side of the house and up the stairs.

By the time I got to the top, my fury had mounted. How could anyone suspect me?

You found the body and your hoe was with him.

Okay, but besides that? Lots of reporters had bad-mouthed Hal through the years, and I only knew about the five years I'd worked at the paper. Except for the time he made me work Thanksgiving night when he'd promised it off, I'd never maligned him. Much.

I walked through my apartment, stopping at the doorway to each of the two bedrooms and scanning them, as if the answer was hiding under the bed or behind the door. Without giving much thought about where I was going, I marched into the living room, grabbed my purse off its spot on a console table by the door, and made for my truck. I almost tiptoed down the steps because I didn't want Mrs. Keyser to talk to me.

Almost on automatic pilot, I drove toward Syl Seaton's place. That was the last place I'd been before my world turned upside down. Since the upending had happened there, some part of me thought if I could see the mulch pile something would make sense.

It was almost dusk, and the sky had beautiful pink and orange hues. Just an ordinary night. Nothing to suggest a murder had taken place in River's Edge last night. Or maybe today.

I tapped a finger on the steering wheel. It was less than a ten-minute drive to Syl's, but would be longer because I was behind aged Harry Finkle. He drives about fifteen miles per hour, unless it's raining. Then it's ten.

I passed Main Street, which leads to the small town square, the hub of River's Edge. It's no longer full of stores that sell things anyone really needs. People drive twenty-five miles to big box stores.

Now, the square has antique stores, an artists' co-op, a bakery, coffee shop, things like that. If it weren't for a store that sells everything for a dollar, there wouldn't even be a shop that sold tissues. You'd have to go to the very small pharmacy just off the square and pay a lot for something to blow your nose into.

When a clothing store and its adjoining shoe store went out of business two years ago, the Chamber of Commerce president almost begged Hal to move the paper from two blocks off the square to the newly vacant space.

Hal said he'd think about it if he could get a free Chamber membership for life. Since that would have led to other demands for free memberships, the Chamber said no. Besides, half of the members would have left if Hal had started coming to the Chamber's weekly luncheons. The paper stayed in its rundown brick building.

Mr. Finkle finally pulled onto a side street, and he'd only had his blinker on for three blocks before the turn.

I made my way to Syl's place. I had anticipated police tape, but had not expected the mulch to be gone. I sat in the driveway, staring at the vacant spot. Syl's truck wasn't parked near there, as it had been yesterday. It was on the grass to the right of the drive.

There will be ruts you'll have to smooth before you plant seed. Who cares about ruts now?

The front door opened, and Syl walked onto the porch. He had on a tailored suit that looked expensive even from a distance.

I got out of my truck, suddenly aware I must look like a woman who had slept in her clothes and hadn't even combed her hair. Both were true.

I walked toward his porch, unsure what to say.

His expression was solemn, but then his lips twitched, slightly. "You didn't mention the Farm and More store would include extras with the mulch."

A macabre sense of humor. Who knew?

"I guess it was a special deal." I tried to smile, but failed.

37

"Sorry, you looked like you needed cheering up. Not something to joke about." He opened the screen door and nodded toward it.

Without saying anything, I walked up the steps and into the entry foyer.

Syl gestured to the living room. "Same chairs?" He didn't wait for an answer. "You look as if you could use a pick-me-up. Do you drink?"

I sat. "Some, but now's probably not a good time. Do you have a soft drink?"

"Does it have to be diet?"

"Better if not," I said.

He walked to the kitchen, and I heard him put ice in glasses and flip the tab on a can of pop.

I glanced around the room. An occasional table was now next to one chair. A couple of manila folders and a pen sat on top of the table, but nothing indicated what the folders contained.

Syl came back with a glass in each hand and handed me one before he sat.

I swallowed. "Um, I'm sorry about what happened."

Syl frowned, and it made his brown eyes squint. "You didn't have anything to do with it, did you?"

"No. No, of course not. But the sheriff just told me my hoe was in the mulch pile."

His brows went up, and he paused with his drink halfway to his mouth. "Was your name on it?"

"Gosh, no. I wonder how the sheriff..." I thought for a moment. "I've been fingerprinted."

"Why?"

"Not for a crime. I did some substitute teaching for a while when I first came back after college. They do a background check."

"Where'd you go?"

It was such an innocuous question that it took a second to realize he was talking about college. I took a long drink of the cold cola. "University of Iowa. Journalism."

"Couldn't you get a job anywhere else?"

There are pros and cons to a direct questioner. Right now it seemed more like a con, and I felt defensive. "I like it here, and my parents died a couple of years ago. I'm glad I had that time with them."

"You're young for that." No sympathy in his tone, but it wasn't dismissive either.

I sighed, sat back, and closed my eyes for a second. "Right now, it still feels young. I... Damn, I should have called my brother."

"Not close?"

What does he care?

"It's not that. I fell asleep right after I got home and didn't wake up until Sheriff Gallagher stopped by a few minutes ago. Then I was more or less distracted by the hoe thing."

He stood. "Finish your drink and let's go outside."

Mr. No Nonsense. I liked that. Especially since I'd been afraid he would be angry at me. I downed the last of the drink and followed him toward the kitchen, where I placed my glass on the counter. We went out the side door, which opened onto the driveway at the back of the house.

"Are we allowed out here?"

"My house. And the sheriff said as long as I don't go behind the yellow tape it's fine."

We stood silently, looking at what was now about a six-by-eight damp spot accented with a few chips of mulch. There were impressions in the damp earth and a few pieces of something small and white. I'd seen sheriff deputies make plaster casts of footprints at burglary scenes when something really expensive had been stolen.

"Why do you suppose they took all of it?" I mused.

"You know that deputy, Granger?" he asked.

I nodded, and Syl said, "I asked him. All he said was forensics."

"Wonder where the sheriff will put it?"

"My impression was that it was going to a crime lab in Des Moines. They put it in different bags. Some had mulch from near the body. A few other bags had the rest of it."

"Ugh." I turned to face him. "Where were you this morning?"

The amused look again. "Checking to see if I'll tell you the same thing I told the police?"

I flushed. "No. I just wish you'd been here."

He turned back to look at the former mulch area. "I'm sorry I wasn't. I'm sure it was hard for you to find Mr. Morris."

Plus, you could have told the police how shocked I was.

I glanced at an area near the short flight of steps that led to the side door to the kitchen. My vomit was gone.

"I'm not about to play amateur detective, but I've heard your former editor was not well liked. Had you and Hal had a particularly acrimonious disagreement?"

"No." I grinned. "Nor any big fights."

He half grunted, half smiled. "My business consulting choice of words."

"So, looks like you had a formal meeting out of town."

"What makes you say out of town?"

He'd told the sheriff he was in Des Moines. I was mostly curious to know what he did. "Usually only people at one of the banks or the funeral home wear suits. Most of the time, anyway."

He smiled and nodded toward my truck and began walking. I fell in step.

"I just got a contract to design new IT infrastructure for a major insurance organization. I left around six. Thought it would be a longer drive."

We're about one-hundred-thirty miles southeast of Des Moines, but it's not like there's traffic. We reached my truck. "Are you from Iowa, originally?"

He shook his head. "Los Angeles."

"Talk about a change of pace." *And you must like it if you bought property.*

"I was looking for that. Takes less time to drive twenty miles here than three in LA." He opened my truck door.

"So I've heard." I slid in and looked up at him, as I shut the door and pushed the button to take the window down.

He leaned on the truck door. "I drove by the Keyser house. The yard is very well kept. You're welcome to keep working, but I'll understand if you don't want to."

"I need the money, and I like this kind of work."

I was putting my truck in reverse as he asked, "Who will run the paper now?"

I hadn't given it a thought.

CHAPTER FIVE

WHEN I REACHED MY BROTHER Ambrose, he'd just had a call from Sheriff Gallagher. He and my sister-in-law had been about to leave for River's Edge. I said I was doing better than I was this morning and wanted to go to bed early, so they'd be better off staying in Dubuque.

"What did the sheriff want with you?" I asked.

"He wanted to know if I'd heard you say anything especially antagonistic about Hal after he fired you, but I think Gallagher mostly called to be sure I knew about you finding Hal."

Neither Ambrose nor his wife Sharon are big critics of my behavior, so I didn't feel chastised. "I'm sorry I didn't call. I fell asleep until a bit ago."

"I should have insisted you come up to Dubuque after Mom and Dad died."

"Like that would have worked."

He laughed. "Probably would have been counterproductive. You can come now, you know."

I explained how Sandi had cued me into the new job. "I kind of like the work at Syl Seaton's place, and I'm only supposed to leave town if I'm on a story. Or I have to tell Sheriff Gallagher where I'm going, or something like that."

He didn't say anything for a moment. "He doesn't really think you did it, does he?"

I said I thought not, but explained about the hoe. That bothered Ambrose a lot, but I was firm about staying in River's Edge. I finally agreed to have the locksmith come in the morning to put in a deadbolt, but I refused his offer to pay for it.

WEDNESDAY MORNING was warm for barely the second week in May. It was supposed to get to the mid-eighties, although it might rain in the late afternoon. I hoped not. If it was a real soaker, I probably couldn't work for a couple of days. Or I could, but I had no intention of getting drenched and muddy for what Syl was paying me.

I left a message for the locksmith, Marion Hardy, and told her I'd left the door unlocked so she could install a deadbolt. I hadn't thought to ask Mrs. Keyser if that was okay, but she's always let me paint whatever color I wanted. Besides, she could hardly argue about better security.

You left your house unlocked for a locksmith. I was giggling as I pulled into the parking lot at Farm and More at seven-thirty.

Stooper-the-Stone-Mason was near the cash register talking to the first-shift clerk, Andy, who was leaning on the counter. Stooper looked sort of sober. They stopped talking as soon as I entered. Andy straightened up, and they both looked uncomfortable.

I stopped near them. "So, I'm here now. You can ask instead of guess."

Andy flushed. "Sorry, Mel. Everyone's kind of in shock."

My turn to be embarrassed. "I shouldn't have snapped. It was a shocker for me, too."

"You doing okay?" Stooper asked, and hiccupped.

Guess he's not sober. "Yep." I looked at Andy. "Can I talk to whoever dropped off the mulch at Syl Seaton's place?"

"Whose?" Stooper asked.

"He bought the Silverstone place," Andy said. "Ordered that batch of mulch 'cause Melanie was going to spruce up the place."

They both just stared at me.

"Andy. Did you deliver it?" I asked.

He sort of gulped. "Yeah. Boss called me back to do it. Wanted it done right away."

"Did you see anything...odd? Out of place?"

Andy looked uneasy. "Am I supposed to be talking to you?"

"You've known me since I was in first grade, why... Oh, did the sheriff ask you not to?"

"Why would he do that?" Stooper asked.

I was beginning to feel as if I was on a merry-go-round. I ignored Stooper.

"It's fine if you talk to me, Andy. All the sheriff told me was not to tell any details to the guys at the News."

"Urrrp."

I backed up two steps. "Stooper, that stinks."

"Sorry. Need to go brush my teeth." He ambled toward the glass door.

When he was outside, I looked at Andy. "Is he driving?"

"Nah. The tavern lets him sleep it off in the back most days. He's not usually in this early."

"Andy," I began.

He's five-six and built like a stocky brick. Andy was in third grade when I started school, and his mother ran the school bazaar every year.

"Didn't see anything special. The guy – Syl you called him? I didn't even know his name. He came out to tell me to put the stuff at the end of the driveway. Seemed kind of stuck up, but then he give me a five dollar tip and I thought he was all right."

"Nice tip," I said. "Anyone ride with you or honk at you when you pulled in or left Syl's place?"

"I thought you got fired from the paper. By Hal," Andy said.

"I did. He thought I took too many pictures. But you know he fired somebody every few months lately, when subscriptions went down."

Andy leaned an elbow on the cash register, ready to chat. "Heard Fred got some part-time work in Des Moines."

"Andy! I don't' care about Fred right now."

"You don't have to get grouchy about it."

I shut my eyes for a moment. "Sorry, I…"

The door opened, and two men in dark-colored suits stood there, looking at me. "Miss Perkins?"

"Yes."

"Sheriff said your truck was here when he drove by. We're from IDI. We need to talk with you for a few minutes."

"Hot damn," Andy said.

The older of the two men was about forty-five, with close-cropped hair that was more grey than its original brown. "Probably at the sheriff's office."

"Sure. Meet you there."

For a couple of seconds it seemed as if the agent who was closer to my age was going to say he wanted me to ride with them.

I couldn't help it, I grinned. "It's not like I could go anywhere else without being seen."

Both men seemed to relax, and the older one held out his hand. "Charles Holcomb. This is David Masters."

I shook both of their hands. "I can lead you down there, if you like."

"No cuffs?" Andy asked.

THE TWO AGENTS were polite, but they spent a lot more time talking to me than Sheriff Gallagher had yesterday. Today, Deputy Granger sat on the same side of the table as the agents, and I sat across from them at the old metal table. Sheriff Gallagher stood against the conference room's door jamb, eyes moving to whomever was talking.

The third time one of them asked me what time I got to Syl's I said, "Do you really not hear what I say, or is this some kind of deal where you're trying to see if I tell you the same thing each time?"

"Melanie." The sheriff's mouth twitched for a second. "It's just how they do their job."

I looked back at the agents. "I get that, and I realize I know I didn't do it and you don't. It just seems to me that you'd catch the killer faster if you looked for him."

Sheriff Gallagher cleared his throat, and Charles Holcomb nodded. "We have to check every possibility."

"So what others are you checking?"

David Masters didn't seem to have his colleague's patience. "We're asking the questions, Miss Perkins."

"Clearly. But a news reporter asks questions too."

"Which you aren't anymore," Granger said.

For the third time we went over why I was fired and what Hal said in the grocery store. Then the agents looked at their notes, apparently trying to come up with something new.

"Sheriff."

Gallagher looked at me.

"Can I leave?"

"They may have more questions," he said.

I looked at the two IDI agents. "I'll answer any new questions. But I'm not answering the same ones again."

"We'd hate to have to categorize you as a hostile witness," Masters said, almost smirking.

"You can categorize me as dumber than a mule, as long as we cover new ground."

When they didn't say anything I picked up my purse from the chair next to me and left.

IT WAS AFTER the breakfast rush and too early for morning coffee breaks, so the diner only had a couple of people in it. I glanced at the woman behind the counter. "The usual, Shirley, if you've got it."

"Coming right up, sugar." She tucked some loose strands under her hair net as she went to get my food.

I sat in a booth toward the back and scowled for a few seconds as I stared out the window. The diner is on a side street off the square. The buildings are a mix of brick and frame, none more than two stories. A couple of vacant buildings, one with several boarded windows, were eyesores, and a plastic bag moved slowly across the street.

What did those IDI agents think they would accomplish by going over the same material three times? And who else were they talking to?

Shirley set half a bagel and two small cartons of grape jelly on the table. She's sixty or so, or maybe fifty. Hard to tell with her skin creased from smoking. She stopped last year when she got an official diagnosis of COPD. Shirley leaned over to whisper to me. "I know it wasn't you, sugar."

"Thanks."

"I knew your Mom and Dad all my life. They mighta raised a nosy reporter, but they didn't raise a killer."

Damned with faint praise. "I appreciate that. Would you mind if I had that coffee? I got up really early."

She popped her gum as she smiled over her shoulder. "You betcha. Be right back."

I pulled a thin notebook from my purse and opened to a clean page. I'd been so tired last night I hadn't even done an idea page. Whenever I worked on a story, I made myself write fresh notes each evening, and I had to put at least one question at the end. Too many questions to even fool with it last night.

I hadn't realized I was thinking about the first item until I wrote, "Where was Fred yesterday?"

I placed my hand over the sentence as Shirley put a mug of coffee, sugar already in it, on the table. "Eat that bagel now. It'll be cold."

"Yes ma'am." I managed a smile.

When she walked away I scratched out the sentence. Still, since Fred had been in town so soon after I found Hal, it was a fair question. I supposed if Sandi had called him the second she stopped screeching he could have been in River's Edge that fast, but I doubted she had. *Was Fred in town when Hal was killed?*

Fred had had a lot more to lose than I did. He'd bought a house just three years before Hal fired him, and he had to rent out two of the bedrooms to guys who worked at the meat packing plant. He stored his coin collection and expensive shoes at Betty's in case the men were not as honest as the shift supervisor at the plant said they were.

I thought for a full minute. I could see Fred gloating all over town if he won his appeal to claim unemployment benefits. Killing Hal would probably just delay processing Fred's appeal. And how would Fred know there would be a fresh pile of mulch at Syl's, much less be able to get the body there?

Fred knows where I keep my gardening tools. So do lots of other people.

It was hard to do a list of people mad at Hal, because so many people were. I thought about a story he did on Blackner's Insurance. Hal had made it sound like they inflated prices for life and health insurance, but he'd run a correction on the front page above the fold. He had to, because Bruce Blackner said he'd sue the bejesus out of Hal if he didn't. It definitely didn't get Hal the firm's advertising budget back.

The *South County News* plopped on the table, and Sandi slid into the booth across from me. "I can't believe you didn't call me."

I frowned. "You know how to find me. Did you need something?"

She looked offended. "I thought you'd have something to say about the article."

I pulled the paper toward me. "It wasn't in the box at home when I left."

"We were late putting it to bed last night, so the printer couldn't get it out by five a.m.. Wish we were still a daily. The Register scooped us by putting it on their web page." She tapped her index finger on the table top. "Read it."

Publisher Found Dead

The body of South County News publisher Hal Morris was discovered at eight forty-seven a.m. Tuesday, in a mulch pile at the Silverstone place (now owned by Sylvester Maximillan Seaton) on County Road 270. Former reporter Melanie Perkins, who had been hired to do some landscaping work on the property, discovered Morris' body. Deputy Aaron Granger, first on the scene, verified that the body was that of the local publisher and editor.

Morris had fired Perkins several weeks ago, but Sheriff Michael Gallagher noted he did not consider her a suspect. When asked if he thought Morris was killed on the Seaton property, Gallagher said he was more than likely killed elsewhere, but the state medical examiner would be the one to determine that.

Given Morris's prominence in the community, Gallagher called in Iowa IDI to work with the Sheriff's

Department. Neither Agent Charles Holcomb nor David Masters were willing to talk to South County News staff.

Farm and More staff delivered approximately thirty cubic yards of mulch to the Seaton property, shortly after six p.m. the evening before Morris's body was discovered. Seaton said he heard no disturbance on his property between that time and when Seaton left for a meeting in Des Moines at about six a.m.

Neighbors reported no unusual activity. "It was as quiet as a chicken coop after a fox finished," reported Audrey Stickler, whose farm is a quarter-mile down the road from the Seaton property.

Sheriff deputies and IDI agents questioned a number of neighbors and local citizens, as well as Farm and More staff and Ms. Perkins. A Hy-Vee shopper, who did not wish to be identified, said she heard Morris yelling at Perkins the night before the murder. Morris was quoted as saying he should have fired her long ago. Perkins' reply was not audible in the next grocery aisle. Manger Calvin Jenkins referred News staff to the corporate office, which had no immediate comment.

Perkins, who was interviewed for this story, was not able to provide any information other than what she told the sheriff. After working in the front of Seaton's property for less than an hour, she had taken a wheelbarrow to the mulch pile. It was then that she discovered Morris, whose head was not visible until she began shoveling.

South County News staff expressed shock at Morris's death, but were not able to provide any information of Morris's whereabouts after he was last seen in the Hy-Vee store.

Ryan had gotten a decent photo of the ambulance and Granger's cruiser, but it wasn't possible to see the body, thankfully, or even much of the mulch pile.

I looked at Sandi. "Thanks for saying I only told you what I told the sheriff."

"No problem. Know more today?"

Shirley placed a cup of hot tea in front of Sandi and then winked at me. "I can vouch for her time for the last half-hour."

"Good one," I said, not meaning it. When Shirley walked back to the counter, I asked Sandi, "Have the IDI guys questioned you?"

She shook her head. "Odd, isn't it? They asked to look through Hal's office, but they didn't take anything but his address book and calendar. Barely said hello to staff, except to ask if we knew who Hal was with last night."

A car door slammed, and Sandi and I both looked at Ryan, who had parked the Fiesta at an angle and was half-jogging into the diner.

"Maybe they found the killer," I said, ever hopeful.

Ryan entered, spotted Sandi and me, and came over. "Move over Sandi." His face was tanned more than yesterday, which probably meant he had pounded the pavement while covering the story. He had also trimmed his collar-length auburn hair.

"Why'd you get a haircut?" I asked. "You look like a reporter instead of an intern."

"Melanie, did you really tell the IDI guys to, well, you know, F off?"

"Mel?" Sandi was wide-eyed.

I folded my arms on the table and put my head on them. "You've got to be kidding."

"Did you?" Ryan asked.

I raised my head and looked at both of them. "I did not tell them to F off. Though," I thought for a moment, "I suppose it was implied."

Ryan laughed, and Sandi furrowed her brow. "Melanie, you have to cooperate with them."

"I am. They asked me the same questions over and over. I told them I'd talk more if they had new questions. They didn't." I looked at Ryan. "Who told you that?"

It was his turn to scowl. "You know I have to protect my sources."

Sandi and I both laughed, which felt good.

"Isn't Bob your mother's cousin or something? He brought coffee in for the sheriff and me yesterday."

Ryan sat up straighter. "I can't say."

"Okay, then tell me why you got your hair cut."

Sandi picked up the paper and turned a page. "You hadn't gotten to page three."

She pointed at a two-paragraph article that had a black box around it.

"Just tell me what it says."

Sandi frowned, but obliged. "Since Hal owned the paper and didn't have an assistant editor...."

"After he fired Fred," Ryan said.

"Fred shouldn't have been...." Sandi began.

"What does it say?"

They both stared at me.

"I think you did tell him to F off," Ryan grinned.

"Anyway," Sandi said, "you know how Hal set up a citizen advisory board after everyone got ticked at him for not covering the Homecoming Parade two years ago?"

I nodded. The Booster's Club had purchased a much smaller ad than in prior years, reasoning that the entire town knew the parade started at six p.m. on Friday of Homecoming Weekend.

"So," Sandi continued, "they didn't really have a chair or anything, because Hal ran the meetings."

I snorted.

Ryan said, "Nobody came to the last one."

"Anyway, the committee decided that Doc Shelton chairs the group now, and Hal's lawyer came over and said unless people complain or something, they can provide guidance until the paper gets sold." Sandi looked glum as she finished.

"Sold!" This shriek was from Shirley. "They can't do that, can they?"

Fortunately, the only other person in the diner was Stooper, who was sitting at the counter trying to quell a hangover with coffee.

"Could we have a little less noise?" Stooper asked.

I looked at Shirley. "Whoever buys it will keep it running. Don't worry."

The bell above the front door dinged, which drew her attention from us.

"Are they really going to supervise or something?" I asked.

"That's the good news," Ryan said. "They asked Fred to work part-time."

"It's not like we couldn't do it." Sandi opened her hand to tick off a verbal list. "Besides Ryan and Betty and me, there's Salty for sports, and Garnett reads the Register to see if we need to put in anything about what's going on at the state house."

"But you're the only full-time person, Sandi." I pointed a finger at her. "And, no offense, but you can't spell to save your life."

I thought for a moment. The only thing Hal regularly did was a column on local soil conditions and weather. Even the few financial items we put in were from a service that sent us a daily feed with stock prices for ag-related companies.

"Betty knows how to fix paper jams in the copier," Ryan said. "Hal did that."

"Poor Hal. His only jobs were keeping track of mud and clearing the copier." I looked at Sandi. "You like Fred, right?"

She looked away for a second and then back at me. "I do. But he was in this morning, and he sounded kind of bossy. Wanted a list of stories we were all working on."

"He probably wants to be the editor, if a new owner will hire him." I looked at Ryan. "So what's with the haircut?"

He opened his mouth, but Sandi beat him to a reply. "Doc Shelton was in. He told Ryan long hair wasn't sanitary."

Ryan shrugged. "Betty told him we didn't prepare food, but doc didn't laugh, so I cut it."

I pushed the remains of my bagel aside. "I have to change into work clothes and get over to Syl's."

Ryan stood so Sandi could climb out of the booth.

"It's Syl, is it?" She sounded like a teasing teenager.

"That's what he said to call him." I glanced at her as I put change on the table for a tip. "And he's closer to my parents' age than mine."

A voice came from near the entrance to the kitchen. "Now that's insulting."

I'd been so intent on the conversation with Sandi and Ryan that I hadn't noticed that Syl had apparently come in the side door and taken a seat at the counter.

CHAPTER SIX

IN A SPLIT second my thoughts went from I just lost another job to I kind of like this man. I also took in the lack of chatter around me.

I looked at Syl and asked, "Does it show?"

"What?"

"The egg on my face."

He threw his head back and laughed, and Shirley winked at me. Sandi, who had frozen with her hand about to push her hair behind her ear, relaxed.

Syl gestured that I should walk toward him. "Introduce me to your friends."

I did, and he said, "Ah, the newspaper mafia."

Ryan pulled out his notebook. "I wonder if I could ask you a couple of questions."

Syl's brow creased. "You can, but I can't tell you anything. I was asleep on the other side of the house, and poor Mr. Morris wasn't visible when I left a little after six that morning."

"Nice o meet you, Syl," Sandi said. "I'm glad you hired Melanie." She gave Ryan a push with her elbow, and with goodbyes to Shirley, they left.

I sat next to Syl, hoping my face was not as red as it was a minute ago. "I never figured you for a regular at the diner."

"First time here."

Something dinged in my brain, but I couldn't tell what it was. "I was about to go home and change, so I could get to work at your place. Okay by you?"

"Sure." He held up his mug so Shirley would bring more coffee, then lowered his voice. "I saw the article in the paper, but it didn't have information on a service. I thought someone here might know."

"You would go?"

"I'm not sure, to be truthful. But I'd at least donate to a charity in his name or send flowers."

"Oh, sugar, Hal was his own charity." Shirley spilled a few drops of coffee next to Syl's mug, something she rarely does.

She's getting a crush on Syl.

"I see," Syl said, as she moved away, but when he looked at me, I knew he didn't.

"Anytime someone asked the paper to donate to a cause, even to buy Girl Scout cookies, Hal said if they'd buy an ad he'd donate."

"He was certainly..."

"Cheap." I was getting a crick in my neck, so I turned and faced the mirror across from the counter. "But it doesn't help me figure out who put him in that mulch pile."

Syl met my eyes in the mirror. "Won't the sheriff do that? Or does he think you did the honors?"

"I don't think the sheriff does, but the IDI guys at least think it's a possibility."

Syl frowned. "It is odd that you were fired, suggested the mulch, and then Hal ended up in it. But you would have needed a lot of help to put him there."

"Exactly!" It was good to hear someone else say what I thought. A glance in her direction said Shirley was listening, which meant Syl's comment and my reaction would be all over town by tonight. "I'm a little tired of thinking about it. I think I'll head out to your place."

"Sure. Looked like you knew what you were doing, so I won't offer advice."

I PREPARED A mental to-do list as I changed. A couple of items dealt with the work I would do first at Syl's, but the rest dealt with Hal.

First, I needed to find out where Hal went after he saw me in Hy-Vee. He had lived alone *(go figure)*, so if he'd simply gone home there wouldn't be much to know. Betty maintained the office calendar, so she might have ideas about where he went. She also looked for and wrote some of the ads, so she'd be the most likely to know who Hal had insulted lately.

If Hal had been really over the top with someone in town, that person might have gone to his home to have it out with him. Didn't seem likely, but maybe a conversation had turned into a shove and Hal hit his head. Maybe the sheriff had found something interesting at Hal's house. But if Hal was killed there, why take him to Syl's?

I hadn't realized how tired I was, so I ended up working for only about an hour at Syl's before I went home and crashed. This potential murder suspect gig was really tiring.

I was almost asleep when I sat up and grabbed my notebook from the nightstand. Hal's car! If it was at his house, probably someone killed him there and hauled Hal to Syl's. If the car was elsewhere, either the murderer drove Hal – dead or alive – to the mulch pile, or Hal left the car where he was killed. So where was the car?

I WAS AT SYL'S place early Thursday morning. No one at the sheriff's office had returned my call about Hal's car, so I took out my frustration by pulling most of the weeds and tall grass on each side of the front porch. I figured I'd put down some mulch and... "Damn. No mulch."

I kicked dirt off my work boots and climbed the porch steps to knock on the screen door. "Syl?"

No answer. I debated knocking again, but when I'd pulled up he said he was working at home for the day. Maybe he didn't want to be interrupted. I debated calling Farm and More to ask them to bring more mulch, but decided it would be just too weird. I'd leave it to Syl.

Instead, I walked slowly around the house, doing a mental inventory, interrupting it to pull down a lot of ivy in back of the house. I could burn it later.

My memory of the garden tour almost twenty years before was primarily of the area behind the house. There had been a curving brick path and a large bird bath. It was the first time I'd seen a hummingbird. Mother had explained that the small feeders almost hidden among flowers had sugar water that attracted the tiny birds.

A wooden deck covered part of what had been the back garden. Why anyone would convert such peaceful beauty to fifty square feet of treated lumber was beyond me.

I didn't notice an almost-buried line of bricks about two yards out from the house until I stepped on one. The bricks told me that the area alongside the house opposite the driveway had at one time been landscaped.

Surely some plants had been perennials. As if the thought had willed my eyes to be more discerning, two small leaves, green with yellow at the edge, peered up at me. I stooped to move dead leaves from around them and unearthed a hosta plant. I moved my hand wide in a circle and found another one, then a third. *At least I won't be starting from scratch.*

I had been about to stand up when Syl's angry voice drifted out the window. "You know why that extra money was built into the contract. There's a tremendous amount of uncertainty in..."

It was twenty seconds before he spoke again, and he was even angrier. "It's not a honey pot for grubby paws." Short pause. "Of course I appreciated the introduc...."

This was not a conversation meant for my ears. Since I was almost under his window I didn't want to stand. After ten feet of crawling toward the front of the house, my right knee hit something sharp.

"Ow!" I stood and brushed off my knee, annoyed that a pinprick of blood had appeared. I don't mind getting down and dirty, but there's lots of bacteria in soil. Those microbes don't always play nice with the human bloodstream.

I squatted to look more closely at what pricked me, and then wiggled what seemed to be a sharp piece of rock. It loosened quickly, and I was surprised to find a stone arrowhead. There are lots of them in Iowa, but usually any in a yard would have been found long ago.

It was slightly rounded and looked to be a Dickson arrowhead. A few years ago, I wouldn't have known what kind it was, but the diner now has a large poster of Iowa arrowheads. I slipped it into the pocket of my cutoff jeans.

I was rummaging in my truck's glove box when the front door opened and Syl stepped out. "Looking for me, Melanie?"

I retrieved the bottle of hand sanitizer that I use as disinfectant and shut the door. "I almost hate to ask, but did you get a chance to order more mulch?"

When his expression relaxed, I realized he had looked tense.

The humor that sometimes lingered beneath the surface appeared as a wry smile. "Anxious to see what will be in the next batch?"

I shook my head. "Hard to top the last one. Mostly I didn't want to call myself. The guys will be into macabre humor by now."

"I'll call. Listen, I apologize for your having to hear me holler."

I grinned. "You do remember who I used to work for? And I didn't mean to eavesdrop. I was checking the flower beds."

He walked off the porch. "There are flowers under all that mess?"

"Come on." I led him to the area that I had cleared. "I only found three hostas, but they're evenly spaced. I bet there will be more perennials under here. We might be able to get the area around the house spiffy in a few days."

"That's not a word you hear a lot in LA, except on older sitcoms."

It didn't sound like a put-down, but I wasn't sure. "We don't recycle vocabulary as often as people on the coasts."

He laughed. "A gardener with linguistic interests." He turned toward the front of the house and spoke without looking back. "I'll call for you this time, and I'll up my line of credit so you can order what you need yourself."

Fair enough. I had no intention of avoiding people, but the idea of ordering more mulch was sort of vomit-inducing at the moment.

I had just put my work gloves back on when my mobile phone buzzed.

Good. Sheriff Gallagher. "Hey, sheriff, did you find Hal's car?"

Gallagher sounded somber. "That's not why I'm calling, Melanie. There's an IDI agent who wants to talk to you again. Now, you don't have to take my advice, but since your parents aren't here to give you a kick in the butt, I want you to think about being real good-mannered to him."

"Which one is it?" I asked, not really caring.

"Not even sure. You mind your p's and q's, hear?"

I thanked the sheriff and hung up. It hadn't made sense to badger him about the car just now. I'd have to do that later. Then I realized Gallagher hadn't said if I should come to his office, so I assumed the IDI agent would call me.

I was wrong. Agent Masters pulled into Syl's driveway. Granger's cruiser was behind him, but only Masters got out. He dangled a pair of handcuffs as he slammed his car door.

"Really? You honest to God think you have a reason to arrest me?"

I heard Syl's screen door open, but didn't look toward him.

"I don't need to arrest you to put you in these. I just need to think you might try to get away."

Masters looked like a man who had slept little and maybe had a bothersome prostate. I pulled out my phone, pushed my brother's speed dial number, and was already talking as Masters walked toward me. "Ambrose, there's an IDI agent here who's trying to intimidate me. Could you have Ken Brownberg meet me... Agent Masters, where is it you're taking me in handcuffs?"

Ambrose's voice carried without the phone on speaker, but I pushed the speakerphone button anyway. "Melanie, where are you? Ken will come to you and escort you. Where the hell is the guy wantin' to take you?"

Masters was beet red, and by this time Syl was on the porch. I saw him glance at the handcuffs and then at Masters.

"Meet my brother Ambrose, Agent Masters." I wiggled my phone at him. "Where should he send our family lawyer?"

"Why does she need a lawyer?" Syl asked.

"Melanie?" Ambrose was at a lower decibel level, but his anger was clear. "Where are you?"

"I'm at the old Silverstone place, where I'm working."

"Tell him I'll drive you down," Syl said.

I wanted to say I'd drive myself, but Mr. IDI would probably pull me over on the way and make me ride with him. Or think of a reason to give me a ticket and arrest me.

Masters' voice held controlled fury. "Mr. Seaton, this really isn't your concern."

"The hell it isn't." Syl held Masters' gaze as he walked down the steps. "A dead body shows up on my property, and you want to haul my employee's ass somewhere to question her when she clearly could not have put Hal Morris in that pile of crap?"

"I don't think it was fertilizer mulch," I said.

Explosion time. "The Department of Investigation can question anyone it believes connected to any crime, especially murder. Now, Mr. Seaton…"

"How many other people will be at your party in handcuffs?" Syl asked, using a mocking tone.

"Melanie?" Ambrose sounded almost frantic. "I've got Sheriff Gallagher on the other line. He thinks this IDI man is taking you to his office. Is that right?"

I raised an eyebrow in Masters' direction.

He almost spat the words as he glared at me. "That's correct. You be there in ten minutes."

I've never seen someone literally turn on one heel. He banged his car door and drove to the end of the driveway to turn around, where he almost front-ended Granger's cruiser, which apparently wasn't backing toward the road as fast as it should. Master's didn't bother to slow down as he pulled out of the driveway.

Ambrose was talking to someone, probably Ken Brownberg, but I couldn't hear what they said.

As Masters sped away, Syl looked at me. "That the brother you forgot to call the other day?"

I nodded.

"I know you're capable and know everyone in town, but I don't like that agent or the fact that the sheriff sent that deputy to accompany him. Tell your brother I'll drive you down, unless you object."

I can't agree more. "Thanks. Ambrose, did you hear that?"

"Yes. That's the guy you're working for? Tell him I owe him a six-pack."

.

CHAPTER SEVEN

TWO GOOD THINGS resulted from yesterday's half-hour of IDI agents' questions, all of which were repeats of the first round except mine about Hal's car, which they wouldn't answer. First, Ken Brownberg said that if the agents needed to question me again, they were to call him to bring me to them unless there were 'exigent circumstances.'

Whatever those are.

Second, I was so damned mad that I was no longer going to presume right would prevail and someone else would be arrested for Hal's murder. I was going to put my five years of investigative skills to work for myself. Not that I really knew what to do beyond the questions I'd already asked at Farm and More.

I'm a good writer, but it's generally not hard to get information in River's Edge. The paper covers a lot of good things going on in town or, hopefully, a new business. Negative stories were about people everyone would agree were bad guys. Meth makers, home burglars, people like that. People were willing to talk about that, if they knew anything.

The stuff people wanted to stay hidden wasn't fodder for *South County News* stories. Lots of folks might want to know whether the chief teller at the bank was sleeping with the woman who sold lottery tickets at the gas station, but Hal never wanted to be sued. He just walked around spreading gossip rather than writing an article.

That's why I was surprised that the Methodist Church was packed for the memorial service.

I was in the last pew because I wanted to see everyone who entered. By the time the service started, about two hundred people were seated, which was close to the church's capacity. I watched the fire chief silently count heads.

Usually a casket sits in the middle aisle toward the front, or a box of cremated remains sits on a round mahogany table. That was likely the small table's only purpose. Who would want to see a stack of church bulletins on it, if their parents or friends had once rested on the table?

But, no box. Probably Hal's body was still in Des Moines for the autopsy. Instead, there was a large photo of Hal on the table. I couldn't tell from where I sat, but Hal seemed to be smiling. That would be unusual. Idly, I wondered if there would be a grave or if his ashes would be scattered somewhere. I couldn't think of anyone who might want his urn.

Reverend Yvonne Patrick told us the opening hymn would be Blest Are the Pure in Heart. I'm not sure I would have picked it for Hal, but Reverend Patrick never worked for him.

Mayor Samuels, jowls jiggling, gave the eulogy. "Hal Morris was a fixture in River's Edge for more than twenty-five years. Anyone who knew him would say..."

This ought to be good.

"..that he never shied away from a story."

Okay, that was pretty much true.

The mayor praised Hal's dedication to his work and willingness to bear any kind of weather to cover a story.

The weather? He has to talk about the weather to find anything good to say about Hal?

I thought about how different my parents' service was. It was so large that the church used a closed-circuit television feed so people could watch from the community hall. The minister stood after twenty minutes of individual tributes, or we would have been in church half the day. The phrase most often used to describe my Mom and Dad was 'generous spirits.'

My eyes started to water, and a tear strayed down my cheek before I could brush it away.

Someone standing behind me squeezed my shoulder lightly, and I looked up to see Fred.

He bent over and whispered, "It'll be okay."

I patted his hand on my shoulder, and he removed it when I turned to face the front again. *Should I tell Fred that the tear wasn't for Hal? Probably not.*

The mayor had finished, and Reverend Patrick asked if anyone else would like to say something. There were a couple moments of rustling, and then Fred strode toward the pulpit.

I supposed someone on the paper should say something, especially since the only family member Betty had found was a second cousin in Omaha. And she hadn't come.

Fred adjusted the microphone and smiled at the attendees. "Since Hal fired me a few months ago, you might not expect me to be up here."

There were titters from almost every row.

"Several people here probably think Hal was hard to like."

A couple more titters, and a few people waved the cardboard fans the funeral home always puts in the pews.

"What Hal was, was dedicated to River's Edge. How many of Iowa's really small counties have a paper as professional as the *South County News?* How many of those send a photographer to literally every high school sports game?"

Salty liked to go to all of them. But it was true, Hal didn't have to pay him for his time.

Heads nodded now.

"A lot of small papers have closed or cut back to one day a week. The News is still at three days, and Hal hired dedicated staff to cover events in our community."

He also fired a lot of them.

"As we move forward to serve the people of South County, everyone at the paper will use the skills Hal taught us."

Except no one will throw staplers.

It sounded as if Fred was campaigning for editor. Especially since he said 'we' and 'us.'

He closed with, "Today we are celebrating the life of a man who was dedicated to River's Edge. If Hal were still here he'd be taking notes in the back pew."

A couple people said amen, and some clapped. A few others turned to see who was in the last pew, and someone gasped. That made more people turn.

I felt myself reddening. Why hadn't I thought that some people might think I really had killed Hal?

People didn't stare more than a second, and the organ started the lead-in to Amazing Grace.

Under the cover of voices raised in song, I pushed open the tall door and walked into the vestibule. Thankfully, Fred had stayed near the front of the church and couldn't follow me.

Betty, red-eyed and clutching a wad of tissues, came out as I was pushing the door that led from the vestibule to the street. "Melanie. Those people shouldn't have stared."

At the paper, Betty always dressed precisely, rarely in slacks. I was surprised at her choice of a royal blue dress with a white pin shaped like a rose. It seemed bright for a funeral. I had on grey slacks, a black turtleneck, and a white sweater. Rarely did I feel more appropriately dressed than Betty.

"Come outside. I want to be gone before everyone comes out." I walked toward my truck, but Betty had stopped.

"Aren't you going to the dinner in the social hall?" She asked this in a tone that implied it would be scandalous if I didn't.

I turned to look at her. "Those gasps kind of talked me out of it. Catch you later." I smiled as I spoke, while concurrently taking my keys from a side pocket in my purse.

In television shows, police often go to a service or burial to see if any potential suspects attend. A sheriff's deputy sat in a patrol car not far from the church entrance. No sign of the IDI agents. The patrol car could have been there to direct traffic.

I had intended to use the traditional after-funeral dinner to talk to some of Hal's neighbors. Maybe one of them saw him after about seven-forty-five the night he was killed. With no autopsy report released yet, it wasn't possible to know when and where Hal was killed or precisely how. I assumed he was killed late at night and not early the next morning.

I pulled out of the church parking lot and headed for Hal's neighborhood. Maybe not all the neighbors were at the funeral.

His home was modest – from the look of it, a three-bedroom ranch – as were those around it. They had been built at different times, so there wasn't a cookie cutter feeling. I parallel parked in front of his house and turned my head to look at it.

Dark green aluminum siding and brown shutters made his house appear drab, but the lawn had recently been mowed and a large concrete planter had pansies in it. Either Hal had a lawn service that was continuing to work or neighbors wanted the house to look lived in. No car in the driveway.

The house to the right of Hal's had a stroller in the front yard, and the lawn was a week past needing to be cut. It looked friendly. I headed for it.

In response to my knock, a boy of about six opened the door and stared at me.

"Andrew! You know you aren't supposed to open the door if you don't know who it is." A woman in her early thirties gently pushed him away from the door and looked at me. "May I help you?"

"Hi, I'm Melanie Perkins. May I talk to you about Hal for a minute?"

"Are you a bill collector?"

My face surely registered surprise. "He has bill collectors? And no, I used to work with him."

She stared at me for a moment, then seemed to realize she knew my name. "Oh, gosh, you found him, didn't you?"

I nodded. "I hoped you could…."

She interrupted me. "Come on in. But please keep your voice down. I just put my daughter down for a nap."

She opened the door, and I stepped into a world very different than my own. The living room seemed to have been divided into thirds. Against a far wall was a toy box, surrounded by about ten things with wheels, at least four of which were dump trucks. On top of the box was a stuffed rabbit that was minus one button eye.

By the wall that led to a dining room was a large yellow blanket. It housed a baby's car seat, above which were strung brightly colored plastic balls about the size of golf balls. A pile of diapers and a diaper bucket completed the look.

Against the wall closest to the front door was a large screen television with two recliners facing it. *Sanity time for mom and dad.*

My survey had taken less than five seconds, just enough time for the woman to take an additional dump truck off one of the recliners.

"Andrew," I said, "I guess you like trucks."

He grinned, revealing a gap where two top teeth had been. "I like to push them on the sidewalk."

"After Stephanie's nap. I'm Jean. Jean Roth." She gestured to one chair and then sat in the one next to mine. "Why are you asking about Hal?"

Because he was murdered.

"I suppose because I found him. It's hard to think that a killer is still out there."

Jean glanced at Andrew. "You can push your trucks in the kitchen. Just don't make them run into the washer. You'll wake Stephanie." She looked back at me.

"I'm sorry, I didn't mean to scare him."

"You didn't. I just wasn't sure what would come next."

"Me either, right now." I smiled. "I worked for Hal until a few weeks ago. He was very private about this personal life. It's been hard to find anyone who knew much about what he did the night he died."

"Hmm. He did go out about, oh, seven-fifteen, seven-thirty. I was on the porch. He had his fists balled up at his side, and he was walking fast. I figured he was mad about something. Or more than usual."

Ah. You must have known him well.

"He wasn't really a bad neighbor. My husband said Hal was probably terse because he had to look at bad news all day."

He created it. I nodded. "There certainly are ups and downs in the news business. Did you see him come back?"

"Oh, yes, he wasn't even gone half an hour. When he came back he had a brown sack, the size of a bottle of whiskey or wine or something."

"Really? We rarely saw him drink."

Jean shrugged. "Maybe he was having company soon." She frowned, as if thinking. "There hadn't been anyone for a while. We figured he must have broken up with his girlfriend."

If Sandi had been with me, she would have shrieked, "His girlfriend!"

"I didn't know her well," I lied. "Are you talking about the one with the light blonde hair?"

"No. Maybe that was before we moved in. This woman was, oh, maybe forty-five, fifty. Not too tall. Always wore a hat."

Betty? Shirley? Impossible.

"Are you okay?" Jean asked.

I must have done a silent version of a shriek. "Fine. I don't think I ever met that woman."

"We never did either. She usually came after eight or nine o'clock. We used to joke that she was probably married, and they were having an affair."

A clunking sound emanated from the kitchen. Jean stood. "Excuse me."

My mind had jumped to Betty and Shirley, but there were dozens of women about forty-five or fifty in River's Edge. Certainly Hal never acted as if he had a special relationship with either of them. He was as rude to them as everyone else.

Jean came back with Andrew in tow. He didn't look happy. "Stay near the toy box."

I nodded as she sat back down. "Did you see Hal leave again that night? Later than you might have expected him to go out?"

"Didn't see him at all. When my head hits the pillow, I'm out until Stephanie cries for her three o'clock feeding, so I probably wouldn't have heard him."

"You said something about bill collectors."

She looked toward Andrew, who was trying to fit the rabbit into the back of a dump truck. "It's just been the last few months. One knocked on our door. I know they aren't supposed to do that."

"That's true." I waited for her to say more. When she didn't, I asked, "Did they say who Hal owed money to?"

Jean shook her head. "No. My husband talked to Hal. He didn't say the guy at our door said Hal owed money, just that someone who acted kind of nasty was looking for him. We thought Hal should know."

She looked expectant, so I said, "Maybe it was for something at the paper."

She shrugged. "Maybe. Seems they would have gone there."

"Mom. My rabbit's stuck."

I hadn't noticed that Andrew had shoved the rabbit into the truck's cab. I stood. "I should get going. Would you mind asking your husband if he heard Hal go out late the night he died? If he did, here's my number."

I handed her half of a three-by-five card, on which I'd written my name and mobile number. I had burned all my South County News business cards with a bunch of brush in the burn barrel behind Mrs. Keyser's house. Plus, it wouldn't have been appropriate to use them now.

My hand was on her doorknob when I thought of one more question. "I suppose a sheriff's deputy or one of the IDI agents talked to you."

Jean shook her head. "No one's been by."

Great. If they were considering anyone else, they'd be getting information from neighbors.

Knocks on two other neighbors' doors brought no response. They were probably at work. I'd have to come back.

I sat in my truck looking at notes and thinking about how Jean's comments might relate to Hal's murder. Knowing he was not just in debt but seemingly late on payments could be important. Still, it wasn't likely that a bill collector would off him. They'd never get their money.

I drummed my fingers on the steering wheel. A credit report would list who he owed money to, but I had no way to do one. The paper did. Hal said he only did them when he was hiring someone, but I always suspected he asked for credit reports on people that he had a beef with. Good old Hal, always looking for dirt. One more reason he irritated people.

Whatever account Hal had used to access credit checks was likely still open. I debated asking Sandi for help, but other staff could possibly see any requests she made. She might get in trouble. If Fred was the interim editor, I'd probably have to go to him. Heck, he could have already done one.

What would happen if I stopped by *South County News*? No one would throw a stapler at me anymore.

Betty was at a desk behind the counter, where a receptionist sat before one of Hal's cost reductions. She had changed into a black dress with white trim, and kind of formal jewelry – a silver pendant and pearl earrings.

She must have decided she was underdressed for the funeral. *It's like she's in mourning.*

"Goodness, Melanie. I wouldn't have... Didn't expect to... Who would you like to talk to?"

"How come you're at the front desk?"

She frowned. "We're taking turns. Half the reporters in Southeast Iowa have dropped by in the last few days. If no one is at the desk, they wander around."

"Good reporters," I said.

Fred's voice came from behind me. "It's slowed down since the memorial service."

"Hey Fred." I turned to face him and was surprised that his face was thinner and he had bags under his eyes. He looked as if he hadn't slept well, if at all. I hadn't really looked at him when he had tapped my shoulder in the back of the church, and I couldn't see his haggard look when he spoke from the pulpit. "You okay?"

"Sure. What's up?"

"I keep trying to think of ways to find out who murdered Hal. I figured you guys were looking into it, too.

He studied me briefly. "Can I assume you won't try to scoop us?"

"I don't think another paper would take an article from me." When he didn't smile, I did. "Of course I wouldn't."

His mobile phone started playing the melody to Joe Jackson's Sunday Papers. He answered it, listened, and then said, "Okay, let me put you on hold while I get to my office." Fred looked at me as he started walking. "Come on back in five, Mel."

I watched him for a moment, before I looked back at Betty. "Has he been sick?"

"Just working too much, I think. The *Register's* said he can still freelance for them while he works here again temporarily. He'll cut back for them for a while, but he has a couple feature pieces to finish."

"How about you? You worked for Hal longer than anyone here."

Her eyes grew watery. "It's not easy." She took a tissue from a box on the desk and dabbed at her eyes. "I should be able to talk about him without tearing up."

I put on what I hoped was a sympathetic expression. "You probably remember him when he was in a better mood."

She smiled. "Oh, yes. The first few years I worked here he had lavish Christmas parties and..." She looked at the now-ringing phone on her desk. "Better take this."

Nuts. I had hoped to lead her into a discussion about Hal's love life. Especially to figure out if it included her.

I walked toward the back of the bull pen, where I could see Ryan trying to load paper into the fax machine. No sign of Sandi.

Ryan looked up as I got closer. "Do you know how to clear a paper jam in the fax?"

"Sure. Let me get where I can reach the back of it." The fax sat on a four-foot-square cabinet that also held the office paper supply. The cabinet couldn't be moved unless we were really low on paper, so I unplugged the fax and turned it partly around.

"So, Mel, you doing okay?"

I glanced at Ryan as I reached my hand into the fax to clear the paper. "Yep. Just wish somebody would look a little harder for another suspect."

"Yeah. It'd be a better story."

I tossed the paper into the trash can. "There is that."

He grinned. "You know what I mean."

I did. I pointed toward Hal's old office. "Fred's probably ready for me."

As I got within a few feet of the office door, I heard him talking in a fierce, low tone. "I told you I'd have it next week." He paused. "It got turned down, but the board that oversees the paper now is going..."

I backed up a couple of feet. He had to be talking about the appeal of the denial of his unemployment claim. I didn't realize he knew results. Last I heard, he and Hal had done separate phone interviews with state employees who make the decisions.

The vacant desk of the former food editor was not far away, so I sat at it. When Fred slammed his phone down, I picked up the one on the desk. That way he wouldn't know I had heard him.

His chair squeaked as he pushed back from the desk. A moment later he was at the door, scanning the bullpen for me. I held up my index finger and smiled at him. "Okay. I'll catch you later." I hung up the phone fast, so Fred wouldn't hear the dial tone buzzing.

"Come on in." He walked back to his desk.

I followed, picked up a pile of other counties' local papers that sat on the chair facing him, and sat down. Fred had cleared Hal's personal items off the top of the desk and neatened the piles of file folders that sat on a credenza behind it.

Otherwise, it was as Hal left it, including an award from the Iowa Press Association several years ago, for Best Breaking News Story for a smaller-circulation paper. Hal was covering rising flood waters in 2008 and caught a photo of staff at a canoe rental company watching their canoes slide down a crumbling bank into the Des Moines River. The interview with the elderly owner was gut-wrenching.

"Have any IDI guys been over to talk to you?"

"They had me meet them in the diner. Can't figure out why they would suspect you. It's not like you could even lift him into your trunk."

My laugh was mirthless. "I'll tell them you were my accomplice."

Fred sat up straighter. "Wish you wouldn't say that."

"Just kidding. So, have you heard anything?"

"Not really. Ryan's been to every farm within a mile of Seaton's place, and Sandi's checked the gas stations to see if he stopped in there. No one remembers seeing him after he left Hy-Vee."

I nodded toward the file folders on the credenza. "Anything he was working on worth killing to hide?"

Fred smiled. "In River's Edge?"

I raised my eyebrows, and he added, "I went through them quickly, to see if he had any draft articles for the next issue. All I found was a piece about the river levels being controlled by Red Rock Dam rather than rainfall or snow melt."

It was an article Hal wrote every spring. Half the town agreed with him, half didn't, so it generated a bunch of letters to the editor. Probably why he brought up the issue every spring.

I made a note on a three-by-five card. "Nothing new there. I went to his neighborhood. Only found one person home, and she saw him probably when he was coming back from Hy-Vee. Nothing later."

I thought about telling Fred that Hal might have had a girlfriend, but decided to try to confirm whether it was Betty. "I'll go back this evening to find some other neighbors. I'll let you know where I go, so we don't duplicate."

"You figure it out, you can write part of the story."

I hadn't considered that and simply stared at him for a moment.

He smiled. "Whoever takes over might want to hire you. It'd be like an audition."

"Good headline. Person of interest cleared. Hired to write story."

"Lawn work isn't going to be too big December through February."

"True. I was thinking of buying a blade for my truck."

Fred shrugged. "Suit yourself. Don't rule it out. Plowing snow is cold work."

"Did you know Hal seemed to have money problems?"

Fred looked amused. "Whole town knows."

"I don't mean the paper, I mean personally."

"Gee, hadn't heard that." Fred pulled a notebook toward him. "Why do you think so?"

"Neighbor thought someone who was looking for him was a bill collector."

"At his house?"

I nodded. "Kind of odd in this day and age."

Here was the chance for Fred to volunteer to pull a credit report on Hal. He didn't.

"Hmm. I'll nose around at River's Edge Bank. Gertie owes me a favor."

The branch manager was spare in giving favors, so Fred must have done her a big one. "What about checking his credit?"

He made another note on his pad. "Not sure how that will work for a dead person. Have to find out."

"Share?"

"As long as you do," Fred said.

Except for the Betty or Shirley possibility, I would.

I WAS AT LOOSE ends until Friday evening, so it made sense to earn some money. I stopped by my apartment and put on a pair of cut-offs and ankle-high work boots, and was at Syl's place by two-thirty. His truck was gone, so I pulled mine to the wide space at the back of the driveway. I avoided looking at the place where the mulch had been.

I was on the side opposite the driveway, toward the back of the house, when a vehicle pulled into the driveway. I assumed it was Syl until someone wrapped on the front door a couple of times. I shoved a trowel into the flower bed I was weeding and walked to the front of the house.

The man at the door turned and stared. "Who are you?" He was tall and tanned, but like someone who sunbathed, not a person who got the back of their neck burned from working outdoors. He had on a collared shirt and dark green tie, but no jacket. Definitely not someone I knew.

"I'm Melanie. I'm helping Syl get the yard in shape." The man's intense stare made me uneasy, so I smiled, thinking maybe he thought I was a burglar or something. "It'll take a while to get it really looking good."

His expression changed to one that seemed like phony friendliness. "I'm a colleague of Syl's. I was in the area and thought I'd stop in and see his new place. Do you know when he'll be back?"

"He goes to Des Moines a lot. Do you have his mobile number?"

"Not with me. You probably do." He walked to the edge of the porch and looked down at me.

"I don't, and I need to get it. I haven't been working for him long, and I usually see him rather than call."

"Know when he'll be back?" He walked down the steps, moved a few feet toward me and stopped.

"No. I've noticed that when he goes to Des Moines he's pretty much gone all day." I nodded toward the porch. "If you want to leave a note, I'll grab you a rock big enough to put on it so it won't blow away."

The phony-friendly look was back. "No thanks. I have his number at my office. I'll give him a call." He turned and walked toward an older Lincoln that sat in the driveway.

"Want me to say who stopped by?" I called to his back and wasn't surprised when he said no.

He got to his car and looked at me as he opened the driver's side door. "Good luck with all the weeds."

Walking back to the side yard, it occurred to me that, since Syl had moved here from Los Angeles, it seemed odd he had a local colleague.

I worked for another two hours, most of it behind the house so there would be less brush against the house. Perfect for termites.

At some point, probably when someone built the deck, a large evergreen bush had been planted. It had apparently become a spot to ditch stuff if a trash barrel wasn't handy. I found the flat part of the tool used to smooth cement, a rusty crowbar, the other part of the cement-smoothing tool, and an empty paint can. It was a big bush.

I put the items in the barn with the growing pile of odds and ends I was finding on the property. Some could be recycled, some would go to a guy I knew who sold scrap metal.

So far, the only decent thing I'd found was the arrowhead.

CHAPTER EIGHT

I DROVE BACK TO Hal's neighborhood about seven-thirty. If neighbor Jean had seen him leave at about that time on the day he was killed, maybe some of Hal's other neighbors had. More important, did they remember him coming and going again or someone else arriving?

My knock on the house directly across from Hal's brought a sour-faced man about sixty-five to the door.

"What do you want?"

Not the usual Iowa greeting.

"Hi, I'm Melanie Perkins and I..."

"You're the one who off'd Hal. Come in."

I sort of sputtered as I followed him down a narrow entry hall to a small living room. "I really didn't. That's why I'm talking to his neighbors."

The man reattached an oxygen cannula to his nose and sat in a large, green, stuffed chair that had an ottoman in front of it. "Humph. Can't give you a medal then, can I?"

I glanced around the room. An oxygen concentrator emitted a low hum, and the television was on mute. The remote was on the arm of his chair, ready to be used. As I sat on a love seat across from the man, I couldn't help it. I smiled. "I used to work at the paper, but Hal fired me a few weeks ago."

"Good motive." He coughed into a handkerchief that had been balled up in his hand. It was a rasping smoker's cough, which explained the oxygen.

"Bunch of people had that motive. Why do you seem not to like him?"

"Nothing 'seem' about it. Remember that dry spell two years back?"

"Sure. Couldn't water even my tomato plants some days."

"'Zactly. Hal was doin' a story about how not everyone watered on odd or even days, whatever it was."

"Varied by your house number," I said.

"Right. Well, you can bet your sweet bippy I stuck to the letter of that. Son Sam works at the water plant in Ottumwa." The man's face began to get red. "But old Hal, he wants names to put in the story. He and I had words many times, so he prints I watered my lawn every damn day but Sunday."

When he said his son's name was Sam, I realized I didn't know his. Not the time to ask.

"Bastard wouldn't print a retraction. So, I called our water plant. They can tell how much water you use every day. Put a sign in my front yard with a copy of what the town water folks told me. Showed I used a bunch less water, when I was 'sposed to." He looked very pleased with himself.

I had no memory of this. This man must not have come into the office to complain, and Hal wouldn't have told his staff if he had to eat crow. "Did Hal retract?"

"Put a tiny note, on the classified page no less, saying there had been a... What did he call it? A transcription error."

I looked up from the three-by-five card on which I'd been taking notes. "More than he did some other times, Mr., um, I'm not sure I got your name."

"Anderson. Morton Anderson. You gonna quote me?"

"No, sir. I don't work at the paper now. I just want to find out…"

"Well, I didn't do it."

I wanted to say I could see he wouldn't have had the lung capacity to haul Hal out to Syl's place. Instead, I said, "Didn't cross my mind. I wanted to know if you saw him at all the night he died."

He shook his head. "Sometimes I looked out the curtain if I heard him start the car or pull in. Had to make sure it was someone supposed to be in the neighborhood. Hal saw me, he'd give me the finger. Not that night."

"Any idea who might want to kill him?"

"How much time you got?"

I laughed. "All you need."

He thought. "Nah. Never met a person liked him. Don't know who'd waste their time killin' him." He coughed into the handkerchief again.

"Just one more question."

Anderson nodded.

"Did Hal park his car in the garage or the driveway?"

"Humph. Garage is full of crap. Couldn't fit a toadstool in there."

"So, did the police tow his car away at some point?"

"Not that I saw. Good question." Anderson looked at me intently. "You investigating so they don't stick the murder on you?"

I ignored the question, but handed him half of a three-by-five card with my name and phone number. "If you think of anything else or hear someone else mention that they saw something, will you call me?"

He studied it and looked up. "You find who did it, I'll chip in for the medal."

FORTY-FIVE MINUTES later, I knew nothing more. Other neighbors were not as blunt as Morton Anderson, but they all said they'd had some kind of run-in with him.

Basically, if even the smallest thing bothered him, like a kid running into the yard to fetch a ball, Hal pitched a fit. A few years ago they had stopped inviting him to the annual block picnic, which was held at a park at the end of the street.

I sat in my truck for five minutes, studying the brief notes I'd taken and the addresses of any houses I'd visited. Basically, I was nowhere. It did seem that if the sheriff, with help from my favorite IDI agent, tried to get the county attorney to accuse me of killing Hal, at least a few people would testify they had given it fleeting thought.

People have a reason or benefit to acting the way they do. Or both. I went to high school with a girl whose mom had died when she was six. It was probably why she wanted attention from other kids' parents. She also had learned that the 'poor little me' demeanor got her sympathy. She milked it.

So, what was with Hal? What benefit did he get by being angry all the time? His temperament was why he had no friends in River's Edge. He was old enough, mid-fifties, that it hadn't seemed odd to me that his parents were dead. I didn't remember anyone who said they'd known him all his life.

Hal's obit said he had been born in Iowa Falls. Maybe I should check newspaper archives up there for the name Morris.

Not that an unknown tragedy would account for regularly criticizing people and exhibiting a mean streak. Certainly not for poking holes in a neighbor's hose because he didn't want water from their sprinkler to reach his yard. And Hal wondered why newspaper subscriptions were down.

I BAKED A MIX of chicken and vegetables and read until it was time for the ten-thirty news. The network television that most often carries news about River's Edge is in Quincy, Illinois. Since Hal was a fellow journalist, they had covered the story, but had lost interest after a couple days of 'no new developments.' That was fine with me.

ELEVEN-THIRTY ROLLED around, then midnight. Sleep eluded me. I tried warm milk, and then soothing music. At one in the morning I looked at the clock, groaned, and got up.

I couldn't believe that Sheriff Gallagher, buttressed by his IDI buddies, would arrest me. But I hadn't expected to find Hal in a pile of mulch, so maybe I should expect more surprises.

Whoever took my hoe certainly wanted the sheriff to think I killed Hal. The hoe hadn't been mentioned in the paper yet. I saw nothing to gain by telling Fred or Sandi, so I'd kept my mouth shut. The murderer knew who put it there.

After pacing the apartment for ten minutes, I had an idea that seemed ridiculous, even to me. What had the light been like the night Hal was killed, and how much of the area at the back of Syl's driveway would be visible from the road? Five days ago there had been a quarter moon, and now it was almost half. More light, but not as bright as with a full moon.

The only way to find out was to see for myself.

Jeans were in order, since the temperature was supposed to drop into the low fifties tonight. Technically, Saturday morning, which it was. I didn't own a black stocking cap or trench coat, but I had a navy blue hooded sweatshirt.

I walked down the exterior stairs as quietly as I could, and I didn't turn on the truck's headlights until I was on the road. The drive to Syl's was fast with no one else on the road. I had gone through town and was nearing the end of the blacktop in seven minutes.

No way would I pull into Syl's driveway at almost two in the morning, so I drove past his acreage and pulled into a driveway near the wide spot in the road where the letter carriers stood to stuff mail into four rural mailboxes that were grouped together. The house that went with the driveway was probably a quarter-mile from the road, so no one would notice my truck.

The walk was roughly the length of one Iowa City block, so it wouldn't take long to get to Syl's driveway. I stayed to one side of the road, where gravel and sand mixed with soil that had traveled there from a field. The soil had been softened from spring rains. If I'd been a criminal, I wouldn't have wanted to leave footprints from my ankle-high boots. But I wasn't, so I didn't care.

As I neared the driveway I pulled a pen light from my pants pocket. On the road I knew what to expect, but not on Syl's property. A larger flashlight was in the center pocket of my sweatshirt, but I hoped not to use it.

There are no street lights where town turns to country, and it felt even darker once I walked off the road. Suddenly it sounded like a cricket chorus. I suppose my presence had alerted them, although I was surprised so many males had wings to rub this time of year.

I stayed to the side of the driveway. When I reached the end, near Syl's truck and back door, I squatted and shone the light around the area where the mulch and Hal had been. I had not expected to see anything remarkable. It was dry now that the mulch had been gone a few days.

I stood and looked toward the street. Assuming the murderer wasn't wearing traffic-safety orange, it would be almost impossible for someone in a passing car to see anyone back here. Maybe if the murderer had been moving quickly, but someone dumping a body would be able to hear a car approach in time to duck either behind Syl's truck or whatever they were driving.

And they had to be driving. It would've been nearly impossible to put a man's body in a wheelbarrow and move it, with arms and legs flailing. I hadn't noticed any small tire tracks or the marks a wheelbarrow makes when you park it, so to speak. Only a weight lifter could have carried Hal any distance.

I shivered. I was thinking about Hal as if I was playing a part in a TV show. I knew Hal. When my parents died he gave me a week off. I should feel sad. An image of him throwing the orange at me in Hy-Vee came to mind, and I smiled. No stapler he could reach for.

I backed a few feet further from the house and slowly surveyed the entire area. The barn behind the house looked almost sinister in the dark. I half expected a horde of zombies to come toward me, parading through Syl's large back yard with their awkward gait.

Ugh.

The crack of a branch made me turn to peer toward a group of overgrown bushes and small trees a few yards from the driveway. I really need to get those trimmed. They'd be a great place for a burglar to hide.

I didn't want to use the larger flashlight. Waving its beam around could call attention to me from quite a distance away. There couldn't be another person here. Deer and opossum are as rampant as raccoons in Iowa. It had to be an animal. If anyone was over there, they wouldn't be anxious to run into me. No need to worry, right?

Get moving. You don't want to hang out here until dawn.

I walked toward the barn. The sheriff deputies and IDI would have searched it well, so there would be nothing to find. I merely wanted to look toward the driveway from the barn.

I stood in the barn entrance closest to the house and looked toward the house and its driveway. This was how it would likely have looked to the murderer. No lights on in the house, no farm dog to bark and rouse Syl. *He should get one.* No indication that anyone would appear to interrupt the untraditional burial.

When I did a half circle turn in the barn, it looked as it did a few days ago, except the tarp was off the tractor in a heap beside it. It was awfully clean for a barn, even given that Syl didn't use it for anything.

In the corner stood an old broom, the kind with long, stiff bristles that everyone's grandparents had. I walked to it and stooped, shining the light on the bristles. They looked clean for a barn broom, but maybe Syl washed it. Or had someone do it. I couldn't see him out here in his snazzy suit.

A small brown spot caught my eye, and I put the pen light closer to the bristles. *Can that be mulch?* I reached for the spot and then pulled my hand back. It had to be the sheriff or somebody using gloves who removed it.

The sound of a person's footstep behind me made me straighten, but before I could turn, the back of my head exploded in pain.

CHAPTER NINE

"MELANIE. MELANIE!"

"Go away."

"Are you okay? What happened?"

I opened my eyes. I was face down, my head turned to the right. The floor around me was a dirt one, so I definitely wasn't home.

"Melanie!"

The voice was insistent, I'd give him that. And familiar. Not my brother. "Oh, Syl?"

"Thank God."

I moved my arms, intending to put my palms on the floor to raise myself up, but he put a hand on my shoulder.

"Stay down!"

"My head hurts." I stared at my hand. My elbow was bent so my hand was about even with my eyes.

"Did you fall?"

"Don't think so. Why am I down here?" I remembered driving to Syl's and parking down the road.

"No idea. I woke because I thought I heard someone outside my window." He paused. "I need to direct the ambulance back here. Promise me you'll stay lying down."

"Not going anywhere." I shut my eyes. It registered that Syl must not have taken a sleeping pill. I heard the sound of a truck or something, pulling into the driveway. No siren, but the driver wouldn't have used it so late at night.

"Back here," Syl called. "Back here."

He was kneeling next to me again in seconds, or so it seemed. "Remember not to move until the EMTs tell you to."

"My head hurts."

"No kidding." He stood. "She's had some kind of blow to the head. I don't' know if she fell or was hit."

"Damn. Mel!" Martin was the same EMT who'd come when I'd found Hal. He started feeling my arms and legs. "Anything broken you think, Mel?" he asked.

"Just my head. This floor's really cold."

"Okay. My partner's bringing a gurney. But I want to put a neck brace on you before we move you."

Martin and John, who was a good friend of my brother's, had me in the back of the ambulance in less than five minutes.

"If you shine that light in my eyes again, I'll bite you."

Martin chuckled. "Guess you'll be all right."

"The light just hurts." I paused. "Can I have some water?"

His tone was sympathetic. "We're almost to the hospital. They'll put an IV in you, get some fluids started."

"I want something in my mouth." I swallowed. "Really dry."

He patted my shoulder. "Almost there."

I had just noticed that I could see street lights out the ambulance's back window. Then it apparently went over the speed bump in the hospital driveway.

"Ow."

"See, we're here," Martin said.

The back door of the ambulance opened, and I heard people running toward us.

"Is she conscious?"

Martin and John lifted my gurney and extended its legs to the pavement.

"Yeah," Martin said. "Said she thinks someone hit her in the back of the head."

"Oh, good Lord." The woman had an authoritative tone. "We may need to airlift her to Iowa City."

"Please don't." I almost sobbed. "I want to go home."

John spoke in a soothing tone. "They'll do their best to keep you here, kiddo. I'm going to call Ambrose."

Oh, crud. My brother would be furious that I'd gone to Syl's at night alone.

Someone ran up as they wheeled me into the ER. "I'd like to come in with her." It was Syl.

"We need to examine..." the woman's voice said.

"I'll stay out of your way."

"See that you do," she snapped.

The next few minutes were a blur of pain and ceiling lights that were way too bright. Someone came in with a portable x-ray and took pictures of my head and neck. Then the woman was back.

I focused on her. She was perhaps forty, maybe Hispanic, with very black hair and dark eyes. "Who are you?"

She smiled. "It's good you care. Can you tell me what day it is?"

"Hmm. I'm not sure if it's yesterday or today."

I heard Syl clear his throat.

"How about the year?"

I told her, and gave her yesterday's date. I remembered it because I'd written it on the three-by-five cards as I took notes.

"Good, good. Now, how many fingers?"

This made no sense. "You have five."

"Mel, she means how many are raised," Syl said, with the amused tone barely hidden.

"Oh, two. Your index and middle fingers."

"Great. I'm going to put some pain medicine in your IV. I wanted to be sure of your condition before I did that."

I heard plastic tear and saw her draw liquid into a syringe from a small glass bottle. "Are you giving me a shot?"

"No, putting it in your IV. It'll help a lot with the pain."

I remembered that I had told her several times that my head hurt. Whoever she was. "Who are you?"

"I'm sorry, you asked me that." She finished whatever she was doing with the syringe and patted my hand, smiling. "I'm Doctor Maria Vargas. We usually have a quieter night around here."

"Dr. Vargas?" I recognized Sheriff Gallagher's voice.

"Oh, Sheriff. I'm not sure. Well... Ms. Perkins, can you talk to the sheriff for just a minute?"

"Why not?" I whispered, feeling like I was going to cry. *That's stupid.*

"Hey, Melanie," he said. "Can you tell me what happened?"

"I went to look at...oh. Did you get the broom?"

"What broom?"

Before I could answer, Syl said, "She talked about that when they loaded her into the ambulance."

I did?

"I have one in the barn, but it only now occurred to me that she might mean that one."

"Okay." Sheriff Gallagher spoke slowly. "Before we talk about the broom, did you fall, or did someone push or hit you?"

"Hit me. From behind." I opened and shut my eyes. "I can look at you, if someone would turn off that stupid light."

"There's one on above the sink," Syl said. He stood and walked toward the door to turn off the overhead light.

I opened my eyes. "Thank you." I looked up at the sheriff. "Am I in trouble?"

He smiled. "I have no idea. We won't worry about that just this minute. Did you see who hit you?"

I started to shake my head and winced. "No. I just wanted to see what it looked like at night, and I... Could I have some water?"

Syl stood and left the room.

"Keep talking if you can," Gallagher said.

"I wanted to see, see Syl's driveway the way the killer saw it. And then I walked to the, oh, the place with the tractor. The barn."

Dr. Vargas came in carrying a Styrofoam cup. "If you can keep an ice chip or two down, the nurse can bring you a tiny bit of ginger ale." She held a plastic spoon with a few chips near my mouth. "I don't want you to sit up."

I chewed the chips she gave me. "Can I have more?"

"A couple." She put them in my mouth, and said, "Let's wait just a few minutes to be sure you keep them." She left.

Like I would give them away.

"So, you went to the barn," Gallagher prompted.

"And I saw the broom. I put my light on it." I felt myself getting excited. "It had a bit of mulch on it."

"Ohh-kay." Gallagher said. "And then what?"

"Um, for just a second I thought I heard someone behind me. And then, well, I guess he conked me."

"A man?" he asked.

"Um. No clue."

A nurse came in, nodded at the sheriff and checked the machine that was annoying me by blowing up the blood pressure cuff on my arm.

"Was the mulch there? I mean, on the broom?"

Gallagher frowned at me. "We'll check."

"It could mean the killer used it to sweep mulch. There might be, whadyacallit? Fingerprints."

"You should have called me." Gallagher sounded annoyed.

"It's not like I knew it was there."

He sighed. "I really, really wish you hadn't done this."

I met his gaze. "Me, too, and not just because I got hit."

He nodded. "It's just suspicious." He stared back. "I still have a hard time thinking you killed Hal, but this isn't good."

The nurse had left, and Dr. Vargas was back. "Sheriff. I think that's long enough."

"Sure thing. You keeping her overnight?"

"At least. Will you be posting anyone?"

"I'll try." Gallagher ran his fingers through his hair. "I'm short tonight."

"I'll stay." Syl turned to Dr. Vargas. "You're locked at night, right?"

She nodded, but didn't look happy.

Gallagher looked at me and shook his head slightly. "My guess, doc, is the person knows she didn't see him. Or her."

"Let's hope you're right. Have someone stop by once, if they can." She left.

The nurse came back. About thirty, she sported pastel pink scrubs and a perky smile. People like her make me think I look like a farm hand.

"Your x-rays are back. They don't see a skull fracture, but they'll have a second radiologist look at them on the day shift." She loosened the cuff on my arm and then tightened it again. "You may have a concussion, which is why you'll stay for a bit. We'll get you moved to a room in a few minutes."

When she left, I looked at the sheriff. "Thanks."

"Later, Melanie." Sheriff Gallagher walked out.

I shut my eyes. It would be good to sleep. The medicine made my head hurt less, and I felt sleepy.

"Mel?"

I opened my eyes.

Ambrose's friend John held out his mobile phone. "Your brother wants to talk to you."

"Oh, crap."

I mostly listened to Ambrose. I could tell he was trying to control a lot of anger, which meant John had told him where they found me.

He started by telling me I was crazy to be in a barn – by myself, at night. "Sharon is coming down in the morning. I have to be in Sioux City for a statewide Farm Bureau meeting, and if you aren't dying I need to make it."

I wanted to say I was fine by myself, but there probably wasn't a solid case for that. "It'll be good to see her."

He snorted. "She's going to stay as long as she thinks you need her. And it's up to her, not you." After telling me he hoped I felt better, Ambrose hung up.

John had gone into the hall. When he returned, I handed him the phone. "Thanks."

He grinned. "He'd a killed me if I hadn't call him."

I closed my eyes for two seconds and opened them. "I know. Thanks a lot."

"You need me, you call, okay? If I'm not home, I'm here or on a call. Leave a message." He nodded at Syl and left.

Then it was just Syl and me.

"Syl?"

"Yes."

"It hurts to turn my head. Can you stand where I can see you?"

"Sure." He walked to the foot of the gurney.

"I'm really, really sorry."

He shrugged. "As far as I can tell, you didn't do anything to me."

"I couldn't sleep, and I thought I might think of something if I saw how it looked really late at night. What people could see from the road, you know?" My voice kind of trailed off.

"Interesting. Reporter's instinct?" His words had a mocking tone.

"Oh, damn. When Sandi gets up, she'll check the crime blotter."

"I think that's the least of your worries."

"Yeah. My brother's going to try to get me to move to Dubuque again."

"What's the crime rate up there?"

"Funny." I shut my eyes. "I might sleep a little."

"Good idea. You'll get in less trouble."

I WOKE UP LATER SATURDAY morning in a hospital room, with curtains pulled around the bed and Syl dozing in a lounge chair next to it. I had only a vague memory of being moved to the room.

Syl didn't snore. Ambrose did, so had my father. Syl's usually perfectly combed hair was mussed, but not a lot. The stubble on his face gave him a more rugged look.

He didn't dress like Ambrose or my father. Instead of jeans he wore cotton slacks, and his collared shirt had probably cost what ten of my Dad's had. His clothes were rumpled, as if he had grabbed yesterday's from the hamper.

Light filtering through the thin privacy curtain told me it was early, maybe six a.m. I had been lying flat on my back, and it ached, so I pulled my knees up and shifted toward my right side.

Someone opened the door to the room and soft-soled shoes squeaked toward me. When the woman pulled back the curtain, Syl sat up with a start.

She ignored him and looked at me. I took in her white lab coat and hand-held caddy of syringes and figured I was about to get stuck.

"Can you tell me your name?" she asked.

"My head's okay."

The woman, who was in perhaps her late forties, with silver-streaked brown hair pulled into a severe bun, smiled. "I need to be sure who I'm taking blood from."

"Oh. Melanie Perkins."

She placed her caddy on a table by my bed and pulled out a syringe. "Is this Mr. Perkins."

"Only if I'm crazy." Syl nodded at her. "Syl Seaton."

The woman didn't smile, but looked at me as she put the rubber tourniquet on my arm so she could get at a vein. "I'm Margaret. This will just be a little stick."

Liar.

We didn't speak until she was done. "Are you from around here?" I asked.

"We moved here because my husband got a job at the plastics plant. We're from Illinois." She turned and left.

"Plastics plant?" Syl asked.

"That kind of boxy building on the south edge of town, on the river."

"What do they do?"

"I did a story on them. They make molds to make, oh, hardhats for beekeepers, sinks, lots of things."

"Who would have thought?" Syl stood and pulled the rest of the curtain back, so we could see out the window. "How are you feeling this morning?"

"My head throbs, but not as much as last night. Or, this morning, I guess it was."

"What were you thinking?"

"I mostly wasn't, I guess."

The amused look again. "That's obvious."

I felt as if I'd explained myself ten times. "I just wanted to see it the way the murderer had. I thought it might tell me something."

Syl stared at me for a couple of seconds. "Do you think you know who killed your old boss?"

"Nope. Lots of candidates."

He shook his head. "If you think you're okay, I'll head home."

"I'm a lot of trouble, aren't I?"

He smiled. "I need that yard work done." He pulled on a dark blue sports coat that he had slung on the back of his chair. "I'm sure your family and friends will be by, but if you really need something, call."

As he got to the door, I called, "Probably see you in a couple of days."

He turned. "But not before your doctor says you can do that kind of work."

I FINISHED a breakfast of Jell-O, broth, and tea and stared out the window. I hoped the nurse would do as she said and find out if I could have solid food.

My door was mostly closed, but familiar voices came from the hall.

"Let me look," Sandi hissed. "If a woman's in the room they might think you're gawking."

Ryan sort of snorted, and it sounded as if they walked by my room.

"I'm in here." I cleared my throat and spoke more loudly. "In here."

The door swung open. Sandi and Ryan more or less gaped at me.

"You don't look so hot," Ryan said.

"Shut the door, you guys."

Sandi did, and they walked to my bed.

"Don't ask me what I was thinking," I said.

"We don't know enough to do that. Stooper left a message at the paper and said he saw an ambulance drop you off here."

"Stooper? What was he doing here?"

Ryan shrugged. "Sometimes, when he's really drunk, someone who doesn't know him sees him on the sidewalk, and he ends up here."

"Great." I told them what had happened in about thirty seconds.

"Are you insane?" Sandi asked.

"I didn't think anyone else would be there," I huffed.

"Are you okay?" Ryan asked.

"Concussion, maybe. Nothing worse."

Ryan gave me a stern look. "That's a lot. Especially if you play football."

"I don't. You guys need to go see if that broom's there."

"Okay," Ryan said.

"Sheriff Gallagher would love that," Sandi added. "Plus, he probably has it."

"He said he was short-staffed last night. Maybe no one's been by."

Sandi grinned. "Call your buddy Syl."

"He might not be home yet."

"Home from where?" Sandi asked.

"He, uh, spent the night in that chair." I pointed.

Sandi grinned more.

"Now that's a story," Ryan said.

"No, it's not," I snapped. "The sheriff said he didn't have enough deputies on duty to leave someone here, and Syl said if the hospital was locked, he'd stay."

"Bet he wouldn't do that if Ryan got hit," Sandi said, in a kind of sing-song tone.

Ryan pulled a notebook and pen from his pocket. "We need to ask you a couple of questions."

"The heck you do."

"Mel." Sandi waited until I looked at her. "You know we have to do an article."

When I ignored her, Sandi continued, "To be clear, you weren't specifically looking for the broom?"

By the time they left ten minutes later, I was drained, and it was only eight forty-five. At least I had my phone, which had been in the pocket of my sweatshirt. My truck had probably been towed into town by now. Maybe Sharon could help me get it.

Sharon. I liked my sister-in-law, but I didn't want anyone around right now. Maybe if I acted meek she'd only stay one night.

A sharp rap on the door announced Sheriff Gallagher. Behind him was Agent Masters, who wore a smirk.

"Melanie," the sheriff said.

"Sheriff."

Gallagher smiled. "You look better than last night. You remember Agent Masters."

"I wouldn't dream of forgetting him."

Gallagher shook a finger at me as he sat in the chair Syl had vacated. "This can be quick or long."

Masters leaned against the wall, opposite my bed and directly in my line of vision. "What were you doing there last night?"

"Doing? Nothing. I just wanted to see the place at night."

We went over everything I had already told Sheriff Gallagher. When I figured they had to be done, Masters added, "This makes you look guilty as hell."

I kept an even tone. "Of what?"

"You damn well know what."

I sort of snarled. "I did not kill Hal Morris. Besides, if I did, I wouldn't be stupid enough to put him someplace where I'd be the one to find the body."

When Masters started to say something, Gallagher cut him off. "Right now, that's the best point in your favor."

"I would think you'd lack forensic evidence, too." I looked at the sheriff as I said it and tried not to sound too snotty.

"Your fingerprints are all over that hoe," Masters said.

"As it's mine, they would be." I held his gaze. "Someone wants you to think it's me. You'll figure out it's not me eventually, but by that time, whoever did do it will be all cleaned up and have gotten rid of anything incriminating."

"If there is someone else," Masters said.

"It's not as if you're looking. You haven't even talked to his neighbors." I wished I hadn't said that as soon as it was halfway out of my mouth.

"Mel." Sheriff Gallagher spoke sharply. "You leave this alone, hear? I don't want to hear about any more visits to Mr. Seaton's place at night. Any more ideas…"

"Hey, did you find the broom?"

Neither spoke, and Gallagher finally said, "No."

"See," I felt excited. "Whoever killed him wanted it."

"If it was ever there," Masters said.

Gallagher cleared his throat as he stood. "Mr. Seaton confirmed that he had one in the barn, but he couldn't remember when he last saw it."

"What about the footprint molds you made the day we found Hal?"

"The day you found him," Masters said. "And that's not for you…"

Gallagher interrupted him. "Assuming you won't repeat this, I'll say it was a very common athletic shoe.

Won't be much use unless we find the exact same shoe, and even then not much."

"Nuts."

Gallagher frowned, "Is Ambrose coming down?"

I felt like a chastised child. "Sharon's coming. Ambrose has some big Farm Bureau meeting in Sioux City."

Masters seemed to want to say more, but Gallagher moved toward the door. "Tell Sharon she sees anything odd at your place, she's to call."

They left, and I leaned into my pillow. I knew I was lucky it was the sheriff himself who'd accompanied Masters, rather than Granger or a deputy I didn't know well. Granger would want to ingratiate himself to the IDI agent, and someone who hadn't known me most of my life could think I'd killed Hal.

I had enough of a headache already.

CHAPTER TEN

SHARON AND I have always gotten along. She didn't start dating Ambrose until their senior year, when I was a high school freshman. Most of their dating time was in college, at Iowa State. Since I went to the University of Iowa, we don't root for the same football team, but I don't hold it against her.

She's very tall. Ambrose likes rodeos so he taught her how to rope cows. From a horse, of course, and only for fun. Not a lot of women have the arm strength or length to do that well. She still looks as if she stepped out of a magazine, always coordinated outfits and naturally curly hair she has only to comb to look perfect. I do kind of hate her for that.

Sharon had assured the doctor I would follow all instructions for a probable mild concussion. We settled into my apartment, me lying on the couch, her bustling in the kitchen to make coffee. It hadn't even started percolating when someone rushed up the stairs and rapped on the door in shave-and-a-haircut-six-bit cadence.

"That's Fred's knock." I raised my voice. "That you, Fred?"

"Yeah, you okay?"

Sharon walked to the door and turned the deadbolt to open it. "She's been better." She stood aside so Fred could come in, giving him a sort of stern look. Fred was in the same high school class as Sharon and Ambrose, so she knows he can be a little pushy. "You're welcome to stay for a bit Fred, but no interviews. Mel said she already talked to Sandi and Ryan."

"Oh, sure."

Fred surprised me by walking to the couch, bending over, and kissing me on the cheek. "I was so worried." He handed me a Peppermint Patty, which he knows is my favorite candy.

"Gee. Thanks, Fred. Pull up one of the kitchen chairs."

"No flowers?" Sharon asked, only half-teasing.

"Mel likes to plant her own." He sniffed. "Can I get a mug of that high-test?"

"Sure."

I could hear Sharon placing mugs on the counter and getting milk from the fridge.

Fred sat next to the couch, looked at me, and shook his head. "I would have gone with you."

"No questions," Sharon called.

"I'm commiserating, not questioning." Fred grinned at me.

"I honestly thought I was just taking a dri.. Hey, do you know where my truck is?"

"In the lot behind the paper. Sheriff had had it towed to his place. Betty went down to his office and said if it wasn't evidence she'd drive it, rather than you getting some kind of storage fee or whatever. Granger hot-wired it for her, of all people."

"I'd have paid to see that."

"Me, too," Sharon called.

"Anyway, give me a key, and I'll have Ryan bring it here. He can walk back."

"You guys are the best."

Fred tilted his head toward the kitchen and whispered. "Anything you can tell me?"

"This percolator isn't so loud," Sharon said.

"C'mon, Sharon. It's not like I'm grilling her."

"It's okay, Sharon. Fred's kibitzing."

"You two," she muttered.

I looked at Fred. "It's just so odd that anyone else would have been out there."

"You don't think it could have been the owner, that Syl guy, do you?"

"Can't see why he'd knock me out. It's his place, so not like he'd have to explain himself to me."

"Knock some sense into you. You still take milk, Fred?" Sharon called.

He turned his head to answer her. "Yes, thanks." He looked back at me. "I was in Des Moines this morning. Ryan and Sandi drove out there, but they said there was a sheriff's car in the driveway, so they couldn't look for that broom."

I sighed. "When the sheriff and the IDI agent came to the hospital this morning..."

"The IDI agent?" Fred asked.

"Masters. I don't think he likes me."

"Is he the one you told off at your buddy Syl's place?" Fred asked.

"How'd you hear about that?"

Sharon called from the kitchen. "From Sophie, sheriff's secretary. At least, that's who I heard it from."

"Sheesh. Anyway, Gallagher said they found no broom. At least we know someone wanted it."

Fred tilted his head back a bit and looked toward the ceiling – his thinking position.

Sharon came in with two mugs of coffee and sat mine on the coffee table near me and the other closer to Fred.

"Sorry, Mel, yours is instant decaf."

I remembered the hospital's instruction and smiled instead of groaned.

Fred turned to look at her. "Thanks. You have any ideas, Sharon?"

She winked at me before she turned toward the kitchen to get her own mug. "I have strict instructions not to encourage Melanie to keep digging into this."

Fred grimaced, and then noted my rising color.

"So, Sharon, did Ambrose say you couldn't talk to me either?" Fred asked.

She walked into the room with her coffee and sat in the recliner. "No, but I won't be much help. I'm not suspicious like you two."

"What about Sophie?" I asked. "Did she have any ideas?"

Sharon shook her head. "Nope. Did you ever get your unemployment, Fred? I heard Hal said he fired you and then you lost the first appeal."

It was Fred's turn to redden. "How could you know that?"

She raised an eyebrow. "I stopped at the diner for coffee before I picked Mel up at the hospital."

I was delighted Sharon had asked the question. I'd know for sure if Fred won or lost his first round of appeals without having to ask.

"Damn," Fred said. "No one has any ideas about who killed Hal, but everyone knows the confidential results of my unemployment claim."

I smiled at him. "If it makes you feel any better, everyone knew you didn't deserve to be fired. We wanted you to get your unemployment." My comment seemed to calm him.

"If you must know, Hal told a bunch of lies, and I got denied. Doc Shelton went to the unemployment office a couple days after Hal died and said the Advisory Committee had looked into it, and Hal let me go so staff salaries would go down. He didn't want to pay unemployment. I heard they're going to speed up reclassifying me as a layoff."

"Do the unemployment people know the committee was mostly for show?" I asked.

"No, but most of them knew Hal, and since he's dead, he can't contradict Doc."

"Good." I gave Fred a thumb-up sign. I felt almost guilty thinking Fred might have been mad enough to kill Hal. Plus, there would be the same issue as with me. Fred might be taller and stronger than I was, but could he honestly have hauled Hal out to Syl's?

After a couple of sips of coffee, I leaned back on the couch again and shut my eyes, while Sharon and Fred talked about a married couple they graduated with who was getting divorced. Sharon was working on their class's next reunion, and since Fred was class president, she tried to goad him into hosting a barbeque at his house.

My mind kept replaying the scene at Syl's the previous night. With the broom gone, besides the night in the hospital, all I had really gained was affirmation that no one could've seen much from the street.

Who could have hit me? There would have been plenty of places for someone to hide. Even though I had been pretty focused on the broom, I was surprised someone had been able to sneak up on me. Maybe the person was already in the barn. Then I wouldn't have heard them strolling through the yard.

My eyes opened with a thought. "Hey, did you do that credit check we talked about?"

When Fred and Sharon stared at me, I realized I had interrupted them. "Sorry."

"You're a hoot," Fred said, smiling. "Turns out only a spouse and Hal's executor could request it. I'm not willing to try to fool the credit agencies."

"Why'd you want that?" Sharon asked.

I shrugged, hoping Fred wouldn't mention the bill collector. "Just a hunch. Thought maybe if he owed money someone would come looking for him."

"You watch too much TV," Sharon said.

I wrinkled my nose at her. "I got rid of cable when Hal fired me."

Fred stood. "Me, too. I'll poke around some more. Have to get back to the paper. I told Ryan he could do the first draft on your story, so I'll probably have to go over it a lot with him."

My story.

I SLEPT MUCH of Saturday afternoon, and got up at about four to take a shower. Sharon stood outside the bathroom, reading a book she'd brought. Ambrose must have told her to really keep an eye on me.

By the time I'd showered and put on clean clothes, I was ready to sleep again. This time I just dozed. Sharon made us grilled cheese for supper. My second favorite comfort food.

Sandi came by after work. I finally realized she wasn't so much interested in who hit me as to why Syl stayed at the hospital.

"I told you already, the sheriff was down a deputy last night. Syl was just keeping an eye on me."

Sharon looked up from her book. "Bet he wouldn't have done that if you were a guy who did yard work."

"Or ugly," Sandi said.

"He doesn't strike me as that shallow." I sighed. "I really don't want to leave my innocence in anyone's hands but mine."

"I'll pretend I didn't hear that." Sharon resumed her reading.

Sandi grinned. "I heard that the sheriff sent Granger and another deputy to talk to Hal's neighbors today. Maybe he really thinks you didn't kill Hal."

I wish I could believe that.

"Are the IDI guys still around?"

"They didn't eat at the diner today like they usually do." Sandi's face showed excitement. "I got a call from the TV station in Quincy about you."

"What did you tell them?" Sharon's tone was kind of sharp.

"That I thought Hal was more likely to put himself in the mulch than Melanie."

Sharon smiled and went back to her book, and I laughed, which made my temples pound so I stopped. "Still no autopsy results?"

"Nope," Sandi said. "If they hadn't sent him to Des Moines, we would have had them by now."

"Anyone seen Hal's car?" I asked.

Sharon cleared her throat.

I ignored her. "Did the police take it?"

Sandi looked surprised. Gee, I figured it was in his garage or the sheriff had it."

"His neighbor told me there was too much stuff in the garage for a car."

Sharon turned a page. "Cover a lot of murders, you two?" She didn't look up.

"Thankfully, no." Sandi stood and looked at me. "Most garages have windows."

"Go for it," I said. "But watch your back."

As Sandi shut the door behind her, Sharon looked up from her book again. "I can honestly tell Ambrose people look in on you. Mrs. Keyser came up while you were napping."

"She's okay, but she would talk for two hours if I'd let her."

Sharon shut her book. "So I gathered. So, what's the plan?"

I rolled from my back to lean on one elbow as I looked at her. "You going to help?"

"Not the way you'd like, but if you promise to always work with Sandi or Fred or one of your other newspaper buddies, I'll tell him you're going to leave the investigating to them."

Sharon is usually in lock step with Ambrose, so I studied her for a second. "You would lie to Ambrose?"

"Of course not. You do have to promise. I'll tell him you're leaving it to them, and you will be sort of a consultant if they have questions. Then I'm not lying."

"Okay. Unless I go to the library to look up something, I'll work with Sandi or one of the others from the paper." *Mostly.*

CHAPTER ELEVEN

SUNDAY MORNING, I felt a lot better, so Sharon left about eight-thirty. She said, as long as I was recovering well, she might as well get home in time to fertilize her tomatoes and make Ambrose order feed for their horses.

I wasn't one-hundred percent, so I scanned the information sheet the hospital had given me. My symptoms were mild compared to some listed. After roughly thirty-six hours, my headache was largely gone, and I was tired. I didn't feel nauseous or dizzy.

It seemed the two most important things were not to do anything too physical and to be aware of how I felt. I didn't expect additional symptoms, certainly not serious ones, but recognized I probably shouldn't do heavy yard work for a few days, maybe even a week.

What a pain.

It would be smart to call Syl. To thank him, of course. I also hoped he would trust me enough to pay me to do some physically easy things, like walk the property to figure out where to trim bushes, to plant flowers, or even to create diagrams for how to lay out a couple flower beds.

After a quick shower, I called.

"Gardeners Unlimited," he answered.

"Excuse me?"

He laughed. "I saw your name on caller ID. How's the head?"

"Much better. Listen, thank you, and I want to apologize again. I shouldn't have been out there without your permission."

"Probably not safe for you to be anywhere alone at night at the moment. Apology accepted."

I took a breath of relief. "It may be a week or so before I can do strenuous work, but there are things I can do to keep things moving."

He listened as I outlined my ideas for prioritizing the work and planning flowerbeds.

"Sure. If you can get on your knees at all, pick up some colorful stuff from your farm place and plant a few things near the house. It'll look a lot better."

"Do you have any preferences for colors?"

"No, you can... Say, why don't you find someone else to do a couple of days' worth of digging weeds or whatever?"

It made sense, of course. Syl would want the work done sooner rather than later, no matter what shape my head was in. "I'm sure I can find someone. I'll ask around." We discussed an hourly rate for the person Syl referred to as 'your helper.'

When I hung up, I stared out the window for a while. Part of my brain was thinking of what I'd plant in the spots near Syl's house, another part was wondering if I would be able to weed at least the vegetable parts of my own garden. The final brain segment meandered through a list of people who might work with me at Syl's.

I thought about asking Andy from Farm and More, but he would gossip to everyone. Stooper kept coming to mind, too. He was usually sober in the afternoon. Plus, I should probably thank him for leaving a message on the *South County News* answering machine.

I had no phone number for Stooper, so I called the tavern. The bartender said the best time to talk to Stooper was when he came in 'to get started' about six in the evening.

My head wasn't up to deep thinking and even reading made my eyes tired. What I could do was get some bedding plants for Syl's place. Andy would be at Farm and More to needle me about being grouchy, so I went to the afternoon farmers' market to look for flowers. I wandered through the aisles, taking in the rhubarb and strawberries, wishing Missouri peaches were ripe.

I knew about half of the vendors. The mall at the edge of town, if you count six stores in a strip shopping center a true mall, lets local farmers use most of its parking area one evening each week and Sunday afternoon.

Most towns don't have Sunday markets, so the River's Edge market has a good draw. Since the occasional person who wanders into a shop at those times represents much of the business the mall gets from April to early November, the store merchants don't complain about fewer parking spaces.

In May, half of the farmers sell mostly bedding plants, plus a few early fruits. There's no room in my apartment for a bunch of pots, so I start ninety-nine percent of my vegetables in the yard. However, buying a couple tomato and squash plants means I get produce a few weeks earlier than from seeds.

"Melanie." John used a sing-song cadence. "Do I need to tell Ambrose you're doing too much?" I hadn't noticed him and his wife, Polly, checking out a bed of strawberry plants.

"No, Sharon won't back you up. She was here 'til yesterday." I smiled at Polly. "Is he this much trouble at home?"

She laughed, showing perfectly spaced teeth that accented her dark pink lipstick. "He can be useful." She raised a canvas tote that was on her arm. "When I get one more bag, he'll do the carrying."

"Yeah, yeah." John looked behind me. "Polly and I need to get to those tomato plants."

I wondered why he was in a hurry, and why Polly didn't protest, until a woman's voice warbled from behind me. "Melanie Perkins. Your parents would be shocked."

I closed my eyes for a second before turning to look at Eliza Wright. She thinks that commenting on others' behavior is some sort of public service. I disagree.

"Morning Eliza. Buying rhubarb?" The tart fruit would be appropriate for her.

She narrowed her eyes, which made her four-foot ten frame seem somehow smaller. "Of course not. No one grows rhubarb to match mine."

Of course not.

"What were you doing at a single man's home in the middle of the night?"

I heard John spew coffee and hoped it didn't reached Polly.

Nobody needs to wait for the Monday paper to get news.

"I'm doing gardening and lawn work for him. My new profession."

She lifted her chin and frowned. "At two something in the morning?"

"Night shade vegetables."

Nearby vendors coughed or laughed, but Eliza had no idea the term referred to specific vegetables, like eggplant or tomatoes, rather than any that needed special care after dark.

"My lands. He should take care of those himself. What is he like?"

At least I can laugh at her. Fred hates her because she repeated some of Hal's lies about why he fired Fred. "Mr. Seaton is very nice, very professional. You'll probably meet him at some point."

"What church does he go to?"

"No idea." With anyone else, I'd have suggested they call and invite him to theirs.

"Did you see a Bible in his home?"

A less suspicious person would say yes or no or that it was none of her business. I recognized the question as her attempt to learn if I'd been in his house. If I said yes, the next question would be what room was the Good Book in. "I usually talk to him on the porch."

It was sixty degrees, but Eliza was wearing two sweaters. She pulled the outer one tighter. "There are lots of good local boys in River's Edge."

I looked at my watch. "Gosh. Where does time go? I need to get some bedding plants, so I can get them in today." I turned and walked toward the end of the aisle so I could turn into the next one.

"You tell Ambrose I said hello, now."

I waved over my shoulder and kept going.

As I passed John, he murmured, "He'll love that."

I whispered, "Shut up," and kept walking.

I bought a flat of yellow marigolds and added four daisies, which were in six-inch pots. The farmer I bought them from loaded my flowers in his wheelbarrow and walked me to my truck. He was from the next town, so didn't know Eliza. Thus, he responded to her wave with a cheerful hello, which she took as a reason to talk to him.

I unlocked the back of the pick-up and waited while they visited about expected rain tomorrow and whether it would be a wet summer. By the time she asked how large his farm was, he had wised up and said he had to get back to his booth. He loaded my plants and made a quick getaway.

When I shut the back of the truck, Eliza was still there. She had a single, four-inch pot of zinnias.

I never buy them in pots. They germinate in no time. "Heading home to plant?" I asked.

"See? Lots of nice local men."

I tried not to smirk. "We chatted on the way out. He and his wife just had a little boy."

She leaned forward a couple of inches. "You don't have to be young to have a love life, you know."

I locked the back of the truck. "Who's hitting on you, Eliza?" *Fred would be proud of me.*

Eliza pulled back a bit, doing her best to look affronted. "I have not been with a man since my dear Joshua died fourteen years ago.

Go figure. "Yes, ma'am."

A smile played at her lips. "I was talking about someone we both know."

I dreaded hearing her gossip. I'd have to decide whether to refute her or warn a friend of the rumor.

"Hal turned into a real ladies' man the year before he died. Did you know that?"

I'll be in debt to Eliza. Who knew? "He seemed happier." *Lie, lie.* "We weren't sure who it was."

She leaned to within six inches of me. "Someone you know well."

"Ryan?" I asked, not smiling.

"Oh my, no." She looked at me with narrowed eyes. "Oh, you're joking."

Ryan will kill me. "Yes, ma'am."

"You know her," Eliza said.

It would kill her not to tell me, so no need to ask. "Maybe we should let Hal rest in peace."

She considered this, and in a voice that dripped honey, said, "Maybe you should ask Betty about that."

I knew to take anything Eliza said with a full tub of salt, so I kept a straight face. "Gee, Betty usually doesn't gossip."

Before she could say more, I told her Syl expected me to put the plants in today and almost hopped in my truck. She had no way to know I was fibbing.

BY THE TIME I left the farmers' market, I realized I would have to spend part of the afternoon napping. It was frustrating. I meant to nap for only a few minutes, but when I woke up, it was time to eat a quick supper so I could find Stooper at the tavern.

I was walking out the door when Ambrose called.

"You behaving yourself?"

"You can ask your buddy John. I ran into him at the farmers' market. He was Polly's bag man."

His tone showed irritation. "I thought you were going to take it easy."

"When's the last time you knew me to sit in my apartment all day?"

"But that was a lot of walking."

"Ambrose, didn't Sharon tell you I pledged to be careful and rely on my friends if I needed them?"

"Yes, but..."

"How was the Farm Bureau meeting? Anything juicy I should pass on to Fred or Sandi?"

"You're trying to change the subject," he groused.

"I appreciate all you do, but did Sharon boss you around when you were twenty-seven?"

After about three seconds of silence, he sighed. "Just try not to have the sheriff on your case when your head's banged up."

I WAS SURPRISED at all the people in the tavern at six PM. The tavern, whose formal name is Beer Rental

Heaven, is smaller than the *South County News* bullpen. Dark paneling makes it seem dingy, though it really isn't. Owner Gary Bradley has a cleaning crew come in every morning, and he keeps the large wooden bar polished.

Shirley sat on a stool near a tall, round table on the far side of the room. When she saw me squinting around the room, she raised her beer. "Come over here, sugar."

There was no sign of Stooper, so I walked toward Shirley. "So, this is where you go when the coffee runs out?" *And by the way, did you come here with Hal?*

She laughed. "You know full well Sunday is Ladies Night. Only way Gary gets people in here Sundays. Beer's half price for us. First one's on me."

I held up a hand. "Not drinking for a few days. The whack on the head is getting better, but I don't want to push my luck."

Shirley was somber, not a side she often exhibits. "You've had some rough things happen to you the last couple years."

"Yep. Trying not to let Hal's death get to me."

"Good for you."

"So, Shirley, can I ask you a question?"

"You ask me questions all the time."

I grinned. "Besides what the special is."

"Shoot."

"None of us at the paper really knew Hall outside work. Did he have any friends at all?"

She took a swig of beer. "Friends? I don't know. The only thing I know is he was always writing something."

"You mean you think he took work home?"

"Don't know about that. I was in Ottumwa one time, at that bookstore on Second Street. Not there anymore. Remember it?"

I nodded.

"They ordered some book for him, and he looked at it and didn't want it. They were hopping mad. Guy said he'd asked Hal to be sure it was what he wanted, because it was expensive. And heavy to mail back to the supplier."

"What was it about?"

She smiled. "Being a private investigator. He saw me when he was storming out, but he didn't stop."

"But you asked him about it?"

"Next time he was in for coffee. He said he was writing some kind of crime novel and he wanted to learn how detectives investigated."

I raised my eyebrows. "I never heard a word about him writing fiction."

Shirley shrugged. "Maybe somebody'll find a draft when his house is..."

A sort of whiney voice reached us. "What was you doin' at that Sylvester's place at night?"

I hadn't noticed Andy at the table next to Shirley. This was probably because his arms had been folded on the table in front of him, and the crease on one cheek told me his head had been on them until just now.

"Early to bed, Andy?" I asked.

Shirley laughed. "He's not snoring yet, sugar."

Andy gave both of us a sour look. "I heard you was maybe where you weren't 'sposed to be."

I tried to keep irritation from my tone, but didn't entirely succeed. "I couldn't sleep."

"My wife tries warm milk."

Shirley put her hand over her mouth to hide a smile.

"I was thinking about Hal. Milk didn't work."

Andy opened his mouth to say something, but the door to the street banged open and he glanced at it.

Stooper stood, not swaying, and surveyed the room. I couldn't imagine why. He knows what it looks like.

He took in me sitting with Shirley, said, "Huh," and made his way to the bar.

I looked at Shirley. "I want to talk to Stooper before he, um, has a few."

She winked and raised her beer mug slightly in my direction. I smiled and moved toward Stooper, who was talking to Gary.

"See, since I'm in here every night, I think I should get half price for ladies night, too."

"Stooper," Gary rubbed the bar with a cloth as he spoke, "we've been over this. If I let you do it, then Andy'll ask. Pretty soon all the guys will get pissy if I don't give them two for one."

I sat on a stool next to Stooper and looked at Gary. "Can I do two for one and give one to Stooper?"

"Sure, Mel," Gary said. He looked anything but pleased as he pulled two beers for us.

I placed a bill on the bar as he set down the beer. "That enough for a tip, too?"

He nodded and walked to the other end of the bar.

I figured I'd really ticked him off.

"Thanks," Stooper said. "I don't think I know anything for the paper."

I met his eyes in the mirror behind the bar. "Don't work there any more, remember?

"Oh, yeah. Gardening stuff." He drank half the mug in one long gulp. When a couple drops made their way down his chin, I handed him a cocktail napkin from a pile on the bar.

He took it. "Thanks. What's up, Mel?"

"I need some help with the gardening stuff."

"Me?"

"It's not a lot of work, and it could be just a couple of hours some days, late afternoon. I hurt my head, so I can't do real physical work for a while. I mean, it's not heavy stuff. Weeding, spreading mulch, like that."

He swiveled to face me. "Guess you don't want to do the mulch anymore."

I sighed. "Mulch is fine, and more's already been delivered to Mr. Seaton's."

Andy spoke from just behind me. "He told me to call him Syl when I brought more."

God give me strength.

I turned to face Andy. "Ditto. Did you need something?"

Andy looked at Stooper. "Don't you think she's kind of grouchy lately?"

Stooper's reply was very serious. "She's not used to finding bodies."

Behind me, Shirley laughed, but I didn't look at her.

"True. Sorry Andy. I'm just trying to talk to Stooper." I swiveled to face the mirror.

Andy muttered as he walked toward the other end of the bar. The only words I heard clearly were "stuck up."

Stooper actually grinned at me. "He likes to know what's going on."

"I've noticed."

Stooper drained his mug. "Sure, I can help you out."

"For money," I said. "Syl's money, not mine."

"Huh. Even better. Not every day."

Our eyes met in the mirror again. "How about tomorrow about four. You need a ride?"

"I live on that end of town. Meet you there. Four is good."

"Thanks. Oh, Stooper. Thanks for calling the paper to say you saw me at the hospital."

"Huh. Didn't think I gave my name." He considered this for a couple of seconds. "I guess I probably sounded drunk."

"Gee, Sandi didn't say that." *It wouldn't have been necessary.*

He looked at my untouched beer. "You gonna finish that?"

AFTER MY FUN TIME at Beer Rental Heaven, I sat in the recliner and made lists of what I knew and needed to find out. Or, to keep my promise to Sharon, what I needed to work with Sandi, Ryan or Fred to find out.

The what-I-knew list was short and wasn't too different than what had been in the paper or what the neighbors had told me.

What I needed to know was:

- Where's the damn autopsy report and will it pinpoint the time of death?
- Where is Hal's car?
- Where was Hal killed?
- Are there security cameras that might have caught his car the night he was killed?

The question about where he was killed would be the start. No one was going to stand up and claim they did it, unless Morton Anderson's medal came with a huge cash prize.

- Did Betty have a fling with Hal, and was she mad it ended?

The question about Hal and Betty was really touchy. If they had been lovers or even close friends, it was their business. Unless Betty had killed Hal, but it didn't seem likely. How on earth would she have gotten him into the mulch? I supposed she could've teamed up with someone else Hal had annoyed. *That'll be a tough list to narrow down.*

Still, if Betty, Shirley, or anyone else had seen Hal outside the office, they could know more about his personal life. I'd have to find a way to get them to talk about their love lives. I wrinkled my nose. It was hard to imagine anyone snuggling with Hal.

No matter what I considered, there was the issue of my hoe. The murderer knew I was working for Syl and knew where I kept my tools.

CHAPTER TWELVE

MONDAY WAS CRISP, and overnight rain had given the air a fresh smell. I decided that was a reason to be optimistic about finding the truth. What I needed were facts, and they weren't going to come from the sheriff or IDI. I thought my best options were research on Hal's past and information from his autopsy report. It was ridiculous that we didn't have it.

I headed for the library. It's in a small building behind the Chamber of Commerce office, just off the square. The brick structure used to house the town's telephone equipment, but many years ago the Rural Electric Cooperative helped River's Edge get a grant for more modern service.

Nowadays, the big phone companies would be willing to string phone lines or provide digital service, but the town is adamant about keeping its own phone company. I used to wonder why, but as phone service prices have gone up around us, I get it.

I parked in the library parking lot and slowly got out of the truck. I wasn't woozy, but the world still had a bit of extra spin.

Kimberly was at the library's front desk. She's thirty-five and still likes to be called Kimi. "Gosh, Melanie, I'm glad to see you're up and around." She waved all five fingers, with their perfectly manicured, bright red nails.

"Hey, Kimi. I'm not top shape, but a lot better. Thought I'd get a book on CD for the truck." I didn't really want one, because sometimes they end up under my seat and I have to pay a fine. It was better than starting the conversation by saying I was here to find out more about Hal's life before River's Edge, though.

"We have some new ones. Mrs. Stevens' son donated a bunch after she died a few days ago."

I followed her back to the audio section. Kimi recommended two new Nora Roberts' books, but I went with Robert Harris's *Pompeii,* which I'd read in paper and thought would be interesting to listen to.

I had followed Kimi to the check-out counter before asking, "Do you know if there was an obituary for Hal in a paper near where he grew up?"

She stopped going through the CDs to be sure they were all there. "Gosh, I'm not sure I know where he was from."

"I think he grew up in Iowa Falls, or at least that's where he was for a time."

"Hmm. We don't have a paper from there, but we have an index of Iowa papers. Oh, it probably wouldn't be in it yet." She brightened. "What am I saying? Go online, the paper up there probably puts its obits online."

She handed me my book, and I headed for the computer. A Google search usually only turned up articles from the last ten or fifteen years. I wanted older articles. The library subscribed to the Iowa newspaper index. The *South County News* did, too, but I wasn't up for asking for access to it.

I found the Iowa Falls paper with no problem, but was disappointed to see its index was grouped in five-year increments. I'd have to search several times for the same topic.

Starting with papers from thirty years ago, I searched for Hal Morris, Morris family, house fires, fatal car accidents, and murder suspect. My rationale was that something bad must have happened to Hal to make him such an ill-natured jerk.

I found nothing except the title and date of an article about Hal buying the *South County News*. It was frustrating not to be able to read the article, but it probably didn't offer clues to Hal's temperament. Either he had been the way he was for some private reason, or he'd been spoiled rotten as a kid and didn't know how to get along with anyone.

Just as I reached for the Off button on the computer monitor, I thought about the Iowa Falls obituaries. They might be available by date. Sure enough, a four-paragraph article began with the date of death and immediately mentioned he was murdered.

The obituary said Hal had been an assistant editor at an Iowa Falls paper for several years. The third paragraph said he had been orphaned in his teens and had stayed with a local family until he graduated from high school, because he had no other relatives.

In one sentence I might have the answer to Hal's anger with the world. Not that I'd ever know. However, it told me there might not be a later event that shaped his temperament. I'd been half expecting to see that he was bilked out of a small fortune or created enemies by recommending people join a pyramid scheme.

I'd been older than Hal when my parents died, but only by a few years. It was sad. But there didn't appear to be a dramatic story behind his rudeness.

I closed the file and decided to learn about Syl Seaton. There probably weren't too many Sylvester

Seatons in the country, but I thought I'd try Iowa before I went to Los Angeles.

It took about thirty seconds to find a *Des Moines Register* article about the contract he got for the insurance company. Except it wasn't with a particular firm. It was with a state insurance industry organization. My eyes widened. It was a $1.2 million contract to compare products each Iowa company offered, rates that were publicly available, aggregate claims data, and a lot more. Syl was described as an experienced business analyst who had worked in several states, including California and Wisconsin.

Insurance is a big industry in Des Moines. I was surprised there weren't local firms that could do the work. Five minutes later, I found two letters to the editor saying that plenty of local businesses could have handled the contract. The final mention of him was a terse statement from the company that awarded the contract saying that a competitive bidding process ensured the best product for the best price. The letters had been several paragraphs. The statement was a one-inch item in the business section of the paper.

While the material gave me a better understanding of what Syl would do, it didn't sound like the kind of work that would entail having henchmen watch his house and hit people over the head.

All in all, I felt as if I'd just wasted an hour of my life.

That meant trying to get information on Hal's death. Since that would not come from the sheriff, I headed for the county coroner. The position is a part-time one, and Iowa law requires the person to be a physician. The official title has been medical examiner, probably since before I was born, but the term is only slowly taking root. It might not have at all except TV shows usually say medical examiner. Since I wanted to talk to the South County examiner, I reminded myself to use the correct term.

Doc Shelton is the local physician most people go to for colds or whatever, but he isn't the medical examiner. Doctor James T. MacGregor, Jr., is head of pathology and hematology at the hospital, but it's not like he's the one who draws your blood. People mostly deal with him if they have some kinds of cancer or an infection gets into their bloodstream. Either way, you might not be his patient for long.

Dr. MacGregor's office is in the hospital, so the only way to get hold of him is to call or go there. I decided to visit, since I had no idea who would get my phone call. I didn't want a rumor about me having some infectious disease. Even more important, I didn't want someone calling Ambrose to see if I was okay. Privacy laws only go so far in a small town.

Southern Iowa Memorial is a twenty-five bed hospital. When I did a story on its fiftieth anniversary, I learned that so-called critical-access rural hospitals get Medicare payments from Uncle Sam that correspond to the cost of their services. Larger hospitals only get to recover a percentage of costs. The full reimbursement policy is supposed to keep smaller-town hospitals open, and I'm glad it seems to work.

I parked in the hospital's back lot and went in the door near occupational and physical therapy, which is close to the blood unit. My mother used to go there to donate blood. I keep meaning to do that.

My running shoes squeaked on the impeccably clean tile floor. Along the beige walls were pastel paintings of peaceful scenes, probably to calm nervous patients. If I had to pick a favorite, it wouldn't be the one that showed pink marigolds. I've never seen even a hybrid in anything but shades of orange or yellow.

I paused outside the wide glass door that opened to the hematology waiting room. Dr. MacGregor's name was on the door, but I didn't know if his office was in the suite. Only one way to find out.

The automatic door swished apart, and I glanced around the waiting room. A very elderly black man was reading a copy of *Family Circle* magazine that was past its prime. A quick look told me it was the only reading option. He didn't look up.

The woman behind the long counter smiled in recognition. "Hey Melanie. Glad to see you looking good." She sombered. "I'm sorry about Hal."

"Thanks, Rosemary. Tough week, but I'm good." I waited for a minute as she took a phone call. She's only about twenty. Rosemary went through a medical assistant program at a business college in Des Moines. She was disappointed that the only job she could get was as a medical receptionist.

She hung up. "What's up, Mel?"

I took a breath. "I wonder if I could talk to Dr. MacGregor for a minute?"

Rosemary doesn't frown, she sort of does a pout of concentration. "Do you have an appointment?"

"No. It's not about me." I lowered my voice. "It's about Hal."

Her puzzled look cleared. "Oh. You mean because Dr. MacGregor's the medical examiner."

No, I mean I wondered what his good cholesterol was. "Yes. You know I don't work for the paper any more..."

She grinned. "Everyone knows that."

I smiled even as I did an internal groan. "It was...odd finding him. I know Dr. MacGregor didn't examine him, but I'd still like to talk to him."

She shrugged. "Since you aren't reporting, I can ask." She stood and walked down a carpeted hallway on the left.

I glanced at the silent man and his magazine, noticing that he had a hearing aid. Good.

Rosemary came back and nodded to me. "See that gate in the wood, on the left?"

I hadn't seen it, probably because no handles or hinges were visible. I nodded.

"I'll buzz you back."

At the sound of the buzzer, the man looked up. "You got right in."

"I'm not getting lab work done. Just talking to someone."

He nodded, seemingly satisfied that I wasn't butting ahead of him, and resumed reading.

It was only a few steps to a door on my right. It was open, and Dr. MacGregor looked up as I walked in. "Have a seat, Melanie. Glad you don't look much worse for wear." He looked at me more closely. "Is that a bruise near your right ear?"

"Yes, sir. I shouldn't have been at Syl Seaton's place after dark." I sat across from him in a chair with a leather seat and back and wooden arms. The formal chairs matched Dr. MacGrgor's stiff posture.

"Goodness." He took off his dark framed glasses, folded them, and placed them on the desk. "I read that short piece in today's paper, but I didn't realize you were seriously hurt."

Thankfully, the article was largely an update on Hal's murder. After the article continued on a back page, it said that this was 'the second crime within a week on the property recently purchased by Sylvester Seaton.' The attack on me and my hospital stay were mentioned, but so was the fact that Syl had hired me to work on his yard. Someone who didn't notice that I'd been hit about two-thirty a.m. might infer that I was knocked out while digging up weeds.

I smiled. "Not badly. But someone else was there, and they didn't want me around."

He shook his head. "Something to do with Hal's murder, you think?"

I was relieved. I'd been afraid Dr. MacGregor would go all doctor-patient privacy on me and not be willing to talk. "Makes sense to me."

"Why were you out there in the middle of the night?"

I told him the truth, but didn't refer to the broom which, thankfully, had not been mentioned in the paper.

He joined his hands as if praying, but brought the fingers to his chin. "I probably shouldn't talk to you, but I knew your parents, of course, and Rosemary said you're not here for the paper."

I nodded. "If you did the autopsy, we'd know the results by now. I suppose they sent him to Des Moines because it was more convenient for the IDI guys."

He shook his head. "Sheriff Gallagher explained that Hal was so universally disliked anyone could have killed him. He didn't want information getting around. I didn't like it, but I had to respect his decision."

"He's a smart guy." I sighed. "It feels as if whoever did it wants the sheriff to think I killed him." *Should I mention the hoe*? No. "That's why I really want to know what killed him."

He stared at me, still leaning his chin on his fingers. Apparently he decided it was okay to talk to me. He lowered his hands to his desk and drummed on it for a few seconds with his right fingers. "Two blows to the head. The first one would have knocked him silly, but he would have survived. Second one led to so much swelling he likely died within an hour, maybe a good bit less. Can't be sure, but there was such a scant amount of mulch in his lungs that...."

"My God. He was alive when someone put him in there?"

MacGregor's tone was gentle. "Barely, but not conscious. He didn't smother, if that's what you hate to think about."

I let out a breath. "I guess it is. But," I rubbed goose bumps on my arms, "it means someone probably knew he was alive. Maybe he was in their trunk alive..."

MacGregor stopped me by shaking his head. "If so, Hal was not conscious. Don't dwell on it. Besides, I'm not convinced he was killed elsewhere."

I stared, eyebrows lifting and eyes widening. "Why would he have been there? I mean, I can't think of any reason why. He barely knew, barely knew...."

"Mr. Seaton?" MacGregor supplied.

Something tripped in my brain, and I thought I remembered that Hal said he'd bought Syl coffee, which he usually did at the diner, since it was cheap. *When I saw Syl there a few days ago, he said it was his first time at the diner. Was one of them lying?*

"Melanie?"

I had been staring at Dr. MacGregor, not speaking. "I'm sorry. I was trying to remember if Hal had even met Syl. Mr. Seaton. What, uh, makes you think he was killed there?"

"That would be too strong a statement. I read the report. Sheriff has it. Probably be released today or tomorrow."

Great. I could have waited. "That's why you're talking to me."

He nodded. "You can come back after you read it." My face must have conveyed surprise, because he smiled. "Your mom brought me meatloaf after my mother died."

I swallowed hard.

Dr. MacGregor became more business-like again. "Neither the heels of his shoes nor back of his pants or the front, for that matter, showed signs of being dragged. That's a lot of dead weight to lift. Two people could have carried him, but even then his back would have been dragged, probably."

Dead weight?

I spoke slowly. "I just assumed he was killed somewhere else and brought there."

Dr. MacGregor shrugged. "He could have been. Most of the bodies I examine are sudden deaths. I verify a heart attack or stroke. Car accident victims, that kind of thing. I read about criminal death examinations, of course. You should talk to Sheriff Gallagher when this is all public."

Oh yeah. He'll talk to a suspect.

I WENT HOME TO rest for a few minutes before going to the paper. Ambrose and Sharon would be proud.

When I got to the *South County News* office, no one was at the front desk. Sandi was standing by the copier, feeding it pages. I called to her.

When she turned to look at me, Sandi's expression was what could be termed frosty. I frowned and shrugged, my way of asking what was going on that she didn't like. She raised her eyebrows and turned back to the copier.

What bee is in her bonnet? I sat in the folding chair next to Sandi's desk and watched her walk toward me. I could do that because she wasn't looking at me.

Sandi slid into her chair and turned over a paper on her desk. "What's up, Melanie?"

"I came by to talk to you guys, and… Why are you acting weird? You turned that paper over so I wouldn't see it."

She stared at me briefly. "I figured you were here to talk to Fred, and I have other work to do."

She wasn't going to answer me directly, so I decided to plow ahead. "I talked to Dr. MacGregor about Hal's autopsy report."

I expected Sandi to exhibit her non-poker face, but she was almost blasé. "Fred'll be glad to hear that."

"What's with the Fred business? What's wrong with you?"

"You don't have to pretend," she said.

I raised my voice. "Pretend what?"

Her aloof front cracked, and she tilted her head as she looked at me. "That you and Fred really aren't working together and alone on Hal's death."

I was flummoxed, and it had to show. "We aren't working alone. We agreed to share information."

The cold stare was back. "Exactly."

"Sandi, if you don't tell me what the hell you're mad about, I'll, I'll…"

"Leave Ryan and me out of the story?"

"Leave you out? What do you mean?"

Her face relaxed. "Fred said you were to work directly with him on anything to do with Hal. Ryan and I should 'go about our usual business.' I think that's how he put it."

I hadn't realized I'd moved to the edge of my chair, and slid back. "That's ridiculous. You guys are all over town. You'll hear stuff."

She seemed more like her friendly self as she leaned toward me. "That's what I said. He was adamant."

"It makes no sense." I regarded her, shoulder-length red hair pulled back in a scrunchie and tan blouse sporting a chunky necklace of what looked like medium-sized brown rocks. "Fred and I never talked about that."

Sandi leaned forward. "So, Dr. MacGregor had seen…?"

The door to the street opened. Sandi hastily picked up papers from her desk and looked toward the door. "Hey Fred, look who's here."

Fred had his briefcase in one hand and a cup of coffee in the other, with an apple balanced on top of its lid. "Melanie. Didn't expect you."

I wondered why Fred didn't want me to work with Sandi, but wasn't about to let on she'd told me that. I gave him my usual smile. "Morning Fred. Didn't know I'd need an appointment."

He stopped a few feet from Sandi and me and gave her an impassive glance. "Just meant I'm not always here this early." He jerked his head toward his office. "Come on back."

"Later, Mel," Sandi said. "Your head okay?"

"Better every day." I followed Fred to his office and stayed by the door as he set down his coffee and pulled some papers from his briefcase. The office looked less like Hal's space.

A couple of cardboard boxes sat near the window. They probably had Hal's personal items or background papers from whatever he'd been working on. He printed everything, unlike everyone else, who downloaded articles onto their computers.

The small bookcase now had books I recognized as Fred's. Among them were his battered Thesaurus, a couple of books on Iowa history, and the style and word usage guides he preferred.

I glanced at him. He'd been watching me, it seemed. I smiled. "Looks like you."

He nodded and gestured to the chair across from the desk. "I almost didn't bring any of my stuff back, but Doc Shelton said it could be a few months before the paper's sold and a new editor's picked."

I sat. "Why so long?"

"Hal didn't have a will, so everything has to go through probate. There's no one to contest the sale, but they have to figure out what to do with the proceeds. No one can find any family."

"Much less his murderer."

Fred met my eyes. "No kidding. Figure out anything?"

I felt like I was talking to a stranger rather than the guy I used to grab a burger with after work. "Sheriff probably still doesn't believe I killed Hal, but my favorite IDI agent acts like he thinks I was at Syl's that night to destroy evidence."

"In all fairness, can you see his point?"

"I can. But I'm not an idiot. Why would I go there at night, when I'd stick out like a corn stalk in a bean field? I can do what I want when I'm there working."

Fred gave a fleeting grin. "You probably don't want to go around town saying that."

"Too true. I did learn one thing." I leaned forward. "Ran into Eliza at the farmers' market yesterday." I relayed some of what she had said. "So, do you know anything about a special friend Hal had?"

"Maybe someone recently committed," Fred murmured, as he slowly shook his head. "Or just let out. You have any ideas?"

"I think I'd have more luck asking around about it. Women could feel more comfortable with another woman."

He nodded. "Plus, technically you aren't a reporter."

And you don't want the other reporters working on this.

"Did Sandi find out anything about Hal's car? I had just walked in and hadn't had time to ask her."

Fred frowned. "How'd you know she was looking?"

I didn't want to say it was my idea. Sandi and I share a lot, so if she hadn't told Fred that, she had a reason. "We both kind of wondered about it when we were talking about his neighbors. Guy across from Hal's house said he parked it in the driveway, not the garage."

"No one knows where it is," Fred said.

"Are you going to mention that in the paper?"

"I'm doing a follow-up piece that will be in the paper at the end of the week."

And you didn't say whether you would talk about that. "Okay, so you need anything I might find out by Wednesday, right?"

At this, Fred appeared to relax. "That would be great. You can email, if you want."

"Sure." As I stood I noticed that the pile of folders was no longer on the credenza. Fred is almost compulsively neat. "I know it's a stretch, but would you mind if I went through those folders that were on the credenza?"

"Uh, let's see. I don't mind. I...should probably ask Doc Shelton, in case there would be questions about you looking at it."

"Oh, sure. Let me know."

Fred nodded, seemingly thinking.

"I'll bug Sandi on my way out."

"Listen, Mel." Fred tried to unlink two paperclips that were on his desk. "Given that there could be a murderer hanging out in town, probably is, I told Sandi and Ryan I wanted to carry the water on this."

"Ah. But if you're not around, I can clue her in on what I found, right?"

He looked at me. "You've got my mobile."

"Sure." I moved toward the door. "I'll talk to you tomorrow afternoon, if not before."

I looked around the bullpen. Sandi wasn't at her desk. Ryan was hanging up a windbreaker on the row of hooks near the small kitchen just off the bullpen, in the back.

"Hey, Ryan."

He looked at me with a passive expression that said he thought I had teamed up with Fred to deliberately leave him and Sandi in the cold.

"Hey to you, Mel. Doing okay?"

"Much better." I walked onto the sidewalk, and someone in a car half a block away flashed their headlights at me. It was Sandi.

I nodded and walked to my truck. When I began to drive in the direction of the diner, she followed me and flashed her lights again. I pulled to the right and she drove around me. Apparently we were going to talk somewhere else.

A minute later she drove into the Hy-Vee parking lot, and I pulled into a parking space a few away from hers. It registered that she was in her own car, a blue Toyota Corolla, rather than the paper's little Fiesta.

She was closer to the store, but didn't wait for me. *What is this? The Watergate parking garage?*

Sandi walked toward the dairy display in the back of the store. When I got there a few seconds after she did, she was inspecting a carton of yogurt.

I took a half-gallon of milk from the refrigerator and walked to her. "I don't really like the Greek yogurt. Too creamy."

"Sorry for the subterfuge," she said. "I didn't want Fred to see us together."

"Sandi, if this is subterfuge, don't apply at the CIA."

She faced me, unsmiling. "It's like he doesn't want us to know what happened that night."

I wanted to say I agreed, but didn't. "Makes it kind of hard to cover the story."

"You know what happened that day, don't you? The afternoon, I mean."

"Fred told Sharon he found out his unemployment appeal was denied."

She nodded. "He called Hal. Fred was in Des Moines, so thank God he couldn't come in right away. You could hear them scream all over the office."

"Both of them?"

"Just Hal. But he yelled, 'Fred, you were never worth a dime of what I paid you.' He said that to Fred, of all people."

"Fred was the best of us. By far." I didn't mind saying this. He was thorough and never sensationalized. Not that a lot of what went on would fall into the sensational category in River's Edge. *Until Hal showed up with a tangerine in his mouth.*

"Why?" Sandi asked. "Why isn't he having Ryan and me all over this?"

"You know what you're not saying, right?"

Sandi started to tear up, but shook her head slightly and straightened her shoulders. "I can't believe he would kill Hal."

"Certainly not on pur..." I stopped, and turned to see who was behind the squeaky grocery cart approaching us. "Damn." It was Eliza.

"Hello, girls," she trilled. "Always good to see my two favorite reporters." Anytime Eliza wanted something, whoever she was talking to was her favorite whatever or her good friend. As is her custom, she had on a heavy, wool coat, far warmer than the temperature required.

"Hello, Eliza. Did you get everything you wanted at the farmers' market yesterday?"

"Oh, yes. But selection is still so limited. I'm here for grapefruit and apples."

Sandi started to walk toward the front of the store with her yogurt.

"Have you two heard the latest about Hal?"

Sandi stopped. Eliza had our full attention.

"What's that?" I asked.

"Don't think so," Sandi said.

She almost sang. "Sheriff just issued a press release. Autopsy results are out."

Before Sandi could speak, I said, "I heard they'd be out today. Guess I'll head for the Sheriff's Office." I started for the cash register, and Sandi scampered ahead of me.

"Don't you want to know more about it?" Eliza sounded almost desperate to impart what she knew.

"Need to read it first-hand." I said this over my shoulder, without stopping. I didn't mind ruining her morning.

Sandi and I had paid and were out the door before Eliza and her squeaky cart got to the register.

As we walked out, she asked, "Will you make me a copy?"

"Jeez, Fred'll have to show you that."

Her phone rang as I was talking and she answered it. "Okay. Sure. At Hy-Vee, getting yogurt for lunch." She listened for several seconds. "Okay. See you there."

"Fred," she said, clearly angry as she put her phone in the pocket of her slacks. "He's picking up the autopsy report and says he'll see me at the office. He wants to be sure it isn't too gory for me to see."

"Kind of hard to know more about how he died without seeing it."

"You'll get it right?" she asked. "Dinner at that barbeque place on the edge of town. Fred hates it."

I stood still while she pulled out of the parking space.

Sandi rolled down her window. "Park a couple of blocks away, okay? Seven."

WHEN I GOT TO the Sheriff's Office, Fred was already standing at the counter that separates the public from staff. He was beet red, staring at Sheriff Gallagher.

Fred's voice rose with every word. "That's ridiculous, sheriff. It's public information."

"Information that was released by the medical examiner in Des Moines. The county supervisors said they want people to get it from him, not me." Sheriff Gallagher's expression was neutral, but his posture said he thought Fred was out of line.

Fred's fists were balled at his side. He opened his mouth, closed it, then opened it again to spit out, "Fine."

He turned so quickly he could have bumped into me if I hadn't stepped aside. "Mel. You won't get any help here."

I nodded. "You want me to drive to Des Moines for you?"

He took a breath and spoke calmly. "No. I need to head up there for a quick meeting at the *Register*."

The door to the street was hydraulic, or he might have slammed it. I looked at Sheriff Gallagher.

He spoke quietly. "Sent a copy to your lawyer, since you're so popular with IDI." He pointed a finger at me. "What I do is my business. You don't need to tell Fred that."

I smiled faintly. "Won't come up."

As I turned toward the door, I saw that Sophie and a young deputy, Newt Harmon, I thought, appeared to have paused in mid-activity.

"And Melanie."

I turned to face Gallagher.

"You probably don't want to look at the pictures.

CHAPTER THIRTEEN

SHERIFF GALLAGHER WAS RIGHT. I looked at the photos and wished I hadn't. But, it seemed important to see them.

The most relevant point, noted after particulars of Hal's age, date of birth and such, was that the cause of death was listed as homicide, blunt force cranial trauma. I thought about not reading more, but forced myself.

The medical examiner's notes started with how the body came to him, so in a black body bag. Hal had been dressed in a long-sleeved blue cotton shirt, khaki twill cargo pants, and black leather shoes.

The body was described as that of a normally developed, well-nourished Caucasian male measuring 70 inches in length, weighing 187 pounds, and appearing generally consistent with the stated age of fifty-eight years. The body was cold and unembalmed with rigor having begun but progressed little.

The only thing that told me for sure was that Hal lied about his height and weight. He wasn't the six feet tall he'd always claimed, and he always said he weighed

170 pounds. Not that it mattered now. What I needed to find out was how soon after death rigor began.

I didn't care what his brain weighed, but did note that his skull was "symmetric and evidences extensive trauma in the occipital region." I looked for a trash can when I read that, "Subdural hematoma and comminuted fractures of the occipital bone are observed."

Fortunately, a few deep breaths settled my stomach. It calmed more when I went to the water fountain for a deep drink and then walked around the conference room for almost a minute.

Hal's cardiovascular system was essentially normal, but while aspects of his respiratory system seemed to be, one thing stood out. "There is no obstruction of the airway, but minute amounts of shredded wood were observed." The medical examiner noted the deceased may have taken a few breaths after being covered in brown mulch.

That information required another walk around the conference room.

Hal's lungs were noted as unremarkable.

Obviously you never had to listen to him yell.

I deliberately did not read about Hal's male genital or urinary systems, but did note that there were "approximately 125 ml of partially digested semisolid food" in his stomach. This seemed like a lot if a person had eaten supper at a traditional time and nothing after that. I wished it had said what kind of food. On television the medical examiner sometimes finds an item sold only at one local restaurant. In Iowa, half the stomach contents would hold part of a pork tenderloin sandwich, so knowing the undigested food might be no help.

Most toxicology results were inconclusive, but the report did note that he had no carbon monoxide in his blood and his blood alcohol level was approximately .14.

"Wow."

Ken Brownberg had apparently been near the door and looked into the conference room. "What's wow?"

"He had almost two times the legal limit for alcohol."

Brownberg nodded, unsmiling. "He certainly would have had difficulty avoiding an attacker."

"Maybe he had a drinking partner that night. Do you know of anyone he spent time with?"

Brownberg shook his head, slowly. "No direct knowledge. I saw Shirley sit with him at the diner a few times."

"You mean to chat for a second?"

He shrugged. "When she's on break she takes off her name badge."

"Good observation, counselor."

He raised his eyebrows as he spoke. "You know, if you do need an attorney for a defense, it can't be me. I do almost all civil work. The occasional under-the-influence case, but that's about it."

I nodded. "I don't plan to need a defense."

"Let's hope. Stop by on your way out, and I'll give you a couple of names, just in case."

"May I make a copy?"

"I can have my secretary do it."

"I don't, uh, want all the photos. Maybe just one of the injury, one of his head." As I said that, I must have blanched.

"Want some coffee?"

"Nope. Not exactly the calm my stomach craves."

He nodded and walked in the direction of his office.

All that was left was the summary, which described Hal's injuries. "Blunt force traumatic injury with multiple cranial fractures resulting in craniocerebral injury. The narrow wound measures approximately 3 inches high x 1/2 inches wide. Subdural hematoma and comminuted fractures of the occipital bone are observed.

Depths of bone fragment penetration range from 1/2 inch to 2 inches. Fatal injury appears to have resulted from a blow administered to the posterior of the head, delivered at an approximate 80° angle to the occipital bone."

I leaned over the waste basket and got rid of the water I'd been drinking.

The most important point was at the end of the summary. Based on the state of rigor mortis, time of death was estimated to be between 12 and 3 a.m.

What had Hal been doing that ticked off someone so late at night?

WORKING IN SYL'S garden would be a good break from thinking of Hal's crushed skull. A glance at my watch as I pulled into his driveway showed two-forty-five. I figured Syl must be in Des Moines. No Stooper, but he wasn't due yet.

I separated plants in eight of the six-packs of marigolds and placed individual plants around the front and side gardens. The daisies being perennials, I wanted to be more certain about where they went. They sat on the front steps.

I surveyed the marigold distribution. They needed to be fairly evenly spaced, but they would soon be ten times larger, spread in any direction they wanted. No spacing would stay precise.

My eyes wandered around the front and side yards. Because of Dr. MacGregor's comments, I had to consider that Hal had been killed at Syl's rather than elsewhere. Why couldn't there be a button from the murderer's coat mixed in with driveway gravel? There wouldn't be. River's Edge wasn't a television show. Besides, between the sheriff's deputies and IDI, they would have found anything lying around.

Did Hal bleed after he was hit? It was hard to imagine that a hard blow would not break the skin, but what did I know? On TV, police sprayed something that made even scrubbed-away blood stains turn bluish green. I wondered whether the area around the former mulch pile had been sprayed? I decided to assume it had. The photos didn't show blood on Hal's clothes, so there might not have been blood on the ground. *Ugh.*

Gravel crunching made me turn.

Stooper was only about three yards from me. "Anyone could sneak up on you."

"You're right." He appeared to have showered, and his hair, which hung just below his chin, was neatly trimmed. His jeans and tee-shirt had holes, but you don't wear good jeans to do yard work. "I brought some bottles of water for us."

Stooper looked slowly around the lawn and flower beds closest to the house. "This how it looked when you found Hal?"

His question surprised me. Partially because he sounded so sober. "Pretty much. I'd cleared some undergrowth near the house. Syl, Mr. Seaton, thought if we spread the mulch and planted a few flowers it would look a lot better."

He glanced at my wheelbarrow, which was near the back of the driveway. "Andy told me he wouldn't put the mulch in the same place."

I sighed, exasperated. "He drove it almost to the barn. We have to cart it further to get to the front."

"Mike at McKinney's Garage said he tuned up that little tractor and oiled the wheels on some kind of cart."

"Everyone knows everybody else's business in this town."

He grinned briefly. "It'll make it easier on my back."

"Of course. I'll show you where...damn! I don't have a key to the tractor."

"Mike said it's taped to the bottom of the seat."

Of course it is.

Stooper and I walked to the barn together, and he started the tractor with no problem. A pin was almost rusted into its spot on the front of cart, but once it came out it was easy to hook up the cart to the hitch on the back of the tractor.

Two cartloads of mulch later, with me almost forcing Stooper to take water breaks, the stuff was spread loosely over the front flowerbed and the one on the side of the house opposite the driveway.

"Stooper, you need another break!"

"Not that hot," he huffed, using my rake to even the mulch near the front porch.

"It's almost five-thirty," I said.

"Don't have a schedule." Stooper sat next to me on the lowest porch step and took a long drink from a water bottle.

I found his comment curious. Maybe if he had something to do Stooper wouldn't focus as much on beer. *What are you, a counselor?* "How's the stone mason business?"

He smiled briefly. "Waiting for Mr. Harper to decide what he wants on his wife's stone."

"Oh, uh, that's... Wait, isn't he in the Alzheimer's unit in the nursing wing at the hospital?"

"Yep. I give him two options. Nurse said he moves them around on his meal tray."

"God, that's sad."

"Yeah," he grimaced. "Pretty soon I'll just do one and take a picture. Tell him it's what he chose."

"You can do that?"

He shrugged. "No kids. Don't nobody care but me."

"That's depressing." I studied my folded hands, which sat on my knee. "Poor Hal. I wonder if anyone will see he gets a stone."

"You liked him?"

I waited a beat. "No more than anyone else."

"My coat got stolen in the bar once. He got me one at Salvation Army."

"You're kidding."

Stooper shook his head. "Told me not to tell no one. Not like he cares now."

"That might be the first truly nice thing I heard about Hal."

Stooper grunted, and he kept staring ahead. "Yeah, he was…kind of rude most of the time."

I turned my head so I was looking at Stooper's left ear. "You have any ideas about who killed him?"

He grinned. "Present company not included?"

"Funny." I took a swig of water.

"Who was he with that night?"

I spewed water and wiped my mouth. "What do you mean?"

Stooper looked at me. "I was on the curb, by the grate near Farm and More. Hal drove by. I think someone was following him. At least, they honked, like Hal should slow down. Hal was kind of weaving." He paused. "Or I was."

My first thought was random. I knew why it smelled near that grate sometimes. "So you saw him that night. What time?"

"After the tavern shut."

That would be after midnight, and it was probably the best time estimate Stooper would be able to give. "Did you talk to the sheriff about this?"

He looked surprised. "He must know."

"Not this, not if it was that late at night."

"Huh. Well, I was pretty drunk. I guess it could have been one car."

I rested my head on my knees, then looked up. "You should probably tell the sheriff anyway."

"He's kind of mad at me now."

"Why?"

"Threw up in the jail last two times I was in there."

We were both quiet for a moment.

"You grew up here, right?" I asked.

"Yep. 'Bout half-mile from here. Bit north."

"Any family besides your parents?"

His tone was bitter. "You remember my old man?"

"Not a lot, just that he, um...."

"Drank a lot."

"I'm sorry. I didn't mean to be, to sound insulting. I was just thinking there must be people who've known you a long time. Who know you're honest."

He did a sideways glance at me. "What makes you think I'm honest?"

"All the years I was at the paper, no one ever said you so much as tried to skip paying for beer or punched anyone at Beer Rental Heaven."

"Not much of a fighter. And I am honest. But no one would believe a drunk."

"Hmm. Sheriff Gallagher might, but the IDI agents may not give you too much credit." I shrugged. "Would you mind telling the sheriff you saw Hal that night?"

"Spose I could. You think it matters?"

"I'm pretty sure no one saw him after about eight o'clock at his house. Do you remember the direction he was going?"

"Let's see. I was on the curb, facing the street. Hal was coming from my left, so heading out of town. West, that would be."

Toward Syl's place.

CHAPTER FOURTEEN

BY THE TIME I MET Sandi at seven Monday evening, I was cleaned up, excited about what I'd just learned, and tired. I also was okay to eat, but not spicy barbeque.

Juanita Sparks is the owner and chief cook. Everyone calls her Momma Sparks, and she sort of gave me the evil eye as we got seated. "You been getting in trouble. You need something to keep spirits high," she said, in her slight Hungarian accent. I have no idea where the Juanita comes from.

I acknowledged her with a nod. "I also need something not as spicy as I usually order. My stomach's doing summersaults today. Any recommendations?"

She tapped a stubby pencil on her order pad. "I take a flour tortilla, instead of bun, and put just a little my not-so-hot barbeque on it. Then I put more strips of tortilla over barbeque before I roll. Lots of bread to absorb barbeque, not so much shortening."

Sandi met my eyes and looked away, trying not to smile. She was obviously thinking of Ryan, who does a really good imitation of Momma Sparks' accent.

"Sounds good," I said.

Sandi shut her menu. "I don't know why I'm looking at this. I'll take the pork special with extra sauce and mashed potatoes."

When Momma Sparks walked away, Sandi leaned across the table. "Fred's not back from Des Moines. What's in the autopsy report? Did you bring me a copy?"

"I've got more than that, but better do the report first." I took the three-by-five card from my purse and placed it on the table. "These are highlights. I'll go to Keosauqua tomorrow to make you a copy." When Sandi frowned, I added, "You can honestly tell Fred you haven't seen it, and I avoided any questions from my lawyer about why I needed two copies."

"I guess I don't have a choice, do I?"

"Sullenness doesn't become you. All the salient items are on the card. I'll walk through the bullet points."

When we were halfway through eating, Sandi pushed her plate to one side. "Why didn't you tell me it was so gory?"

"Would you really rather not know?"

She shook her head. "I just wouldn't have ordered barbeque."

"Get a take-out box."

Sandi slapped herself on the forehead. "How could I forget? Ryan's mother heard from her cousin that nothing in the house was disturbed. No blood anywhere."

"Huh. Unless the sheriff finds a good friend of Hal's who's been in the house, how would anyone know if a throw rug or paint tarp is missing?"

Sandi sighed. "I've been thinking along those lines."

"Here's the bigger news. Stooper's helping me with heavy...."

"Stooper!"

"He might not want you yelling his name."

"Is he sober enough?"

"Yep. He came about four today, and we worked a couple of hours. Something Gary at the tavern said made me think Stooper's most sober just before he starts drinking in the evening."

"So why....?"

"Listen!" I leaned across the table so I could almost whisper. "Stooper might have seen Hal late that night, along with someone who was following him."

"What?!?"

"Quiet! He also told me he might have been so drunk it could've been one car that looked like two."

Sandy squinted. "So why didn't he tell anybody? Or did he?"

"He didn't realize Hal hadn't been seen since maybe eight o'clock. He said he'd tell Gallagher."

"Stooper might not be considered...reliable."

I nodded. "Still, it could help."

Sandi shrugged. "It's all kind of far-fetched. Like TV."

"Stooper talked about Hal's car weaving. I didn't realize Hal was that big a drinker."

"Me either," Sandi said. "Maybe he just drank alone at home in the evening and didn't usually go out."

We were silent for several seconds, then I added, "I only asked Brownberg for a copy of one of the photos. For sure you don't want to see many. If Fred ever gets around to showing you the full report, make him describe the photos rather than making you look at them."

Sandi's eyes widened. "That bad?"

"It's way worse than TV. The ones of the wound itself are grisly, but they could belong to anyone. Several have Hal's face. Those are the ones you really don't want to see."

"What do I miss by not looking at them?"

"Good question. Since neither of us are forensic scientists, who can interpret from a picture, probably not much." I took a drink of my ice water. "Hear anything about the car?"

She shook her head. "I went to every gas station or garage in town. No one had it for servicing, and both the guys who tow said they never got a call about it."

"Maybe a farm pond?"

"Not too likely. Some of them would be deep enough in the middle, but you'd have to roll a car through a lot of mud to get it that far."

I thought some more. "Be awfully hard to get it in the river. You'd have to drive almost two miles from Syl's, if Hal or his killer even had the car there. Someone might've noticed a car on the road that late at night."

"Would your buddy Syl let you look more on his property?"

"You mean in case the sheriff or his deputies walked by a car or murder weapon and didn't notice them?"

Sandi scrunched her nose, a thinking pose for her. "I haven't heard anyone say they walked every inch of his property."

"I can ask Syl, but he wasn't there until hours after they found Hal."

"After you found Hal."

TUESDAY MORNING I STOOD on the South County Memorial Bridge and looked first south and then north scanning every inch of the Des Moines River that I could see. The segment of the river that goes through River's Edge is about thirty meters wide, free of large rocks, and about twelve feet deep. That would be deep enough to hide a car, but there would be the same issue with the farm pond – plus it's only that deep in the middle.

It was six-thirty, and although the sun had been up for almost an hour, no one had driven by in the last couple of minutes. I listened to the water lap gently against the bridge abutment and wished the rest of my day would be as peaceful as this moment.

My eyes went from the river itself to the shore line – a park not more than an acre located on the far southern end of town, where it floods too often for anyone to want to build there. At least once every year in late spring or early summer, the city public works guys move all the picnic tables and trash cans to the city garage for a couple of weeks.

The park's boat ramp is supposed to be for kayaks, canoes, and small fishing boats – no power boats or sailboats. Not that there's much wind in this part of Iowa. Since it was before Memorial Day and it hadn't been unseasonably warm, I doubted the ramp had been used much.

I walked off the bridge, passed my truck parked outside the ice cream shop, and made my way to the park. The boat ramp was on its far side. It hadn't rained since Hal died, except for a quick shower. Still, the ground retained its spring sogginess. If someone had driven a car through the park, I'd see tire tracks.

By the time I reached the ramp, my sneakers were wet and muddy. The only tracks I saw were other people's footprints. The ramp is angled so someone can slide a boat into the river. I knelt on it, and immediately wished it were made of metal instead of wood. My knee was wet.

No matter how much I stared at the briskly running water, no car hood showed itself. "Nuts."

I had just left the park and was walking toward my truck when Sheriff Gallagher slowed his squad car and lowered the window.

"You're out early."

It would be fair to say he looked as if he was suspicious of any reason I'd have for being on the street before seven a.m. "I'm always up at six. Just antsy, since I can't do a lot of work at Syl's for a while."

He almost smiled as he pushed the window up. "We already checked the river."

I STOPPED AT FARM AND MORE to see how much a couple more hosta plants would cost. Stooper and I had uncovered seven of them, but they were unevenly spaced. Mr. Silverstone had been frail for several years before he died. The missing plants had probably died after years of neglect.

Andy was at the register near the door. "You not arrested yet?"

I came to a full stop and frowned. "And I won't be." *I wish I believed that.*

"Jeez, Mel, you gotta quit being so grouchy."

"I'm tired of hearing you say that. I'm going to the garden area."

I wish stores would put plants that do well in shade together and vice-versa for those that require a lot of sun. Syl's yard had a lot of both, so I bent over the Lilies of the Valley to see if they could tolerate full shade.

A weathered, handwritten sign reminded gardeners that certain plants don't do well if placed near walnut trees. It's been up there for years.

I stood still. Walnut trees.

My dad had traded home-churned butter for a bushel of walnuts every fall. A group of the trees sat near one of the creeks that fed into the river. A car sitting in that grove, at least a quarter-mile walk from the gravel road, would never be seen. Maybe in January, but not with leaves on the trees.

I picked out two hosta plants in six-inch containers and walked to the register. It wasn't staffed, so I called, "Hey, Andy. Can you ring me up?"

Footsteps came closer, from an area I knew was near a coffee table that provides free drinks for customers. And, apparently, Andy.

"Sure, Mel. Watcha got?"

I pointed to the two plants. "Six bucks each, I think."

"Yep." He punched buttons on the cash register. "That'll be twelve eighty-four."

"I'll sign for it, on Mr. Seaton's account."

Andy frowned. "Who says so?"

I hung my head for a second and then looked him in the eye. "Syl Seaton. I don't think you want to get him out of bed to confirm."

Andy smiled and sort of smirked "How do you know he sleeps in?"

I turned and walked out of the store.

"Mel. Mel! Just kiddin'." Andy's voice grew fainter as I got closer to my truck.

I forced myself not to speed as I headed out of town. There was a nursery on a farm two miles north of town. I'd go there later and give Syl the receipt.

The grouping of walnut trees wasn't too far beyond Syl's place. I turned off the gravel road onto a narrow lane that didn't have a street sign. Probably wasn't considered a road, since it ended at the river and there were no houses along the quarter-mile stretch. I'd seen tractors and balers use the lane to get to the huge field of hay that abutted the small copse.

I parked at the end of the lane and trudged toward the trees and the undergrowth that surrounded them, suddenly feeling a chill. What if I did find the car? Would someone think I put it there? *You should have thought of that.* I stopped.

As I debated options with myself, the sound of a car coming down the lane reached me. I stared as the black sedan pulled up behind my truck. A late model Ford, I thought. *Why would they block me in?*

Then a Sheriff Office cruiser pulled in behind the truck, and I knew why. Deputy Granger and Agent Masters seemed to take more time than needed to exit their cars and walk toward me.

I held Masters' gaze. "Are you guys actually following me? I bet Masters had to get up at the crack of dawn to be here this early."

Masters' smile was thin-lipped. "Just got into town to brief the sheriff and heard you were out and about."

"I can't believe the sheriff told you to follow me."

The two men stopped a few feet from me. "What are you doing out here?" Granger asked.

I pointed toward the trees. "I want to see if Hal's car is in there."

"What makes you think it is?" Masters asked.

"It'd be almost impossible to get a car in a farm pond, and Sheriff Gallagher said you guys already looked in the river." I shrugged. "It's flat country. There aren't a lot of places to hide a car."

They looked at each other and then me, before Masters said, "Wait here."

I watched them walk the short distance to the trees, getting some satisfaction because their leather shoes squelched through the terrain.

It was less than a minute later that Granger's voice drifted to me. "I'll be damned."

That meant Hal's car was amid the trees. And I had led them right to it.

CHAPTER FIFTEEN

THE ONLY TIME I'd been in a cell was when my sixth grade class took a tour of the county jail. I certainly wasn't locked in the cell then.

The door that led to the office part of the sheriff's building opened, and Sheriff Gallagher stood still for a moment, looking at me. Then he shut the door and walked toward my cell. My cell!

"You're lucky you didn't end up in Des Moines."

"Why didn't I?"

He sighed. "Because I called IDI in on an assist, not to take over the investigation."

When he said nothing more, I began, "I just wanted to see…"

"It doesn't matter what you want!" He wasn't shouting, but his tone was fierce. "I've told you to come to me first. This looks suspicious as hell. I almost believe you killed Hal."

I whispered, "I didn't."

"Ken Brownberg is trying to convince a lot of people of that. Your bail's gonna be pretty high. You better call Ambrose." Gallagher turned and walked out.

With my phone in a bag of possessions in Sheriff Gallagher's office, I couldn't call Ambrose. It was just as well. I wasn't an errant child who needed to call her big brother. Unless I wanted bail money.

I sat on a metal bench and studied some black splotches of paint on the walls. They probably covered rude words. Someone else must not have turned out their pockets all the way.

Deputy Granger came into the cell area about half an hour later and stopped in front of me. "You want to tell us what you hit him with?"

"Give me a break. I didn't kill Hal, and you know it."

"I didn't believe it at first, but you look guilty as hell to me now." Granger pulled a set of keys from his pocket and unlocked the cell. "Gallagher said you can walk to the courthouse without cuffs. If you stray so much as two inches from my side, I'll taser you."

I could tell he meant it.

Masters was not in the office area. He and Granger had brought me to the jail more than four hours ago, so I figured he could be back in Des Moines by now.

Instead of going out the main entrance, Granger and I walked out a side door that opened to what I'd heard deputies call the 'sally port.' I'd seen them bring drunks into the jail through this entrance. It was also close to the side door of the small county courthouse.

Granger opened the courthouse door with a key, and I knew to turn left, toward the judges' chambers and court rooms. I hadn't thought to ask what the charges were, and now didn't seem the time.

We walked into the smaller of the two courtrooms, one generally used for misdemeanor cases, usually traffic-related. It has the dark-paneled walls that have been there since the courthouse was erected in the late eighteen hundreds. There's no jury box, and the judge's bench isn't elevated much.

Ken Brownberg sat at a table near the front, talking to the county attorney, Myron Smith, who stood next to him. Brownberg looked toward me and nodded, so I did the same back.

I noticed an older man, a farmer judging from his bib overalls and sunburned face, standing next to Smith. He was in his early seventies. I didn't know his name, but had seen him at Farm Bureau meetings when I covered those for the paper.

"Ms. Perkins," Smith said, and moved to a table next to the one Brownberg occupied. I sat next to Brownberg, and Granger sat behind the county attorney.

A side door opened, and Judge Kane came in walking briskly, robes flapping, with his bailiff behind him. Kane more or less glared at Smith. "And what is this? You know court's in the morning."

The judge sat behind his bench, and Smith cleared his throat. "Your honor, Ms. Perkins was found on private property this morning, without permiss..."

"Are you telling me this is about a damned trespass charge?"

I figured the judge had to know why I was here, and his questions and irritation were mostly for show. He's very strict about court procedures. If someone is late for a court date, they're in for two minutes of chastisement.

Judge Kane looked at me. "You understand, Ms. Perkins, Mr. Brownberg, that this is not a trial of any sort. This is a hearing to determine if you can be released on bail." He glared at Smith. "Once I know details of the charge."

Brownberg and I nodded.

"As you know, your honor," Smith said, "Hal Morris's car was found in a group of trees on Mr. Nelson's property this morning."

That's the farmer's name, Jeb Nelson.

Judge Kane rolled his fist, index finger out, clearly wanting Smith to get to the point.

"I didn't know it was there, Tom," the man interrupted, speaking to the judge.

Judge Kane gave him a sort of benevolent smile. "Not a problem, Jeb."

He must be a campaign contributor.

Smith flushed. "Ms. Perkins drove down the private road on Mr. Nelson's property. She then got out of her car, clearly headed for the area where the car belonging to the late Hal Morris was found."

Judge Kane looked at Jeb Nelson. "And you had a problem with this?"

He shook his head. "I didn't know about it, until the Sheriff's Office called to see if I could come down."

Judge Kane glared at Smith. "Who is the complainant?"

Smith swallowed. "An IDI agent, with the sheriff's..."

Judge Kane gestured around the room. "Since when do IDI agents bring cases to my court," he raised his voice, "for trespassing?"

"The complainants," Smith continued, "believe the car's location is an important piece of evidence in Mr. Morris's murder, and that Ms. Perkins may have placed the car there."

Judge Kane glared. "A matter for criminal court." He looked at Jeb Nelson. "Did you want to press charges against Ms. Perkins for trespass on your property?"

Nelson looked confused and shook his head. "Is that why I'm here?"

Judge Kane looked at me. "It isn't relevant in a simple trespass case, but did you know that car was there?"

"No, sir. It's been missing, and since no one's found it in the river, those trees seemed a good place to hide it. I just wanted to look."

Judge Kane stared at me for several seconds before looking back to Attorney Smith. "So, the property owner does not seem to be the complainant in this *civil case*, and I'd bet my lunch there is as yet no basis to file any criminal charges that have arisen from Mr. Morris's murder."

Smith's face had reddened. "That's correct, your honor."

The judge picked up his gavel and banged it – hard. "Then you're wasting my time." He lowered his tone. "And you, Ms. Perkins, you get permission before you go on someone's property. You're lucky Jeb here didn't want to file a complaint." He looked back at Smith. "Not that I would have expected a simple trespass charge to even make it to me."

Brownberg stood. "Thank you, your honor."

By the time I stood, Judge Kane was almost out of the court room, his bailiff holding the door to his chambers so the judge could precede him.

No one said anything for several seconds. I looked at Smith. "May I leave?"

His reply was curt. "Yes, Ms. Perkins, you may." He gestured to an unhappy Granger. "Deputy, come with me back to my office, would you?"

They walked out, leaving a confused Jeb Nelson, Brownberg, and me.

"Mr. Nelson."

He faced me.

"I'm very sorry I went on your property without your permission."

"Not anyone asked my permission to tow that car off my land either." He studied me. "I knew your father well. You sure this is how he and your mother would want you to act?"

My eyes burned hot. "Maybe not." I drew a breath. "But they did teach me not to let anyone bully me."

Nelson put his ball cap on. "Good advice." He walked out.

I stared at Ken Brownberg and then drew the back of my hand across my eyes. "I'm sorry, Ken. I didn't think I was doing anything wrong."

"I understand. But you really, really need to stay away from all this. Call Sheriff Gallagher if you have an idea." He picked up a folder from the table. "This didn't take long, so it won't be a huge bill."

No one in the Sheriff's Office said anything to me when I went to reclaim my phone and purse.

I AVOIDED THE DINER and went home to make a second cup of coffee and a sandwich. Anger made me feel hot, but I had to admit I was as angry at myself as much as Aaron Granger or Masters. I'd given them a reason to think I was guilty.

Why in the hell were they following me? I felt like asking Sheriff Gallagher if he knew they were, but decided not to put myself in the middle of anything else. If I had to bet, it would be that Gallagher mentioned to Granger that he saw me by the river. Granger, always anxious to get ahead, intercepted Masters as he arrived and the pair went looking for me.

It wouldn't surprise me if the formal trespass charges were brought so the Sheriff's Office didn't look like they had put me in a cell without much basis for it. Or maybe to teach me to mind my own business, but people don't usually risk Judge Kane's disapproval to send a message.

Stooper and I were meeting at four, and it was only about one o'clock. I paced the apartment, while my grilled cheese cooked, and planned how I'd spend my time until three-thirty. If I didn't have anything to do I'd just mope.

As I ate, I thought about calling Fred. He'd probably asked Doc Shelton whether I could look at

Hal's folders. Plus, I told him I'd let him know what I was doing related to the murder. I hadn't expected any aspect of a story to be about me.

Instead of going straight to the paper, I drove the fifteen miles to Keosauqua to make a copy of the autopsy report. The copier at the paper was out, obviously. The River's Edge Library is so small you have to put your folders or papers on the floor while you make a copy, so it would be hard to hide what I was doing there.

It was a beautiful day, and much of the drive I could see the river. Some days it moves quickly. Others it's as still as plate glass. Today the still river shimmered in the sun.

About a mile from Keosauqua, a large maple tree lurched into the water. More of the river bank had fallen in since I'd last driven this way. Pretty soon there wouldn't be much land between the road and the river, so there would be some fancy engineering to reinforce the bank. Still, it would be cheaper than moving the road. Stop thinking like a reporter!

On the way back to River's Edge, I took a highway that was more than a mile in from the river. There were fewer curves, so I could drive faster.

I walked into the *South County News* a little after two, as Ryan was walking out.

"Holy crap, Mel. Were you really in jail? And you're out?" Notebook in hand, Ryan had apparently been on his way to the Sheriff's Office.

"I was on Jed Nelson's property to look for Hal's car, but Mr. Nelson didn't press trespassing charges."

By this time, Sandi and Fred had walked out of his office. Betty was still at her desk in the back of the office, apparently immersed in thought and not paying attention to anything else.

When the three of them started asking questions, I held my palm toward them. "Just let me tell you what happened."

Fred's reaction surprised me. "Damn it to hell, Mel. You didn't know what was in those trees."

"That's why I was there."

"You should have called me!" Fred was red-faced.

I kept my tone even. "I said I'd share information Fred, not tell you everywhere I was going."

Before Fred could speak again, Sandi said, "You don't have to tell anyone anything, but if you're going to a dead-end dirt road, maybe text me when you get there." Her lips twitched. "We'll know where to send the dogs to start trailing your scent."

"Funny." I looked at the three of them. "So you didn't even know I was going before Judge Kane?"

Fred shook his head. "No open meeting requirement for bail hearings, which is how that was listed. Shirley called a few minutes ago."

"Shirley! How did she know?"

Sandi shrugged. "Maybe someone from the Sheriff's Office had lunch there today."

Fred looked at Ryan. "Check in with your mother's cousin. See where they've taken the car."

Ryan got up, and Fred missed seeing Sandi and me exchange a glance. It seemed that Fred was willing to let someone else ask simple questions about Hal's murder when he had to.

Fred frowned. "We're going to have to interview you. No way you can contribute to any stories about Hal's murder."

He was right, of course, but I didn't like his tone. I decided to ignore it. "You read the autopsy, Fred?"

He frowned at me. "After I drove to Des Moines to get the damn thing. You?"

"Brownberg got it for me."

Fred nodded at Sandi. "Sandi wasn't keen on seeing the photos."

"Good option." I sighed. "I didn't see anything in there that said who might have killed him."

"Not a real short person," Sandi offered, and grinned. "Unless they were on a stool."

Fred and I nodded, and I turned to him. "Did you ask Doc Shelton if I could look at those folders?"

He stared at me. "Not yet. They don't pertain to the murder, but I better let you look, and ask forgiveness later. He'd say no, at this point."

"Jeez. His father delivered me."

Sandi grimaced. "Yes, but back then he didn't think you'd maybe grow up to be a murderer."

SANDI SAID FRED HAD not given her a copy of the autopsy report, so after surreptitiously sliding a folder under her blotter, I sat in the back of the bullpen. A bookcase stood in front of the desk, because the former food reporter didn't want people staring at her. Or so she had said. I think she thought it made her less of a target when Hal was in a throwing mood.

The folders formerly on Hal's credenza were now in three piles, two being larger than the third. One group dealt with ag issues, including crop projections and a farm subsidy program. Another dealt with weather and the river. As Fred had said, Hal appeared to have been relating river depth to rain cycles and releases the Corps of Engineers made from the Red Rock Reservoir. I thought he just recycled river articles written in previous years. Apparently he actually looked at new information.

The third pile had three slim folders. If I hadn't known Hal, I might have seen the notes as innocuous ideas for articles. Two I could figure out.

Apparently, when he went out for coffee, he also checked to see which cars were at expired parking meters. He had license plate numbers and dates, and next to a few were names of a car's owner. I didn't need a crystal ball to know he was planning to write something that accused sheriff deputies of playing favorites in writing citations.

The three names he had were the mayor's wife, a deputy's personal car, and the florist, Tim Coker. For some reason Hal had always despised him. Probably no one had ever sent Hal flowers. In any event, Hal was going to annoy a lot of people. No surprise there.

A second folder dealt with the town's summer festival. It takes a lot of work, but almost everyone in town helps with it and has fun. Then and for a few weekends in fall, when the leaves are colorful, are the best times for local businesses. Hal had the vendor list for the past six years.

To the untrained eye, it might look as if he wanted one of us to do a feature on this summer's plans. However, he had placed a check mark next to Lions Club-sponsored booths and an X next to Rotary displays. I happened to know that there had been no separate Rotary booth the last three years because they split the cost of a booth with the Chamber.

Hal hated the Lions because they wouldn't let him into the annual pancake breakfast for free. Knowing Hal, he was going to write something saying the Visitor's Bureau gave preferential treatment to the Lions by giving them a separate booth.

The third file was probably a list of topics that hadn't been developed enough to merit a separate folder. Among items was a brochure about the new nursery in the hospital's Obstetrics and Delivery wing. What negative aspects there were to that I couldn't imagine.

A *Des Moines Register* article described historic districts in small towns, which included a two block segment in River's Edge. That part of town has several magnificent homes built from 1850 to about 1890 and a brick creamery building that no longer operates.

I've heard talk that the creamery building would be a good location for an indoor craft and antique mall. That sounded like something that Hal could write a negative article about. He would've complained about a business that catered only to tourists.

A couple pages of almost-indecipherable handwritten notes seemed to be random thoughts. 'FB August' probably referred to the county Farm Bureau's annual meeting. They let Hal in free. He liked them.

Hal had also doodled a fire cracker. He had bugged the Chamber for years about making the Fourth of July display a lot bigger. He seemed to ignore the rationale that insurance costs would be too high.

Hal had drawn a line across the bottom quarter of a paper, apparently so he could use it for a separate set of scribbles. There seemed to be a title. Ins O...something. I couldn't make out the word. Maybe ins and outs?

Another couple of words were profits and bids. Bids was underlined. Finally I realized that a few words, when put together with correct spelling and better penmanship, were the name of Hal's least favorite local independent insurance company, Blackner's. Was Ins insurance?

Since Hal had skewered Blackner's Insurance and had to retract the piece, it seemed odd that he would tackle an insurance company again, much less that one. There were several in town, a couple independent agents as well as State Farm and Allstate. What could Hal have been talking to Bruce Blackner about?

Had Hal written some of what he probably planned, more people might have wanted to kill him. But the articles hadn't come to fruition. I shut the folder, thinking of the past two hours as wasted time.

It was late afternoon. Fred was still in his office, and I didn't hear him talking. I walked in, intending to put the folders on top of the pile of boxes. As I entered, I realized Fred had been listening on the phone, so I mouthed "sorry" and backed out.

I placed the folders on the vacant desk outside his office and looked for Sandi or Ryan. Neither was in sight. I sat at Ryan's desk and wrote a note, which I placed under his blotter, just sticking out. "Did you check security cameras for Hal's car that night?" I figured that was safer than leaving the note on Sandi's desk. Fred often jotted her notes and might see mine.

I walked back to Betty's desk. She looked up when I got closer, and it was clear she had been crying.

I stopped. "I'm sorry, Betty, I didn't mean to bother you."

She tossed a wadded tissue into the trash can and pulled another from a box on her desk. "No problem, Melanie. You had quite a day." She blew her nose and reached in her desk drawer for a lipstick.

"Great to know it's all over town."

She smiled. "No one really thinks you did it. Yet."

I pasted a smile on my face. "Good to know. Listen." I stopped. I hated to make her cry more, but the only way to find out if she and Hal had dated or whatever was to ask. "So, Betty. Maybe you can help me figure out something."

"Sure."

I sat in the folding chair next to her desk, and she listened as I described Jean Roth's thoughts that Hal had a special friend.

Betty started to turn pale.

"So, you knew Hal longer than anyone here. Do you know who an evening visitor might have been?"

She turned to stare at her computer screen. Betty was in profile, back straight and chin raised. "I never heard him talk about a girlfriend."

Clearly we were done talking. I stood. "Um. Okay. Thanks."

She never heard him talk about one. That didn't mean she wasn't his girlfriend or friend with benefits. I tried to remember something she said the day I found Hal. Something about knowing people who might want to kill him, but not anyone who knew how to do it without getting caught. Was she talking about herself?

CHAPTER SIXTEEN

CONFUSED AS I FELT, I recognized there had been some progress. Hal had not driven his car into the woods. The killer must have driven Hal to Syl's place after killing him and moved the car. And then what, walked home?

It was the most logical explanation. To be sure they weren't seen, someone would have had to walk in the ditch alongside the road and duck into yards in town. And there was no guarantee the murderer walked into River's Edge.

And when would the murderer have retrieved my hoe? Planting it in the mulch pile was deliberate. *Somebody must really hate me.*

Or maybe I was simply a convenient foil. At first it seemed that only Sandi and Syl knew he hired me, but I'd explained the genesis of Hal's temper tantrum to Calvin Jenkins.

Even if the store manager hadn't blabbed to others, a lot of people heard Hal hollering. Anyone could have walked to a nearby aisle to see what was going on and stayed to listen to me talk to Calvin. Plus, the store manager probably had to explain Hal's outburst to some of his staff.

Still, while a lot of people would have heard by nine a.m. the following morning, very few people would have known in time to kill Hal and frame me by probably five a.m. If the sheriff or IDI wanted to, they could develop a list of people on what I thought of as the Hy-Vee grapevine. If anyone was trying to figure out who knew Hal threw fruit at me in Hy-Vee, I hadn't heard about it.

It just didn't make sense. What were the odds that someone, who had wanted to kill Hal for a while, heard he was angry with me and used the chance to frame me? I didn't know why I bothered to try to make sense of anything.

WITHOUT REALLY THINKING about it, I walked toward Blackner's when I left the paper at about two-forty-five. It was only two blocks, and I thought the walk in seventy-degree sunshine might clear my thinking.

Blackner's is only one building off the square, so it's a busy part of town. I was almost there when honking drew my attention to a large Buick, vintage 1970s. Mrs. Keyser waved and slowed down, which made someone in a sleek Volvo honk at her.

People don't honk a lot unless it's to alert one of the town's older residents that they missed a stop sign or to encourage a dog to get out of the road. Mrs. Keyser sort of waved into her rear view mirror and kept going. I watched the Volvo tailgate her. Must be from Des Moines.

Inside the insurance office, a thirty-something man sat behind the reception desk. I didn't know him.

I pulled the door shut, but not quite in time to keep a large fly from buzzing in. "Hey, I'm Melanie Perkins. I wondered if Mr. Blackner is in."

He smiled. He was slight, with sort of honey-blond hair and a carefully knotted yellow and blue tie. "Would you settle for a son-in-law?"

I sat in a seat next to the desk. "Sure. Let's see, you must be Cynthia's husband, right?"

He nodded. "Thought we'd try a slower pace than Cedar Rapids for a while. We just had twins ten months ago."

"Wow. I take it you mean a slower pace outside of your house."

He laughed. "Yep. If we'd stayed in Cedar Rapids, Cynthia would've had to go back to work. Child care costs would have taken up almost sixty percent of her salary. We can manage on one income down here."

"Did I miss your name?"

"My fault. Cynthia's husband isn't quite enough, is it?" When I smiled, he added, "Henry Rensler. Grew up near Cedar Rapids. She and I met at UNI."

"Ah. I went to Iowa." I paused. "I'm actually not here to buy insurance. I used to work at the paper…"

He snapped his fingers. "Oh sure, that's why I knew your name. Must have been a shock to find your old boss. You doing okay?"

"Mostly. I don't think as much about finding him as I did the first few days, but it'll never go away."

Henry raised his eyebrows to imply sympathy.

"So, I don't work at the paper now, but Fred and I, you know Fred? He's acting editor."

"Met him just a few weeks ago, when he was here on the weekend. I thought he moved to Des Moines."

"Kept his house. He's been in and out of town, and he'd be a really good choice to be a permanent editor. Anyway, I've been helping him decide which files of Hal's to keep, what to put in storage or somewhere." *That's close enough to the truth.* "I was just going through a file that had notes on articles Hal planned to write."

Henry laughed. "From what I heard, he already wrote something about Cynthia's dad."

"He sure did." I grinned. "And retracted it. From his recent notes, it looked as if he talked to someone here in the last few weeks. Maybe doing research for a story. Do you know anything about that?"

Henry frowned. "Don't think Hal had an appointment, but they could have run into each other somewhere. If you can hang out a few minutes, Bruce'll be back pretty soon."

I said I'd wait and went to the grouping of chairs for clients. A magazine cover said, "Insurance is Financial Planning." I thumbed through it. At some point, Ambrose and I would be able to sell our parents' farm. Until then, my financial planning was limited to making sure I had enough in the bank so all my automatic payments were covered.

The door opened. Bruce Blackner saw me and came to a full stop. "Melanie. What a surprise."

"Thought I might be in the pokey?" I stood, and we shook hands.

"It's all so strange, isn't it? Can I help you with something?"

I repeated what I'd said to Henry.

Bruce literally did an eye roll. "Hal had some questions for me. Come on back."

I smiled at Henry and followed his father-in-law down the hall and into a lavishly furnished office. His desk was fully five feet long, and its burnished cherry finish looked expensive. I sat across from him.

Bruce leaned back in his leather desk chair and shook his head slightly. "I have no idea what he was working on. No telling how Hal's mind worked. He said he was doing 'investigative reporting' about an insurance industry association."

"None of those in River's Edge."

He nodded. "He said it was a story that would bring a lot of attention to the paper, help keep the *South County News* in business. In fact, that was his hook to get me to talk. I'd have been happy to see Hal, personally, go out of business, but the town needs a paper."

I nodded. "I hear Doc Shelton and Hal's attorney are going to find a buyer for the paper. I hope they keep the staff."

"Hard to keep a paper profitable in a small community. Whoever takes over will be easier to deal with. Might help the advertising revenue."

I grimaced. "Anyone would be easier. Obviously the sheriff and his staff are investigating this. I thought I'd see if anything Hal was working on would have made someone angry. Or more angry than usual."

"He asked a lot of questions about insurance regulation in Iowa. You know we're state-regulated for the most part. He wanted to know what kind of oversight the Iowa Insurance Division has, especially over larger firms."

"That's odd. I never heard him talk about anything like that. Except," I smiled, "to cuss you out when he had to write the apology."

"Bit of cussing around here at that time, too." He shook his head. "He was such an unhappy man."

"All of us who worked for him, except Betty and Salty, were a lot younger than Hal. You have any idea why he was so darned miserable with himself?"

"That's a good way to put it. All I ever heard is that he lost his shirt in some get-rich-quick scheme in the 1990s. Not sure that was true, but I heard he put everything he had in it and it went belly up."

"Interesting. Hal was always mad about something. So, did what he asked about lead to anything about local insurance companies?"

He shook his head. "Not that I recall. He was mostly interested in whether I'd heard anything about bids for computer systems for a Des Moines company. But he didn't say which one."

I know someone who recently got a contract for an insurance organization in Des Moines.

BY THREE-THIRTY I was back at Syl's. My head felt quite a bit better, but when I bent over to tie my work boots, it made me slightly light-headed. Probably best to leave heavy stuff to Stooper.

Sitting on the steps were three hosta plants, each in a six-inch pot. A soil-stained note under one of them said, "No charge. Hope you feel better," and was signed by Farm and More's owner, Jody. Maybe he'd heard Andy had royally ticked me off. I'd have to thank him.

I'd been turning over what Bruce Blackner had said for more than an hour. I hadn't thought about Syl's angry phone call with someone since the day I'd heard it while crouched under his window. It could have been a routine business disagreement, but it had sounded like more than that. I couldn't think of a reason to ask him about it, especially since it happened a few days ago.

As I finished taking a rake, shovel, and hand tools out of my truck, Stooper entered the driveway and walked toward me. I raised a trowel at him.

As he drew closer, he smiled, something he rarely does. "Heard you had a good day."

"Nuts. Is it all over town?"

"Oh, yeah." He sombered. "Most people know Hal's car was found there. Make's 'em wonder how you knew."

Because it seemed that Stooper was telling me rather than asking for an explanation, I told him what had drawn me to Jed Nelson's property. "And I really didn't expect to find it. It just seemed a logical place to look."

Stooper had climbed into the pick-up to get to my wheelbarrow, and I grabbed the front of it while he slipped off the tailgate with the handles. It was only then that I noticed his hair was better trimmed and his eyes seemed more alert.

"I don't mind telling people you didn't do it. But you should be more careful."

"No kidding." I pointed toward the barn. "You want to use the wheelbarrow for the last of the mulch or get on that tractor?"

He answered my question by grabbing the wheelbarrow's handles and walking. "Syl's going to get a riding mower. I told him it'd use less gas than that old tractor if we were hauling lightweight stuff. Plus, he needs a mower anyway."

I stifled my surprise. "Did he appreciate the advice?"

"Yeah, he said he paid a guy from town seventy-five dollars, plus gas, to do it a couple of times. I said I'd do it for forty, and you and me could get a five-gallon gas can and keep it filled." He glanced at me as we neared the barn. "You don't mind driving me for gas, do you? I hate to put a full gas can in my trunk. Sometimes my muffler drags and makes sparks."

If it had been anyone else, I'd have been angry. I would've liked to make money mowing the lawn. But I hadn't thought to talk to Syl about it, and Stooper looked happier than I'd ever seen him. "No problem. I doubt anyone would steal the gas can, but we should be sure to find a way to chain the mower."

"I'll think on that. Bolt cutters work too easy on a chain."

We spent the next two hours working, with Stooper tackling the mass of weeds around the barn. I planted hostas and made a diagram of what was in the flowerbeds and what I thought should be added – a mix of perennials and the cheaper annuals.

Stooper and I were standing in the driveway considering what to do next when Syl's shiny pickup pulled in and parked. Syl was in a dark blue suit, with tie loosened and top shirt button unfastened. He carried a brown briefcase with one hand and held the other up in greeting. "Be out in a minute."

Stooper looked at me and frowned. "He don't stop to say hi?"

"Probably it's the end of a two-hour drive and he has business inside the house."

Stooper grinned and walked the few yards to Syl's truck, which he inspected as if he planned to make an offer on it.

Syl came out of his side door, bearing three bottles of water. Stooper and I took one, and Stooper immediately asked Syl if he wanted to look at the area around the barn. I trailed the two of them in that direction.

"See, Syl, all those weeds are gone. You can see that barn from a lot of your back windows. It'll look even better after Mel and me put down some more mulch."

Mel and me?

"Her favorite commodity," Syl said.

Stooper didn't get it.

Stooper had me tell Syl which of the now-visible flowers around the barn were daisies and which were day lilies. Syl's mouth twitched, but he simply thanked me.

"So, Stooper," he said, "I was thinking maybe you could pick out the mower for me."

They spent a couple of minutes going over the price range. Stooper glanced at the sky and said, "Gotta be headin' home." He turned and walked toward the road.

Syl and I were silent for several seconds.

"Nice flowers." He didn't hide a smile as he lowered his voice. "Your friend wants your job. Not enough headstones to make?"

"He works by appointment only," I said, dryly. "If it were anyone but Stooper, I'd be mad, but I don't think he has a devious bone in his body."

"No." The maddening twitch was back. "He's very direct." Syl started walking toward the house, and I fell in step.

I sighed. "It's okay if he mows the lawn regularly?"

"Sure. Plus, if you end up in prison, he can substitute until you get out."

"Thanks. If you'd been in town this morning, you would've thought I was on my way." I gave a brief version of events.

Syl's anger surprised me. "You went alone? Anyone could have been back there."

"I'm pretty sure whoever parked it wasn't coming back to check on it."

He frowned, but adopted his usual tone of voice. "There's a killer out there. At least take someone with you next time you go running down leads."

"I've already promised that to several people, including Fred."

Syl looked puzzled.

"Sorry. He's the guy running the paper for a while." I grinned. "I'm surprised he hasn't been out here to interview you."

"Ah. He's left two messages. You like him?"

"He's a straight shooter. Doesn't sensationalize. Plus, you get to tell the story your way."

"How many times did you use that line when you were a reporter?"

"A bunch. Speaking of the paper, can I ask you something?"

"Don't think I know much about the paper, but sure."

"Fred asked me to look at a bunch of Hal's folders, to see if he needed to do anything with them. Article ideas and stuff."

"He paying you?"

"We're friends. Fred still has to do some work in Des Moines. He's swamped."

Syl nodded. "So laid back here, even more than Des Moines."

I smiled. "It is. Anyway, one of the less legible papers mentioned interviews he'd done with a local insurance agent. It seemed he was looking into some sort of bidding process, but I don't know if it was local or statewide. Anything out of the county would seem odd."

Syl gave me an inscrutable look and glanced away. "I know something about insurance business in Des Moines, but not a damn thing about South County."

"Right. And the only thing local I really know is that Hal ticked off some of the local agents with a story he wrote a few years ago."

"Consistent, wasn't he?"

"Absolutely. It probably doesn't relate to anything. I thought if I could find out if Hal had irritated more people than usual I'd pass that to the sheriff."

Syl shook his head. "I should have guessed. You should tell the sheriff and let him figure out who was mad at Hal."

"You sound like everyone else I know." I almost said "except Sandi," but I saw no point in drawing her into the discussion.

Syl touched the rim of my hat. "Could be a tougher knock on the noggin next time."

We had reached the house. Apparently, if Syl knew something more about the insurance industry in Des Moines, he had no plans to talk about it. "I was lucky. So, I'm still on light duty. Think I'll pack up. Probably come tomorrow to do some planting. Not sure about Stooper."

"I'll be in Des Moines again. Are you well enough to be out here alone?"

"Yes." I realized my reply had been abrupt. "I appreciate that you asked."

He grinned as he started up the back porch steps. "No, you don't."

I WATCHED THE TUESDAY EVENING news, thankful that the Quincy station didn't mention that I'd been in jail for a time this morning. They did mention a development in Hal's murder, citing the car being found in a nearby wooded area.

Sheriff Gallagher or IDI must not have been in the mood to be quoted, because there was no interview. In fact, the reporter seemed to think someone in law enforcement had found the car. Interesting.

I drank some iced tea, but didn't feel like eating yet.

My phone was still in my purse, so I got it, sat in the recliner, and leaned back to call Sandi. She didn't answer until the third ring.

"Hey Mel. Busy day?" Her words were clipped, so she was either busy or with someone.

"Worked at Syl's. Did Ryan learn anything from his mother's cousin?"

"Only that Sheriff Gallagher wanted the car to be examined here rather than towed to Des Moines."

"Have they looked at it yet?"

"It's at McKinney's garage. They'll have to finish soon. The sheriff doesn't want it to sit on the lot, so it's taking up one of the bays where McKinney works on cars."

Mike McKinney probably wouldn't charge the county for holding the car briefly, but he wouldn't forgo income. That meant Gallagher or a couple of deputies would probably finish a once-over by tomorrow.

"We should hear something soon," Sandi continued. Fred asked for an exclusive. Gallagher said that was a big-city word, and he'd talk to Fred first."

"I'd love to be a fly on the wall for that one."

"Me, too. Seems Fred would have to tell us, since other people in town will know. And you be sure to call me if you plan anything else dumb."

I ignored the barb and said I would. As I hung up, I wished I could be as sure as Sandi was that Fred would tell all.

When I got into bed, I made a list for tomorrow:

1. See what Fred finds out re car.

2. Were there security cameras besides the two banks and Hy-Vee?

3. Call Ambrose. How could I forget to do that?

CHAPTER SEVENTEEN

I DIDN'T START WEDNESDAY with number one on my list. Instead I called Ambrose about seven-thirty. He might not have heard anything yesterday, but he would today.

"You got lucky," Sharon said. "Ambrose is in the shower."

"Why is that lucky?"

"Because Fred just called here. He told me about yesterday. You should have called."

I did a mental sigh. "I'm not trying to hide anything. I was just glad to get back to working in Syl's yard and focused on that."

Sharon blew out a loud breath. "I won't tell your brother about Fred's call 'til Ambrose is at work. I don't have to say Fred called first."

"Thanks. I'm sorry if I sound snotty, but I'm whipped. Would you ask Ambrose to call me when he's dressed?"

"Yep. Behave yourself, or he'll hire someone to tail you. Bye now."

There'd been a touch of sarcasm in Sharon's tone, but she didn't sound really mad.

I was the angry one. What business did Fred have calling Ambrose? They saw each other around town if Ambrose was here, but they weren't in regular touch. A glance at the clock told me Fred wasn't at work yet. Just as well. I needed to keep all the pieces of my mind to myself for now.

By the time Ambrose called back, I had practiced being contrite. I told him what happened as fast as I could.

"Damn it. Brownberg should have called me."

"Ambrose, he was representing me. Wouldn't that have been a breach of something? Lawyer-client privilege?"

He was silent for a few seconds. "Why don't you tell him he can talk to me about anything going on with you?"

I agreed, managing to keep reluctance out of my tone. I would tell Brownberg he could talk to Ambrose about anything, but that I wanted to give permission first.

I showered and was at Syl's property by eight-thirty. Brownberg wouldn't be in his office yet, and I could call later on my mobile. Fred I wanted to talk to in person.

My head was better, and I wanted to get some work done before it got too hot. I wished I had started earlier. It might get to eighty-five degrees today.

Syl's truck was gone, so I pulled to the end of the driveway. My wheelbarrow was in the barn, which kept me from having to load it into my pickup every day. I was almost at the barn door when I heard a whimper. I stopped mid-stride and listened.

Was it a child? No, sounded like a dog. I went to the door to look in. It was bright outside, so it took several seconds to adjust to the darker interior. The whimper came again.

A bedraggled, multi-colored dog sat under the wheelbarrow. I couldn't even think of a breed to call him. Maybe a mix of schnauzer, small Labrador, and terrier. He was dirty and looked as if he was too tired to move. His fur had a few burs, but wasn't matted. He hadn't been in the elements for too long.

I approached slowly and stooped next to the wheelbarrow. He moved just his head back, so I held out my hand and let him smell it. He did, and it brought one thump of his tail. It didn't look as if he would bite me, so I patted the ground in front of me.

Slowly, eyes on me the entire time, he crawled from under the wheelbarrow. He looked too tired to stand, and he didn't protest as I picked him up and slung him over my shoulder. At most, he weighed ten pounds.

I started toward my truck, where I had a cooler with water and a ham sandwich. It was lunch meat, not fresh ham, so I knew I couldn't give him much. He was filthy, so I took the sweatshirt that sat on the seat, spread it out, and plopped him on is.

His look said, "Is that all? Aren't you going to help me?"

I smiled and opened the cooler. He sat up and stared as I first took out a bottle of water. I didn't have a bowl, so I poured some in my hand. He lapped and slobbered a lot of it onto the sweatshirt. I kept pouring water into my hand until about half of the bottle was gone.

His eyes stayed fixed on my hands as I refastened the bottle top and pulled out the sandwich. He barked, just once, and moved to the edge of the seat.

"Okay, buddy. Let's start small." I took half of the sandwich out of the plastic bag and tore off a piece of the ham. He almost ate my finger with it.

"Okay...hey." He head-butted my hand, so I tore the rest of the ham into two pieces and fed him. He was about to stick his head into the small cooler when I put the lid back on it. He stared at me and thumped his tail.

"Too much sodium." I sighed. "Come on. You belong to somebody. We'll go to the vet."

So much for working before it got too hot.

JOSHUA MARSHALL WAS THE large animal vet my dad always used for our cows and horses. I figured he or someone in his office did house pets. His flat-roofed cinderblock building sat on the opposite edge of town from Syl's place, so it was more than a ten-minute drive. By the time we got there, the small dog was asleep on my lap.

He woke up and thumped his tail twice when I turned off the engine. Apparently we were friends.

I put him over my shoulder and held him in place with my right hand while I opened the truck door with my left. When he realized where we were, he gave a small whimper.

"You know this place? Have some shots here? That's good." It would mean Dr. Marshall or someone else might know the dog.

He squirmed a little as I opened the door and walked into the waiting area, but didn't try to get down.

The woman behind the counter stood and clapped her hands. "It's Mister Tibbs!"

She was about thirty-five and had on a light blue smock. The dog seemed to not only know her but like her, and I was about to hand her to him when I remembered how dirty he was.

"He was in a barn on the far west side of town. I'm glad you know him."

"Sweet boy." She held out her arms and I handed him to her across the counter.

Dr. Marshall came into the waiting area from a hallway that led to a lot of now barking dogs. "So, he showed up."

Mister Tibbs didn't look as eager to see Dr. Marshall, but he let the vet take him from the woman. I glanced at her name tag and saw she was Annette.

I leaned on the counter and watched Dr. Marshall run his hands over the dog. "Who does he belong to?"

"Past tense, I'm afraid. Did you know the Stevens? Not far outside of town. He died a few years back, and his wife passed a week ago." Dr. Marshall stroked the dog and handed him back to Annette. "I don't feel any obvious injuries. Let's get him cleaned up before we call Animal Control."

"Animal Control! Why? Don't they put them to sleep?"

Annette carried Mister Tibbs into the hall, and just before they vanished, the dog put his head on her shoulder and looked at me. I took it as a thank-you.

"He's a nice little guy. They'll likely find someone."

Dr. Marshall's tone wasn't unkind, but I knew this was a subject he dealt with a lot. He cared about animals, but he couldn't care too much.

"Where do you suppose he's been for a week?"

"He ran out when the ambulance guys opened the front door to get Mrs. Stevens. She'd called 9-1-1, but she was gone before they got to her. They said Mister Tibbs was frantic."

"Oh, that's sad." I felt my eyes start to burn. "Isn't there family who can take him?"

Dr. Marshall shook his head. "Afraid not. She has a son who lives in Colorado, but he's gone back. He said if Mister Tibbs turned up he'd pay an initial vet bill, but he couldn't take him. Travels a lot for his job." He smiled. "Mrs. Keyser let you have a pet?"

"I don't know. I'm not always there either. Maybe he could come to work with me."

Dr. Marshall nodded. "Saw you were doing some landscaping."

"Oh, yeah. And you saw who I found my first day doing it."

He shook his head. "Poor Hal. Such an unhappy person. Got a lot worse after his cat died."

"Hal had a cat? I don't believe it."

Dr. Marshall looked puzzled. "Never talked about old Sammie?"

The door dinged, and a man entered with a collie on a leash.

"He didn't. Hard to imagine him, um, taking the time."

"They were best buds." Dr. Marshall turned his attention to the new arrivals.

I walked out slowly. Hal, good to a cat? A cat probably no one at work knew he had? It didn't make me less mad at Hal for his insults and stapler-throwing, but I had begun to realize there was a side of the man he didn't often let others see.

Part of me wouldn't mind a dog, especially a small one. I thought of Mister Tibbs' mix of black, brown, and white fur and his tail thumps, and smiled.

I sat in my truck for several minutes, thinking. The collie's owner walked out, and I went back in.

Annette was at the front desk, now in a pink smock. She laughed. "Dr. Marshall said you'd be back."

"Sorry you had to change your smock."

"I do it ten times some days."

"I'm not sure Mrs. Keyser will let me keep him." Ultimately, she might be the one to make up my mind. I wouldn't move for a pet, not when my garden was growing so fast.

Annette winked. "I'll call her."

My eyes widened. "She'll listen to you?"

"I went to high school with her daughter. You know Clara?"

I thought Mrs. Keyser's daughter was in her early forties, meaning Annette must take really good care of herself. "Not really. I've met her a couple times when she visited. She's in Minnesota, right?"

Annette nodded. "And Clara had a little terrier for years. I bet she'll let you keep Mister Tibbs."

I leaned my head back and looked at the ceiling. *What was I getting myself into?* I looked back at Annette.

She spoke softly, "He'll be good company for you. Since your parents… Well, you're alone a lot, aren't you?"

Presumably her branch of the town grapevine meant she talked to Mrs. Keyser.

My eyes burned again. "I'll talk to her late this afternoon."

Annette smiled. "I'll keep my fingers crossed."

.

CHAPTER EIGHTEEN

I WAS AT SYL'S when Sandi called early Wednesday afternoon. She was tripping over her words. "You have to come. You have to come."

"Where? Are you okay?"

"Yes." Her voice was softer. "Ryan. Where?"

She was with Ryan. That was good.

"Can't be the diner. Make it the barbeque place," Ryan said. Sandi hung up.

I hadn't had a chance to tell her where I was and that I had to clean up at least a little. I stowed a rake and hand tools in my wheelbarrow and almost ran to the barn with them. Then I jogged to a spigot near the driveway. Syl had told me where a key was in case I wanted to go in to use the bathroom, but I hadn't done that yet. Besides, I was dirty.

The water was cold, and I splashed some on my face, hands, and arms. I was about to turn off the water when I noticed my knees were brown, so I used more water and rubbed. It did little good. *Oh, well. So I look like I work for a living.*

I was not far from the barbeque restaurant when the phone buzzed again. It was in a pouch attached to my dashboard, and I pressed the speaker button. "Almost there."

Sandi was doing a loud whisper. "Change of plans. Your place."

I couldn't imagine what was worth all the subterfuge. When I got home, Sandi and Ryan got out of her car and walked toward me.

"What?" I asked.

"Worth waiting for," Ryan said.

Mrs. Keyser opened her front door and stepped onto the porch. Apparently she had not had her hair done today. "Melanie? Is it a nice dog?"

Sandi and Ryan chorused, "Dog?"

I stopped and faced her. "He really seems it. Did Annette tell you it belonged to someone who just died?"

Ryan pulled his notebook from a shirt pocket.

"Yes," she called. "I knew her. As long as he doesn't go in the house, it's fine." She looked at Sandi and Ryan. "Come up through here."

Sandi started to say something, but I said, "Great, thanks." When Sandi half-glared at me, I murmured, "I want the dog."

"Better be a good dog," Ryan muttered.

As I suspected, when we walked through the front door, Mrs. Keyser showed no sign of letting us get to the inside stairway quickly.

"Melanie, Melanie. The county jail. Tsk, tsk."

Who says tsk, tsk nowadays? I tried not to stare at the huge ladybugs on today's housedress. "It was a misunderstanding."

"Hello, dears." She did a brilliant smile for Sandi and Ryan. Lipstick smeared a top tooth. "I thought I might read about that in the paper."

Sandi adopted her professional pose, which means she straightened her spine and leaned forward a bit.

"The real story was that the car was found. The fact that some people initially thought Mel should be charged with putting it there was just a distraction."

When Mrs. Keyser opened her mouth, seemingly to protest, Ryan said, "We'll probably never do a story on law enforcement overreach, but if we do, that's an example."

Sandi sort of turned green.

"Anyway, Mrs. Keyser. I really appreciate being able to keep the little guy. Did you know his name is Mister Tibbs?"

"Oh, that's one of my favorite movies." She patted my arm. "He'll be good for you."

Sandi and Ryan said nothing as we climbed the stairs. I unlocked the door. I hadn't asked if I could change the inside lock to my apartment, so now I had two house keys.

The interior stair entry to the apartment opened into the hall with the bedrooms. When we walked in and I'd shut the door, Sandi hissed, "Law enforcement overreach? It'll be all over town."

Ryan shrugged. "It was."

"I think it was more the IDI agents," I said.

Sandi and I sat on the couch, but Ryan pointed to the kitchen. "Let's use the table."

"Our intern is all grown up," I said.

"I asked Fred to call me a reporter now. I've only been the intern because I didn't graduate yet."

It also meant Hal could pay Ryan less. I had no idea what Fred would do.

We sat at the round table in my kitchen's breakfast nook. Ryan opened a manila folder he'd been carrying. "You won't believe this." He placed two photos on the table. They'd been produced on a regular printer and were kind of grainy.

I pulled them toward me. "Hal's car! Ryan. Where did you get these? I didn't really think there were cameras on buildings he might have driven by."

"Not commercial buildings. After I got your note I started walking streets that could lead out of town, you know, to where Hal was found. Most home security cameras I saw pointed at the spaces in front of entry doors." He put a finger on one of the pictures. "Except for some people who moved here from Kansas City last year. They also had cameras pointing at the street in front of their house as well as the side yards."

"Good job," I muttered. "Fred will make you a reporter for sure."

Neither of them said anything as I took in the photos.

Judging by the date stamp on the bottom right, Stooper had definitely seen two cars the night Hal was killed. I was certain the car in the first photo was Hal's. The face was unclear, but the driver looked to be male and his head was shaped like Hal's. Despite Stooper's possible blurred vision, I decided to assume he was right.

The second car was a dark Toyota – a Camry, I thought. Fred has a dark blue one. I squinted to look more closely. A car dealer could probably say if it was the same year and model. I tried to give Fred the benefit of the doubt. Maybe it wasn't Fred's car, or it was and he wasn't the driver. I angled the photo toward the window. I couldn't make out the driver.

Had Fred lied? It seemed he was in town near the time Hal was killed and had driven behind Hal's car in the early morning hours.

"It could be anyone's Toyota," Sandi said.

I thought she was trying to convince herself. I looked at Ryan. "Did you give these to the sheriff yet?"

"I'm not going near him. The people who own the house moved here to avoid crime, so they wanted to help." Ryan shrugged. "I sort of let them think I was working with IDI. When I stopped by to get the photos I said who I was. They were kind of mad, but they still let me have them."

"The *Washington Post* will hire you in no time," I said.

"Or the sheriff will put your tailbone in a sling," Sandi said.

Ryan grinned at both of us. "Sheriff's already mad at Melanie." He focused on me. "He might be more mad at you, but he'll get over it."

I stared at the photos some more. "I don't mind giving them to him, but I'll have to say you got them."

"Yeah," Ryan said. "But if he's into kill the messenger, it'll be you."

Sandi blanched and took the photos from me to stare at them again.

"How do we approach Fred?" I mused.

They both said, "You do it."

"He'll be mad at all of us," I said.

"Yeah, but he can't fire you," Ryan said.

I glanced at the clock above my stove. It said four-fifteen.

"Might as well get it over with." I stood, and they followed suit. "Where are you guys going to be?"

"I'm supposed to be tracking down the Chamber director about rumors a telephone service center is coming to town." Ryan shook his head. "Can't imagine they'll get enough workers here."

"Work ethic and lower wages, maybe." I said looked at Sandi.

"Nowhere specific. I'll...let's see, I'll come in about twenty minutes after you go into the paper. Unless I hear gunfire."

"YOU'RE TRYING TO SAY I killed Hal?" Fred was red-faced as he stood behind his desk.

"Keep it down." I shut the door. Only Salty had been in the bullpen a minute ago, but anyone could have come in since then.

"Keep it down? I thought we were friends."

I kept my tone even. "You act as if you thought you'd be in photos with Hal's car. I never thought that. And until I saw your reaction, I didn't know it was you."

Fred seemed to realize his reaction was all the verification I needed. He sat down and put his head in his hands, elbows on the desk.

"Fred."

He looked at me, elbows still on his desk. "What?"

"I don't know if you killed Hal, but I don't think you would frame me."

He straightened and put his hands in his lap. "I didn't try to."

I raised my eyebrows.

"Kill him or whatever."

"But?"

"I saw him – after."

"What?!" I stood up.

"Keep it down."

I sat back down. "Tell me everything."

His voice was low. "I went to Hal's. That night. To have it out with him." He stopped.

"Because you found out your unemployment appeal results that day?"

He nodded. "They also shared what Hal told them. He probably didn't know I was entitled to hear it. He didn't criticize my writing or say I'd made a mistake." He drew a breath. "He said I was lazy, and he couldn't rely on me to hand in stories when I said I would."

I thought Fred looked as if he was going to cry. "You didn't know you could maybe get a lawyer?"

He calmed himself. "You're being logical."

"Terrible fault for a reporter."

"Whatever. I had to finish working in Des Moines. It was, oh, maybe eight o'clock before I could leave for here. By the time I'd driven for close to two hours, I would have at least tried to hurt him."

"So, you went to Hal's?"

"First time he didn't answer. I mean, I didn't know if he was in there. I went away and drank a couple of beers."

"Always fodder for good decision-making."

"Yeah, well, I needed to get my nerve up. I wasn't drunk."

But you were buzzed. "So, you went back?"

"I knocked on the door. After a minute I realized some taillights I'd seen when I was near his house might have been him leaving. So I drove in that direction. I was about to give up when I saw taillights weaving. A lot."

"Huh. And we never saw him drunk."

"Yeah, weird. Don't know if he did it a lot. Anyway, I almost caught up to him, but he made it through a light and I didn't."

"You lost him?"

"Yeah, but there were only a couple of ways he could have gone, so I kept driving around. I was at the edge of town, almost at the end of the blacktop, going to turn around. Then I saw taillights, and they turned off the road."

"At Syl's place?"

He nodded. "But I thought it was vacant until I saw it wasn't just Hal's car in the driveway. There was a truck. Something made me park on the road, a bit down from there. When I started to walk onto the driveway I heard yelling. One of the voices was definitely Hal."

"And the other was Syl?"

He shrugged. "I keep trying to meet the guy. I listened to his voice on his answering machine. He hasn't been there the couple times I've gone by."

"Did the machine sound like the person you heard?"

"I don't think so. The person arguing with Hal had a deeper voice, not like the outgoing message."

"Syl didn't come outside?"

Fred shook his head. "Not that I saw, assuming it wasn't his voice. There could have been a third person, maybe near the mulch. But I never saw them." He stopped.

"Did you hear what they said?"

"Just a few words. Something about Hal working his ass off and some talk about hiring. That was from Hal. The other person only said one thing I understood clearly. He said, 'You don't matter.'"

"So you think Hal was meeting someone there?"

"Don't know." Fred closed his eyes and opened them again, looking at a point above my head. "And then it was quiet."

"Hal probably wouldn't have gotten quiet on his own."

"Yeah, well, he didn't. After a minute something told me I should go look. Hal was, he was by the mulch pile. I could tell he was dead. Something about the way he was lying. And his eyes were…" His voice trailed off.

If the autopsy report was correct, Hal was dying, but not dead. Mortally wounded, soon to die. "What did you do?"

"I ran. It was really dark. I got to my car and drove away from town. Sort of toward your parents' old place."

"You never saw the other person?"

He had his head in his hands again, but he wasn't crying. "No, but if they'd walked straight back, toward the barn, they could have been hidden by the pick-up or Hal's car."

After a few seconds, I asked, "What did you see when you drove back by there?"

"I didn't. Drive by there. I drove west and came into town that back way."

I stared at him, and Fred finally met my eyes. "I was beside myself with horror. I'm sorry. I could have, I should have told…"

"Yeah, you should have! Why didn't you?"

"I thought it would look like I did kill him. It would be my word against, well, against anybody I told. Like the sheriff." He ran his fingers through his hair. "I can't think straight!"

My heart was beating fast, and it made my temples pulse, probably because of the almost-gone bump on my head. I fought against screaming at Fred. I stood and walked toward the door and back again. Fred still wasn't looking at me, so I stood next to him.

"You want me to tell, right?" he asked.

"You're damn right I do."

He looked up, eyes pleading. "I'll never get work again. And what would it tell the sheriff?"

"Gee, maybe that I didn't do it?"

He sagged into his chair, tilted his head back, and stared at the ceiling. His eyes looked vacant.

I was angrier than I'd ever been, even angrier than when Peter Frost filed the lawsuit against Ambrose and me. If I said everything I thought about him, Fred might not tell the sheriff. If he didn't admit it and I repeated what he said, he could deny it. My story would sound like fiction.

Finally he looked at me. "Is tomorrow okay?"

"And what in the hell is wrong with right this very minute?"

"I'd like to write resignation letters. And my cat, you know? I need to find somebody. And I'd like to tell my parents myself. They're in Florida now. I mean, I can't go there, but it won't be an easy phone call."

I didn't care about his letters or cat, but the bit about his parents got to me. I didn't know them well.

The longest time I'd spent in the same room with them was at the town dinner after Ambrose, Sharon's, and Fred's high school graduation. Fred's parents were a lot older than mine. Probably close to seventy-five now.

I sighed. "First thing tomorrow. If you don't do it, I will. You don't want to be some sort of fugitive."

"Thank you, Mel. I'm...."

I walked out. It made no difference how sorry he was. Fred had put me through hell.

CHAPTER NINETEEN

SANDI WAS COMING toward me as I got to the sidewalk. She turned without saying anything, and we walked toward the paper's small parking lot. After a few steps, I said, "It was him."

"He killed Hal? Oh, my God!"

"Hush. He says no, just that he followed him."

"I can't believe he didn't tell me! Did he see anything?"

Given that Fred was keeping her mostly in the dark, I didn't know why she'd expect him to tell her anything. We had gotten to our cars. I'd promised Fred to wait until tomorrow to go to the sheriff. Could Sandi keep a secret that long? No.

"He saw Hal turn into the driveway at Syl's place."

"My God. Hal was killed there." She stared at me. "Does he know who killed him? Did Fred see anyone else there? Was Syl outside?"

My mind raced. Technically, the answer to each of her questions was no. "He has no clue about any of that. And..."

A car horn honked as Ryan pulled into the lot.

I faced Sandi. "If we stand here kibitzing, it'll look odd if Fred comes out. Come on to the diner."

"Are you kidding? Why aren't we going to Sheriff Gallagher? Is Fred already there?"

I looked at Ryan and pointed down the street. He rolled down his window.

"Meet us at the diner."

He nodded and put his window back up.

I looked at Sandi. "When we get to the diner, I'll tell you what we talked about. Just don't screech when I do."

She almost stomped to her car, ponytail swinging, and flung open the door. I let her back out and, driving more slowly, followed her to the diner.

My mind was jumbled with fury at Fred for letting me look like a possible killer and pity for what was about to happen to his life, because he had chosen not to call the sheriff the night Hal was killed. Would I have called? Absolutely. And not just because I'd have been terrified. It was the right thing to do and crazy not to do it.

Fred had been high school class president, and everyone in town seemed to like him. Respect him, too. Recent experience had taught me what it was like to be considered a good person, however that's defined, and that it's hard to be thought of negatively.

But, hell, if Fred said what happened and people thought he was a weasel for not speaking up sooner, so what? Hard feelings would be over in a day or so. Maybe not mine right away, but everybody else's.

Fred must have had another reason for staying quiet. But what? How could I fudge with Sandi and Ryan so they'd wait a day to learn more? And why was I willing to do that?

My mind went over a bunch of things super fast. My first week at the paper, Fred introducing me to the two county supervisors who had come on board when I was in college. Fred standing up to Hal for me, until I learned how to do it myself by the third week on the job. Fred at the funeral home, holding me while I cried because Ambrose had his hands full with my father's two sisters who were also bawling.

"Nuts." I pulled to the curb and called Fred's mobile.

"Melanie?"

"Yeah. Ryan found the cameras that had the pictures. You should probably make yourself scarce unless you want him to hunt you down tonight." I hung up without saying goodbye.

Sandi and Ryan had parked and were standing by the entry to the diner. I parked and Ryan rolled his index finger, indicating I should hurry.

"Okay, okay." As I got closer I said, "There's not much you can do until tomorrow."

Sandi was white-faced. "You don't know that." She led the way into the diner, and we walked toward a booth.

Shirley was behind the counter. "You guys need menus?"

I didn't want her to linger talking to us. "How about a round of iced tea?"

Sandi and Ryan nodded. They slid into one side of a booth, and I faced them. "Good job with the photos, Ryan."

He leaned across the table. "What did he say?"

I told them Fred had gone to have it out with Hal and followed the taillights. Without saying so, I let them think he had not followed Hal into the driveway."

"What the hell was Hal doing out there?" Sandi asked.

"From the sound of things he was drunk. I guess Fred thought so to." I shrugged. "My guess would be Hal went to scream at Syl for pulling the ad. For pulling a thirty-five dollar ad."

Sandi almost whispered. "You think Syl killed Hal?"

"It seems almost impossible to me, but that's not for us to find out."

"Gee," Ryan's sarcasm was clear. "How many folks would have been in that driveway in the dead of night?"

I kept my tone even and voice low. "Again, I have no idea, and this time I'm leaving it all to the sheriff."

"So what's Fred waiting for? He should call the Sheriff ASAP." Ryan sat up straighter. "Maybe I could go with him to talk to Gallagher."

Sandi lifted her eyes from where she'd been staring at the table for a few moments. "I can't believe he didn't say anything, Mel. If Hal drove himself out there and you weren't with him, it really lets you off the hook."

I nodded. "Fred feels bad. I guess he thought he'd look guilty, and he was afraid of losing his job or something." Sandi started to interrupt, and I continued. "I told him I'd give him time to call his parents and write resignation letters."

They both sat back. "Resign?" Ryan whispered.

"He should have told, but..." Sandi stopped, and her freckles stood out even more on her pale face.

I met her gaze. "Are you going to throw up or something?"

She shook her head as Ryan moved a few inches away from her.

Ice sloshing in glasses meant Shirley was approaching. "Hey, kids. You three look like you got expelled."

I turned my head to look up at her as she placed the three iced teas on the table without spilling a drop. She tossed a sugar packet at me.

"Just a really long day."

Shirley stared at me. "You have dirt on your nose, sugar."

Sandi handed me a napkin. "Can't take her anywhere."

Shirley cracked her gum and studied us. "Okay, I'll let you talk." The swish of her back end as she turned to walk to the counter said she was annoyed at us.

I added sugar, and we sipped our tea for almost thirty seconds before we spoke. When Shirley was safely behind the counter, I said, "He's upset."

"And you aren't?" Sandi hissed.

"You sound like a goose," Ryan said.

"I'm upset, I'm angry, I'm hurt."

Their expressions changed from irritation to something more neutral, and Sandi got some color back in her face.

"I know," Sandi said, "I don't get why you aren't hauling his butt to Gallagher yourself."

"If you'd seen him, you'd get it. I told him he'd have tonight to talk to his folks, and if he didn't get to Gallagher in the morning, I would."

"Sheriff'll be mad at you for waiting," Ryan said.

"I don't plan on mentioning the delay."

Sandi looked at her watch and then Ryan. "I need to find Fred."

"You mean *we*," Ryan said.

They both looked at me, and I shook my head. "Not me. I can't tell you what to do, but I'd lay off him for a few hours. I'm going to buy a six-pack and enjoy an evening watching TV, thinking that no one will try to arrest me tomorrow."

MY PHONE RANG AT six-forty-five Thursday morning. I knocked over my alarm clock reaching for it. "Who?"

"Melanie?"

Sheriff Gallagher's voice got me to sit up. "Yes. What's going on?" I asked this in reporter mode, before I remembered I was a gardener.

"Fred with you?"

"Huh?" I swung my legs over the edge of the bed. "Haven't seen him since yesterday, early evening. What's up?"

"Found his car near the river a few minutes ago. Stay where you are." Gallagher hung up.

I was immediately so cold my teeth chattered. I stood and pulled the quilt around me, which made me stumble as I walked into the kitchen. The two beers I'd had the night before roiled in my stomach. I wanted a Tums and some hot tea.

Fred. What have you done? Maybe it was nothing. Maybe Fred left his lights on, and it called attention to the car. Maybe he was fishing further down the river. *You idiot. Fred doesn't fish. Maybe he does. Please, let Fred be fishing.*

I turned the gas on under the tea kettle, remembering to shake it to be sure it held water before I went to the bathroom. By the time I finished brushing my teeth, the kettle was boiling. I took a teabag from the cupboard above the sink, but before it landed in my mug, heavy footsteps on the stairs announced someone.

The steps were too rapid for Gallagher. I peered from behind the curtain on the glass part of my outside door and looked straight into Aaron Granger's eyes. "Give me two seconds to put on a bathrobe."

I ran to my bedroom, took a robe from the foot of my bed, and was at the door again in less than a minute.

Granger walked in. "I thought Sheriff called you."

"He just did. He told me to sit tight, not get ready for visitors."

Granger walked into the living room and faced me. "Where's Fred?"

I blew out a breath. "Talk to me while I pour tea." I turned toward the kitchen.

"Melanie, this is serious!"

I didn't stop. "I know that. But you want me awake, right? You want some?" I lifted the tea kettle and poured hot water over the bag. "I talked to Fred last night, but not since then."

"You sure?"

I slammed the kettle onto the burner. "Damn it, Granger, of course I'm sure. Do you know who you talked to last night?"

"I don't need your..."

"No! I don't need your prejudice and rude crap. This isn't some television show, and I don't go around killing people or hiding my friends." It was the first time I'd totally lost my temper, and it felt good.

"You're acting guilty as hell."

"Oh, bull. When have you ever even met a murder suspect? You don't know what guilty looks like any more than I do." I picked up my still-steeping tea. "Now you want to have a seat and talk about where the hell Fred could be and how we can find him, I'm all over that. You want to act like some dipwad actor, and we don't have any more to talk about."

For a few seconds, Granger was as still as a bird that doesn't want a cat to see it. "Gimme some tea."

I handed him my mug and turned to make more for myself. "You want sugar or cream?"

"No, thanks." He walked to the trash can at the edge of the kitchen, tossed the teabag, and went into the living room to sit in the recliner.

I filled another mug and added sugar. Before carrying it into the living room, I tightened the cord on my bathrobe. When I sat on the couch to face him, I debated apologizing, but decided he and anyone else who suspected me of killing Hal or hiding Fred could kiss my grits.

"We're starting over," Granger said. "What time did you see Fred last night?"

"At the paper, about four." It didn't seem like the time to fib about anything, so I swallowed and told him Fred had seen Hal pull into Syl's driveway, really late.

Same as I did with Sandi and Ryan, I didn't mention Fred had seen Hal's body. I knew I should, but that was something Fred was going to have to tell Sheriff Gallagher himself.

"But Fred didn't tell me that until right then, yesterday. I wanted to make him go right to Sheriff Gallagher, but he said he wanted to call his parents in Florida and write resignation letters. And find somebody to take care of his cat."

Granger had paused with the tea almost at his lips. He finally took a sip and then placed the mug on the coffee table. He appeared to be making a great effort not to rage at me. "Okay. We're going to go over everything Fred said and why he talked to you about this. But I'm gonna let the sheriff know the basics of what you just told me before we go into all that."

Granger walked into my kitchen to use his phone. Yesterday I'd had misgivings about waiting until today to talk to Gallagher. Today I felt like a total fool. I got a sense of the sheriff's opinion from Granger's clipped responses and figured the conversation with Granger or whomever would take place at the sheriff's office. I stood and walked back toward my bedroom.

I really wanted a shower, but there wouldn't be time. I grabbed a pair of cotton slacks and a short-sleeved knit shirt and made for the bathroom. It sounded as if Granger was off the phone, so I called to him. "I'm getting dressed. You want me to ride to the office with you?"

He didn't say anything for a moment. "You can drive yourself, but follow me in."

IT WAS TOO EARLY for my least favorite IDI agents to be in River's Edge, so it was the Sheriff and Deputy Granger sitting across from me in the office. Unlike the time Gallagher had interviewed me about Hal, today he took a lot of notes. He had already had another deputy call Sandi and Ryan, and I knew they were on their way in.

Gallagher stared as he spoke. "So the photos Ryan found led you to him. Why did you believe Fred? He's telling you he saw Hal pull into Syl Seaton's. Not telling me that earlier could mean he wanted to make it look like you killed Hal."

"He didn't say he did that, you know, stole the hoe and put it there. He just said he was really shook and drove back to town. He was afraid you'd think he did it."

"Sure, Melanie." Granger's tone could not have held more sarcasm. "You want us to believe some third party strolled by, saw the body, and then went after your hoe?"

I tilted my head back a bit and rolled my neck before looking at them again. "I screwed up by not forcing him to come here or coming here by myself last night."

"True," Gallagher said, staring at me.

"My thinking was if I told you it would sound made up, and I didn't want to do anything to make Fred change his mind about telling you himself." And I felt bad for his parents, but I didn't say that.

I looked at Gallagher, unflinching. "When did you find his car?"

"'Bout five-thirty this morning," he said.

"And, uh, you knew it wasn't there all night, right?"

A split second of a smile made it to Gallagher's lips before he stopped it, but it was Granger who spoke. "I found it. Wasn't there when I came on duty at eleven last night."

"If his cat's at home, that would be good, right?"

Granger shrugged, and Gallagher said, "It could mean something or nothing. And it is there."

"With a lot of extra food?" I would feel better if it looked as if Fred had planned an exit from River's Edge. I might go after him with my replacement hoe when we found him, but maybe leaving extra food for the cat meant Fred wasn't dead or something else awful.

"If we haven't heard from Fred in an hour or so, we'll do more than look in his windows." Gallagher studied me for several seconds. "Probably need a warrant. Cat looked fine. Mrs. Keyser say you could keep the dog?"

Damned town grapevine. "Looks like it."

Gallagher stood, and Granger followed suit.

"I have no idea what's going on with Fred or whether he killed Hal or saw something that would worry someone who did," the sheriff said. "You know my admin gal, Sophie." When I nodded, he added, "Tell her where you'll be today. I suggest you not spend time alone at Mr. Seaton's place."

I nodded, stood, and walked toward the door. Before I shut it, I turned. "Did Stooper tell you he saw Hal late that night?"

Granger looked surprised, but Gallagher nodded. "I should have paid more attention to him. He wasn't sure if he saw one car or two, so I figured he wasn't any kind of reliable witness."

"I told him to call you." I shut the door.

I hadn't told Sandi and Ryan that Fred said he saw Hal's body, but if I didn't tell the sheriff and he later found out Fred told me that, I'd be back in a jail cell on some charge – whatever somebody could think of. My throat tightened. *How could Fred do this to me?* If he was gone, no one would believe me. Again.

I bent over to take a sip at a water fountain not far from the sheriff's private office. Sophie wasn't in yet, so I scribbled a note with my mobile number and said I was going home and then to the diner. For all I knew, Shirley would have heard not only that Gallagher was looking for Fred but where he was.

SHOWERED, DRESSED AND FED, I felt better. I stayed in a back booth at the diner, listening. It didn't seem that anyone knew Fred's car had been found at the river.

Three by five cards were on the table in front of me. I couldn't spread them all out, or there wouldn't be time to grab all of them if someone tried to sit with me. Instead, I had three crisscrossed piles, which I had mentally labeled as Reasons to Kill Hal, Hal's Timeline, and Fred's Schedule. There were probably thirty cards. There would have been fewer if I hadn't put the reasons to kill Hal on separate cards.

A new card said simply Fred. I was mad at myself for scratching him off the list I'd started almost two weeks ago. I still didn't have answers to the most important questions about him.

In addition to where he was now, I needed to find out if Fred saw more the night Hal died than he had told me. What reason would there be to hide that now, when he'd admitted he had seen Hal after he died? Or admitted it to me, anyway.

And why hadn't I asked him how my hoe got there? The only excuse I had was that I'd been so flabbergasted it was like being in shock. Almost as bad as when my parents died. Well, not quite.

And where was Syl in all this? Some sleeping pills were so strong they made a person do things and then not remember them later. Could Syl have found Hal on his property, killed him, and gone back to bed?

Wait, he would have buried him. That would have taken an hour or more. And when he got up in the morning, there would likely have been bits of mulch everywhere. Oh, and a murder weapon. If Syl had killed Hal, surely even strong sleep medicine wouldn't hide that fact from himself. But why would he? What did Hal ever to do Syl?

Someone opened the diner's glass front door with enough force that I looked up. *Think of the devil.*

Syl saw me and walked rapidly toward me. Without asking he sat across from me. "What the hell is all this Melanie?"

At least he didn't yell. "I'm trying to piece it together. I take it the sheriff called you?"

"I just got off the phone. Told him he could go all over the property again." He leaned across the table toward me. "But all he said was someone may have seen Hal at my place that night."

Shirley was a couple of booths down, taking an order. She looked toward us. "Now, I haven't heard that." Her look was accusatory.

"I'm sorry, Shirley. What little I know I'm not supposed to talk about."

She gave a pointed look at Syl, whose back was to her, and went back to taking the order.

"All I know is Fred finally told me he'd followed Hal out there that night, and…"

"To my property? What the hell for?"

"Fred wanted to tell off Hal for lying to the unemployment people about why Fred was let go. He went to Hal's, but no one answered." I described Fred's efforts to follow Hal's taillights and that he saw Hal turn into Syl's driveway.

Shirley, order pad in hand, had been walking toward Syl and me and heard the last few words. "Sugar, don't I share what I know?"

I ducked my chin on my chest for a minute and raised my eyes to look at her. "I swear, Shirley, there's lots of questions but no answers yet. Bottom line, Sheriff Gallagher wants to see if Fred saw Hal really late the night Hal was killed, and I'm not supposed to talk about it."

Her eyes widened, and she whispered. "You mean he thinks Fred kilt Hal?"

Syl's posture telegraphed impatience.

"I highly doubt it." *And if I find out Fred did, I'll push him off the bridge.* "Fred's car was parked in town in an odd spot, that's all. Sheriff wants to talk to him."

She stared at me for a full two seconds and then smiled, widely, at Syl. "Now sugar, you probably need some high test to listen to all this."

"Had coffee at home. Better be decaf to go."

"Black right?" Shirley had already started to walk away.

"Unless you have bourbon."

I'd never heard Shirley giggle.

Syl looked back at me. "That's all it is? Are you sure?"

"The only thing I'm sure of is that it's looking a bit less like the sheriff thinks I did it, and that makes me happy." *And if Fred has hurt himself, I'll be really sad.*

Syl's stare was intense. "But this Fred, he's your friend."

I nodded and wished my throat wasn't constricting. "I'm…angry, but also sad."

"Well, I won't make you talk about it. I can't imagine there's anything else to be found on my property, but I really want to have this finished."

I nodded, not sure enough of myself to speak.

"Where's that brother of yours?" Syl asked.

"Oh, damn. I should have called him."

Syl's laugh was contagious, and I started to giggle. "At least, this time, it's good news." I stopped. "I hope."

Syl had been gone less than one minute when Shirley came over. "What's this about Fred?"

"All I know is his car was by the river early this morning." I swallowed the lump in my throat.

She stared at me and apparently decided to believe me, because her tone became less strident. "Andy just called. He said Gallagher called Farm and More, so they'd post a sign saying sheriff and the fire department were organizing a search party. Meeting in the park."

I almost whispered, "I should go help."

I left money on the table rather than stand by the cash register where people might ask me questions. I beeped open my truck and slid in, but before I could start the truck my phone buzzed. Caller ID said it was the vet.

"Oh. Mister Tibbs." I pushed the answer button. "Hi, Dr. Marshall"

"He's yours if you want him."

I didn't say anything for several seconds.

"You can keep him awhile, and we'll help you find another owner if it doesn't work out."

"Okay, thanks. See you in a bit."

My first thought was that Mister Tibbs might be good company, and the second was that the dog was going to rearrange my life. There wouldn't be a vet bill today, but there would be later. I stopped at the dollar store and bought dog bowls and a leash, but by the time I got to the vet I was convinced that getting the dog was a bad idea. Dr. Marshall would understand.

The barking began as soon as I entered the office. Mister Tibbs was in a dog crate on the counter, and he stuck his nose through the plastic grate.

Annette laughed. "I thought you might have gotten the heebie-jeebies, so I brought him out."

I shook my head, but I was smiling. "I guess I'll be up at five a.m. from now on." I touched his nose, and Mister Tibbs literally jumped as he barked. "Shhh. Good boy."

Annette laughed. "He's a girl."

"You're kidding."

"Mrs. Steven's dog before Mister Tibbs was Mister Ed. She picked out a male pup from a litter, but when she went to pick him up, the boy had been given away. The only one left was this cute little critter."

"Obviously not an experienced breeder," I said, dryly.

"Not hardly. A farm dog, but the family said they couldn't keep four puppies. Anyway, she'd already decided to name him Mister Tibbs, and she just couldn't get the name out of her mind."

I peered into the crate. "And I thought it was a neutered boy."

"He was so filthy you couldn't tell. I mean, she."

"Spayed?"

She nodded emphatically. "Dr. Marshall won't see them past a year if they aren't."

"No kidding." That sounded more like a city vet than a country one.

"He'll handle a big emergency, of course. He gets some senior-level DVM students to help him do a spay and neuter clinic here a couple times a year."

"Good for him. Okay, show me what kind of food to buy, and we'll be on our way."

CLEANED OF DOG slobber and in a fresh University of Iowa tee shirt, I was back in my car with Mister Tibbs on a blanket in the very narrow back seat of my truck. We had spent ten minutes with him trying to walk across the middle console into the front seat and me gently pushing her back, saying no. She was now tuckered out and content to sit on a blanket in the back.

All parking near the river was full. It looked as if half the town had come to search for Fred. I parked on a side street two blocks from the park and took the leashed Mister Tibbs out of the truck.

When we got to the park, I stood on the edge, scanning for people I knew. Hy-Vee had set up a table with coffee and water bottles. Several sheriff's deputies had on yellow vests, and a woman in a police uniform I didn't recognize had a dog with its K-9 police vest.

"I can't do this."

Mister Tibbs looked up, apparently assuming we should be moving on.

"Melanie." It was the youngest sheriff's deputy, Newt Harmon. He walked toward me. "Hey, I was just looking for you."

"Do you have…news?"

He shook his head as he pushed his sunglasses from his eyes to the top of the head. "No, Sheriff Gallagher asked you to be sure not to do any of the river searching."

My eyes widened. "Why not?"

"Sorry. Should have said that first. He'd like you close by in case you can help him, you know answer questions or something."

I knew this wasn't true. Gallagher would have called or had someone call me to say that. Apparently, if I showed up, I was to be sent away.

"Sure thing." I jiggled Mister Tibbs' leash. "Just picked up this guy…girl, probably too much excitement for her anyway."

Mister Tibbs stood, wagging her short tail, clearly available for petting.

"Heard you were getting him. Her." He bent to stroke the dog and then stood. "You take care now, you hear?"

CHAPTER TWENTY

SHERIFF GALLAGHER CALLED me about three-thirty to say Fred's body had been found leaning against the bank of the river just after the town of Farmington, Iowa. I registered that this meant Fred's body had traveled about ten or eleven miles and blocked all thought of what he might look like now. Or tried to block.

"I can't talk now," I said, ending in a sob before I hung up and threw myself onto the couch.

I've never cried that uncontrollably before, not even when my parents died. A metallic sound registered, but didn't deter me.

Mrs. Keyser burst into my living room. "Melanie! Melanie!"

I gulped sobs. "I'm okay."

She was breathing hard. "You are not. Is it Ambrose? Is Ambrose all right?"

I put my hand over my mouth to stifle sobs. "Fred. Fred...drowned." And then I sobbed more.

"Oh, my." She walked away from me, and I heard her turn on water in the kitchen. She was back in just a few seconds. "Here, sit up. Just sit up, and get your breath."

I wanted to say I could breathe however I wanted, but even as hopeless as I felt, I knew she was trying to help me. I sat up, snot running from my nose and tears everywhere.

Mrs. Keyser reached for a tissue box on the coffee table and snatched two or three and shoved them at me. Then she sat on the recliner, still short of breath.

I blew my nose and gulped a few times as I tried to stop sobbing. "I'm sorry I scared you."

"That's not important. I wouldn't have used my key, but you didn't answer." She stood and shoved a mug of water into my hand.

"I didn't hear you. All I could think..." I swallowed some water and whispered. "Does drowning hurt?"

Her eyes filled with tears, and she spoke gently. "I think it's over pretty quickly. Did he...do you know how it happened?"

Someone ran up the side steps and banged on my door. Mrs. Keyser stood and opened it.

Ryan came in, looked at her, and ran to me. "Mel. God, you're okay."

"No, she's not." Mrs. Keyser returned to the recliner.

Ryan flushed. "I meant, well, we didn't know where she was." He sat next to me and put an arm around my shoulder.

I cried for maybe another two minutes and then fought to control myself. Mrs. Keyser was in the kitchen, from the sound of it boiling water for tea or instant coffee.

I wiped my eyes and blew my nose again. Ryan picked up the tissue box and held it out for me to take a few more. I looked at him with swollen eyes. "Thanks. Do you know what happened?"

He shook his head. "I'm not sure anyone does. People looked for him by the river all day, and the sheriff asked the Coast Guard to keep an eye out in case he... If he made it to the Mississippi."

"But he didn't, right?"

Ryan frowned and lowered his voice. "I heard a couple miles beyond Farmington."

I spoke in a low voice. "So that'd be what, twelve miles on the river?"

Ryan took a breath and squared his shoulders. "Yeah. No one said he got to Missouri. It would be easier for his parents if he... his... if he stayed in Iowa."

I nodded. "If an Iowa ME handles an autopsy, his parents might, um, get him faster."

"I can't think about it," Ryan said.

My instincts went back to reporter mode. "Why would he do this? You think he was, uh, upset about yesterday?" *Duh.*

Ryan shrugged, and Mrs. Keyser's voice reached us. "Upset about what?"

I leaned into the couch, wishing I had some of Betty's cucumbers for my eyes. Betty! I looked at Ryan. "Are Sandi and Betty okay?"

"No one is okay."

Mrs. Keyser came into the living room holding two mugs of tea. "His poor parents. Aren't they in Florida?"

I accepted the tea, and she looked at Ryan. "There's more hot water in the kitchen."

He stood. "I need to see what's happening. For the paper. Sandi and I figured Mel would be alone." He looked at Mrs. Keyser.

"I'll stay up here as long as she wants."

It occurred to me that Mrs. Keyser didn't sound as if she was fishing for gossip, which was her usual mode. I was glad she was here.

Ryan left. I cradled my tea and stared at the wall near my parents' photo. If I looked at them, I'd lose it again.

"Melanie, do you want me to call anyone?"

I looked at her and sipped tea before speaking. "I'll call Ambrose in a bit. He and Sharon were in Fred's class."

"That's fine, but is there someone you want to come over?"

I blew my nose again. "I'm probably better off if I get cleaned up and go out in a bit. If I sit here, I'll just cry."

"Poor, poor Fred," she tutted. Her tone changed subtly. "Did he have a break-up or something?"

She had moved to beauty-shop-gossip mode, but I couldn't be angry. Fred's death would be the focus of most conversation in town for days. All I said was, "Maybe he left a note."

She stood. "You knock on my door if you need anything."

"Thanks. Thank you for coming up." My voice was shaky again. I needed to get out of my apartment.

I walked to the bathroom and leaned over the sink to splash water on my face. I didn't bother looking in the mirror. Who cared what I looked like?

I dried my face and turned toward the hall. Thankfully, I didn't shriek at the sight of Mister Tibbs, whom I'd totally forgotten. I scooped her into my arms. "I'm so sorry, buddy. Or should I call you girlfriend? I scared you, didn't I?" She snuggled into my shoulder, as if Mrs. Stevens carried her around like a toddler.

I put her on the floor next to the couch, near the old pillow and blanket I wanted her to think of as home base. I sat next to her and rubbed her belly for almost a minute. "You need to stay here while I go out, but I don't think I'll be too long."

After finishing the tea and some apple juice, I started to think more clearly. I wasn't sure I could talk to Ambrose without losing it again, so I texted him and Sharon. I apologized, but said I didn't want to cry more.

It was a given that Ambrose or Sharon or both would be in town by tomorrow morning at the latest.

Should I assume Fred committed suicide? Probably, but it would help if he left a note. It would help me if that note repeated everything he had told me about seeing Hal's body. If he didn't admit that he was nearby when Hal was killed and I was not, I'd still be a person of interest, probably. Or maybe his suicide could lessen suspicion.

Forget all that. Fred is dead!

I looked for a clean top and decided on a dark peach knit shirt rather than a tee shirt. Not that anyone cared what I looked like, but the news crews from Des Moines and Quincy would be in town. I didn't need to look like a vagrant. *Sunglasses. Where are my sunglasses?* Probably in my truck's glove box.

My crying jag had worn out Mister Tibbs, so she didn't fuss as I left. I was unlocking my truck when Granger's cruiser pulled into Mrs. Keyser's driveway. *If he says something about me hurting Fred, I'll figure out how to shove him into the river.*

For a change, Granger was almost solicitous as he got out of the car. "How you holding up, Mel?"

"Better than thirty minutes ago or so." I took a breath. "Did you get his parents?"

Granger nodded as he leaned against a front fender. "Yeah. Hard on the sheriff when he has to make those calls."

"You need me for anything?"

"Probably not. Sheriff wanted me to ask if you knew anything you hadn't thought of earlier, but if you don't, no need to go down tonight. Tomorrow's soon enough."

I shook my head. "I'll probably think better in a few minutes, but not sure what I know right now. Did he," I took a breath, "leave a note?"

"Think there was an envelope on his keyboard at home. Not sure what it was."

"I was going to the paper. Just to be with, be with the guys."

He nodded. "Come on down about eight-thirty tomorrow. Sheriff'll call you if he needs anything before that."

I started to ask if the IDI guys would be around, but I didn't really give a damn.

THE *SOUTH COUNTY NEWS* OFFICE was crowded, and a tray of cookies sat on the front counter. I stood just inside the door for a few seconds. When Hal had died people had stopped by, but nothing like this.

From where I stood, I could see yellow police tape on Fred's closed office door. If it hadn't been for that and the twenty or so people sitting in chairs around the bullpen, it would look the same. But everything was different.

I walked toward Sandi's desk, and a couple of chairs squeaked as people moved back.

Someone said, "I'm sorry, Melanie."

I didn't acknowledge them, but knelt next to Sandi, who had her head on her folded arms. I put my hand on her shoulder. "It'll be tough, but we'll all make it."

She raised her head. Her eyes were puffy, and her face was basically one red blotch. She seemed surprised to see the mascara all over her sweater, when she sat up. "He's been so withdrawn, but I didn't know what was bothering him. I would have helped him."

"We all would have."

I looked up to see Bruce Blackner and nodded. "Yes." I gave him a half smile and turned back to Sandi.

"You want to go home or stay and help me put the paper to bed?" Until the words were out of my mouth I didn't know they were coming.

She puffed her cheeks and blew out a breath. "Whew. What time is it?"

I glanced at the clock above the front door. "Three-forty-five. We have at most an hour and a half."

A woman's voice asked, "What kind of help do you need?" Peg Boynton owned the small bakery on the square. She had probably brought the cookies.

I stood from my squatting position and faced what was now a group of about fifteen people. "It means a lot that everyone came. And it's fine if you want to hang out, but maybe in the back or that meeting room near the bathroom for a bit. That way Sandi..." I scanned the room "and maybe Ryan and whoever can finish. We send the paper by computer to the printer."

There were murmurs, and Bruce Blackner said, "I'll sit by the door. I can direct folks to the conference room while you two finish working.

I noticed Stooper, who was sitting in a chair behind the others. He stood. "I'll go down to the tavern. Gary'll want to send over some sodas or something."

People started to walk toward the door. Peg Boynton blew a kiss, and I heard a woman's voice, I wasn't sure whose, say, "...and one of those cheese and cracker trays at the Hy-Vee."

I looked down at Sandi. She gave the barest smile and straightened her shoulders. "A mini-wake." She stood. "Okay. Come back here to the big computer screen, and we can finish layout. We'll have to add, to add..."

"At least a small piece about Fred," I finished.

Sandi and I were used to working together. We would know instinctively what to move off the front page to make room.

After a minute of looking at the screen, I said, "Maybe leave the picture of the mama goose and her brood, and put the article about getting them out of the sewer on page eight."

"Agreed. We can make the picture smaller if we have to. People'll need to see something happy." Sandi looked toward the door and back at me. "Ryan's supposed to be out seeing what happened. I just...couldn't."

The front door opened, and Doc Shelton walked in. He spoke briefly to Bruce Blackner and walked toward Sandi and me. "I'm sorry. It was so busy this afternoon. I couldn't leave patients."

Sandi was at the desk chair, and I was standing behind her. Doc Shelton gave me a peck on the cheek and put a hand on her shoulder. "Tribute to Fred that you're going to make the deadline."

"Thanks," Sandi said, her voice husky.

I looked at Doc Shelton. "It was mostly done. We're moving a couple of things, and as soon as we get more from Ryan, we'll put a short article on the front page. Unless he's found out a lot more."

He pulled a pen from the breast pocket of his shirt. "I'll write a short quote, something from the Advisory Committee."

I hadn't thought about getting comments from anyone besides what Ryan would bring back from the sheriff. Boy, are you rusty.

Sandi and I had just turned back to the computer screen when the door opened again. Ryan didn't look like an intern any more, and it wasn't just the haircut. His jaw was set, and his eyes focused only on Sandi and me.

When he was almost to us, he said, "I wrote a draft. You want to read my handwritten version or type it in first?"

"Easier to edit if you type it." When he raised his eyebrows at me, I smiled. "I'm not saying it'll need editing, just that you don't want Sandi and me leveling suggestions at your handwritten copy."

"Too true. Afternoon Doc." Ryan walked to his desk and turned on the computer screen.

Sandi and I had everything done except the blank left hand column on page one when Ryan called, "Go to the active folder."

Sandi swiveled and turned on the computer with a standard-sized screen that sits next to the larger one we use for layout. She went to the active folder and opened a file that simply said, "Fred."

> For the second time in a month, a South County
> News staff member has died. The body of Fred
> Simmons was first spotted by a pleasure boat
> approximately one mile south of Farmington.
> River's Edge residents had been looking for him
> since a sheriff's deputy found Simmons' car
> near the river at about five-thirty yesterday
> morning, May 17th.
>
> Circumstances surrounding Simmons' death
> are unknown, but Sheriff Michael Gallagher has
> said that a note was found in Simmons'
> residence. Details have not yet been disclosed.
>
> Simmons' death occurred just two weeks after
> that of Hal Morris, South County News
> publisher and editor, who was found murdered
> on the property of River's Edge resident
> Sylvester Seaton. County Sheriff Gallagher
> stated there is no immediate relationship
> between the two deaths, but he had been about
> to talk to Simmons to see if he knew more about
> Morris's whereabouts the night Morris was
> killed. Gallagher stressed that, at this point,
> Simmons is not a suspect in Morris's death.
>
> [insert Shelton quote]

> *Sheriff Gallagher has said his office will*
> *continue its investigation with possible*
> *assistance from the Iowa Department of*
> *Investigation. Findings will be released as they*
> *are available. Funeral arrangements are*
> *pending.*

Ryan had a separate article titled "box" that was a brief sketch of Fred's career.

Sandi whispered, "I was okay until I read about the funeral arrangements."

"It's very good," Doc Shelton said.

I hadn't realized he had come to stand behind Sandi and me.

Ryan walked toward us and looked at me. "What do you think, Mel?"

"Pertinent and to the point. I'm not sure I could have done as well today."

"Thanks." He met each of our gazes for a moment and then glanced at the front page layout. "I'm pretty drained. You care if I go home as soon as we're done?"

Sandi spoke, "Mel and I really only need to paste the text into the publishing software." She looked at Doc Shelton. "Done?"

He nodded and handed us a handwritten piece of paper, which Sandi and I scanned quickly.

Fred Simmons has been a stalwart member of the River's Edge publishing community since he edited the high school newspaper almost fifteen years ago. While he left the *South County News* for a stint at the Des Moines Register, he agreed to step into the role of interim editor and provided solid leadership during a trying time. He will be missed. The paper's Advisory Committee and staff extend its sympathies to Fred's parents, Harvey and Rose Simmons.

Sandi turned away, and I nodded. I might have added something about how Fred mentored all the new reporters but, really, nothing much mattered.

CHAPTER
TWENTY-ONE

USUALLY I READ my articles when they are published, but I didn't even look at Friday's paper. I awoke feeling numb and nothing penetrated.

It wasn't until I was making a second cup of tea that I realized Mister Tibbs was sitting in front of the apartment door, so that I would take her out to do her business. I leaned down to pet her. "I'm not being a very good human to you, am I?"

Her tail thump indicated disagreement, but a few days ago she was living under a wheelbarrow, so her judgment was skewed.

Sharon did not sound thrilled about staying in my guest room now that Mister Tibbs shared the apartment, but Ambrose laughed so hard about the mismatched name and sex that it made me more comfortable foisting the dog on Sharon.

I should never have taken the dog. I like having someone at the foot of my bed. And how much will I spend in vet bills?

Ambrose was able to get a neighbor to feed his cows for a few days and Sharon took off a half-day, so they had arrived in River's Edge about three-thirty on Friday. An hour later, Doc Shelton called to see if Ambrose could pick up Fred's parents at the airport Saturday. The friends Fred was closest to in high school weren't coming into town until late Saturday or Sunday.

That made Sharon cry, because Mrs. Simmons taught her math in middle school and she knew how Fred's parents doted on him, as she said. Ambrose, ever one to try to lift someone's spirits, wanted the three of us to drive to Des Moines to eat lunch and maybe visit the Botanical Gardens before going to the airport. I just couldn't, and he didn't push.

Before we finished our first cup of coffee Saturday morning, my mobile phone buzzed. Caller ID showed Doc Shelton's home number, and I flashed the phone at Ambrose before I answered.

As usual, he didn't let me finish saying hello. "Got a proposition for you Melanie. How would you like to be the temporary editor for..."

"No. Sir. Thank you, but no."

Perhaps it was my abrupt response, but he didn't try to persuade me.

"If you bring in someone and you want me to meet them or answer questions, I'd be happy to help."

We ended the call politely, and I looked at Ambrose. "Did you know he was going to ask me to be temporary editor?"

"Nope." He looked at Sharon. "You?"

She shook her head. "Our radar must be set wrong."

I shrugged. "Probably not. Doc kind of makes decisions and charges ahead."

Ambrose and Sharon looked at me as if they expected more.

"I just...can't. Everything bad that's happened in the last few weeks is centered at the *South County News*."

Ambrose started to say something, probably about a steady income, but Sharon cut him off. "Good choice."

By the time they left about nine on Saturday, Sharon had steeled herself so she could support Mr. and Mrs. Simmons. Much as I love Ambrose and Sharon, I thought the break in togetherness for a time was a good thing. Usually we're with each other to do something specific or celebrate Thanksgiving or Christmas. Hanging out to wait for a funeral has its own stresses.

SUNDAY MORNING WAS overcast, and it seemed fitting. I checked the weather forecast for Monday, and thank God, it was going to be sunny. I figured I could handle the memorial service if it was cloudy, but didn't think I could make it through a trip to the cemetery in the rain.

Fred was being cremated, and his parents wanted to bury his ashes near the plot they had already bought for themselves. Sandi had heard that Stooper was busting his butt to have part of the stone inscribed for Monday. He could finish it later.

Ambrose, Sharon and I went to the ten o'clock Sunday service. It was almost like a party. About ten of their classmates were in town already, and most of them attended the Methodist Church. Reverend Patrick said it looked as if we were celebrating Fred's life in two services. Fred's parents weren't there, maybe because it would be too hard to accept condolences on two days.

After the service, we stood just outside the church for about twenty minutes as people shared Fred stories or showed each other pictures of their kids. I mostly listened. I was friendly with these people, but hadn't been close to any of Ambrose's classmates except Fred.

"So, Mel," an Irish brogue rose above others, "do you have any newspaper shenanigans to share about Fred?"

I kept a smile as I turned to face Patrick Brannon, the class clown of Ambrose and Sharon's senior year. What I wanted to do was scream that this wasn't a party, but instead said, "Gosh, where to start?"

"Ah, c'mon. You got something."

"Okay, you know how people in parades throw candy at the crowd watching them?"

"Sure," Patrick said, "and Hal kept writing that it was just an excuse for litter, right?"

"Yep. Fred would stand on the opposite side of the street from Hal and try to hit him with candy." This was true, and it was one of my most light-hearted memories of Fred. "Sandi and I each gave him a quarter every time he hit Hal."

This sent Patrick into hysterics, and I used this diversion to kiss Sharon on the cheek. "I'll catch you guys later this afternoon."

With Patrick's voice calling for more stories, I made for my truck. We had driven separately because Ambrose and Sharon were going to lunch with some of their friends and I was meeting Sandi. I hadn't seen her since Thursday evening at the paper, sort of an unspoken agreement not to meet in person unless one of us needed something. Sandi seems to need a car battery jump almost monthly, so I had half-expected a call.

THE DINER WAS packed, but it's the only eatery open on Sunday mornings. Sandi was already at a back booth, and with her was Ryan. Sandi's sunglasses were on the table within easy reach, and she looked nervous. I blew her a kiss and swung in across from them.

"So, how was church?" she asked.

Ryan rolled his eyes.

"Shorter than usual and actually nice." I told her about the story sharing outside after the service.

"Gee, I should have gone."

"Gee," Ryan said, "I told you so."

I shrugged. "It could have been maudlin. I only went because Ambrose and Sharon are here."

Ryan leaned across the table and spoke in a low voice. "I want to get whoever killed Hal. As far as I'm concerned, he killed Fred, too."

Sandi put her sunglasses on, and I nodded. "It's all I thought of for two weeks, and Hal has hardly crossed my mind since, well, you know."

"Me, too," Ryan said, "but this morning I'm back on track."

I placed my purse on the table and pulled out the three by five cards. "These were my Thursday ideas."

Sandi drummed her fingers on the table for a second. "Can we order?"

I handed the cards to Ryan, and he went through them as we ordered from the Sunday food server.

When she left for the kitchen, I did a quick mental summary. Hal in the mulch, me on the hot seat, an unknown person who didn't want me to find the broom with mulch on it, and – because of his car's location – greater certainty that Hal was killed at Syl's.

That was it. No clear suspect, no evidence in sight beyond the car.

Ryan interrupted my thoughts. "What about the guy you're working for? I've dug up background. He looks like a geek. I don't find any record of him even owning a gun."

I raised my eyebrows. "You've been at it."

"You don't have to sound so surprised." His brief grin said he hadn't taken offense. "But Mel, I have to ask. Did Fred leave you a note or talk to you more?"

I shook my head. "If he'd left me one, I'd share." I looked at Sandi.

"He wouldn't even talk about the case with us. Why would he have left a note about it?"

I noticed she didn't say Fred had not left her a note.

Rather than a funeral home visitation, Fred's parents received friends in the church for the hour before Monday's memorial service. Ambrose, Sharon, and I arrived promptly at ten a.m., because they wanted to be sure to greet Fred's parents. I had proposed a later arrival, hoping not to. I'd written them what I hoped was a considerate note.

As the three of us moved forward in line, I glanced at Fred's parents several times. Mr. Simmons shook hands with vigor. Mrs. Simmons was perched on a short stool and rarely stood. She was seldom teary, but her soft handshakes seemed to take all of her energy.

An urn with Fred's ashes sat on the same table that had held Hal's photo less than two weeks ago. When I saw that, it made me too choked up to speak, so I shook Mr. Simmons' hand and kissed Mrs. Simmons' cheek. She was wearing a lot of perfume, and I stifled a sneezed as we walked toward a pew.

People chatted quietly, and eventually Sandi and Ryan arrived. They were friendly at the paper, but as far as I knew didn't spend time together outside of work. For now, Sandi seemed glued to Ryan's side.

After ten minutes of somber greetings with mostly Ambrose and Sharon's classmates, I realized some of them thought I dated Fred. At least I inferred that from the emphasis on certain words as they spoke to me.

"How are *you* doing, Melanie?

So glad Ambrose and Sharon could be with you, Mel."

When a woman I remembered as Student Council president in their year walked away, I looked at Ambrose and whispered. "Why do they think I dated Fred?"

"You can thank Mrs. Keyser," he whispered back.

Crud. I'd have to set her straight.

The service was grueling. Every time someone rose to the pulpit to share a story about Fred, they would end with, "If only I'd known," or "I would have done anything to help Fred."

After the service, I waited on the sidewalk while Ambrose and Sharon said goodbyes to friends who were leaving town that afternoon. Sandi and Ryan walked up to me, and it was the first time I had a good look at Sandi.

Her back dress was stylish, like you might wear to dinner at a fancy restaurant in Des Moines. She wore a simple silver cross, but what was most striking was that her eyes were glassy.

"So, Mel, we made it by…I mean through it."

She's had a sedative or something.

After Hal's innumerable staff meetings, Ryan, Sandi and I had learned to telegraph non-verbal opinions to one another. Mostly insults aimed at Hal. This time I gave Ryan a questioning look, and he did the barest nod.

I was about to ask Sandi if she felt okay (as if any of us did), when Doc Shelton made a beeline for us. With him was an African American man about fifty-five. I didn't recognize him, which meant he was likely from out of town. There are more Hispanic residents in River's Edge all the time, in large part because of the meat packing plant. I doubted there were more than ten black families.

"Good morning, crew," Doc said.

We returned the greeting, and I resisted telling him I was not on the paper's crew anymore.

Doc gestured to the man. "This is Scott Holmes. He's active in Lions, too, and he just retired as an assistant editor of the Iowa City Gazette.

We shook hands. Given Doc's call about me being temporary editor, I figured this was who he had gotten. Sandi and Ryan couldn't hide their surprise as Doc told us, but they recovered quickly.

Sandi asked, with only the briefest slur, "So will you work from Iowa City or move here for a while?"

"My wife and I have driven down a couple times to see the colors in October. This will be a great chance to get to know life along the river."

I took in Scott Holmes, as Doc assured Sandi and Ryan that Holmes would be a steadying hand and they would enjoy working with him. Holmes was almost six feet and trim, something not all sedentary reporters can say.

I said good-bye to Sandi and moved toward Ambrose and Sharon. Just beyond them were Sheriff Gallagher and his wife. I felt myself getting flushed. I wished I had told what Fred said about seeing Hal's body. *Why did I leave that for Fred to tell him?* If I told him now, he'd think I had some ulterior motive or, worse, arrest me for withholding information.

CHAPTER
TWENTY-TWO

THE DAY AFTER Fred's funeral, Ambrose and Sharon left at five-thirty, so Sharon would be on time for work in Dubuque. I felt somewhat better, maybe because I went to bed determined to be less sad. More normal. Whatever the new normal was. Between that and Mister Tibbs' constant presence, I was working toward an emotional mend.

Memorial Day weekend was only a few days away, and it was eighty-five degrees in the shade. My father always added the shade part when he wanted to say he thought it was too hot.

Ambrose wanted me to come to Dubuque for the weekend. I didn't feel like going to a barbeque with their friends and seeing some newly released movie, but I was more grateful for my brother now than I had been even after our parents' deaths. He might be more than one-hundred-fifty miles away, but wherever he is, Ambrose is by my side.

Car tires scrunched on the gravel in Syl's driveway, and I looked up from where I was planting a bunch of begonia plants near the front steps. The dark green Ford Taurus shouted rental car and not just because it had a rental company sticker on the back window. It was way cleaner than most cars that have been driven on country roads.

The man who got out was the same one who had stopped by previously to see if Syl was home. *Stopped by before Fred was dead.*

He stayed by the car. "Thought Syl might be home when I saw the truck."

I studied him. "Syl's is much better looking."

"Okay, I'll catch him later."

Without so much as a goodbye, the man got back in his car and began backing down the driveway. I thought about calling out to get his name, but if he didn't care to give it, I didn't care to ask. That kind of 'so what' thinking has been my norm since Fred died. I've been trying to care more about everyday things, but I don't.

At least I had the work at Syl's. Sandi was mad at me. She had heard that Doc Shelton asked me to serve as interim editor for a while, but I turned him down. I told her if they needed freelance work to fill in gaps, I'd do it because of her and Ryan.

Before I left for Syl's, Sandi emailed me that Scott Holmes was already at the paper. His handsome thirty-something son drove down to help Holmes move in his personal office chair and a couple of boxes. In spite of her grief, Sandi's email made it sound as if she was less annoyed at me.

At the reception after Fred's funeral, Mrs. Keyser introduced me to a new family practice physician, who also gets her hair done at Marvie Marvel's Beauty Shop. The woman is in an apartment and about to buy a house in town. Mrs. Keyser appears to think she is my booking agent.

I was getting bags of topsoil from the barn when more tires crunched on the driveway. This time it sounded like something heavier than a pick-up. Thinking Syl might have ordered furniture or something, I dusted my hands on my cut-offs and walked to the front yard.

The back end of a white van faced me. It took a minute to realize it was from the TV station in Quincy. *Oh, crud.*

I pasted a smile on my face and walked toward the van. A carefully groomed, slender woman about thirty and an older man in jeans and canvas boat shoes got out. *Let it be a feature story about Californians moving to Iowa.*

The woman saw me first, and she must have used the same kind of glue I did to widen a smile. She said something to the man, and he pulled a camera from the sliding door that gave access to the back seat area.

"You're Melanie, right? I'm Candi Spright."

Of course you are.

"I am. Are you looking for Mr. Seaton?"

"Not really." She nodded her shoulder-length blonde hair, in direct contradiction to herself. "I wondered if we could have a word about the press release the South County Attorney's Office issued this morning?"

That's the last time I leave my mobile phone in the truck. As a former reporter, I knew she had a job to do and a deadline. My goal was to be as uninteresting as possible. "Gee, I've been out here for several hours. What's up?"

Her face lit up. This was a television reporter's dream. Get the interviewee's first reaction to an event. Preferably one that made them cry if the camera stayed on long enough.

"County Attorney Smith stated that no charges would be filed against you in the death of your former editor, Hal Morris. How does that make you feel?"

Good thing I've played poker. "Puzzled, I guess. I had no clue that Mr. Smith was considering filing any charges."

Candi looked taken aback, but recovered quickly. "I believe that since you found his body, there was speculation that you might have killed him."

I was beginning to enjoy this. "There was some macabre humor about how he was found, and he did fire me for taking a lot of pictures of flowers. But I never heard any official, what did you call it, speculation about my being a murderer."

Her face turned pink, and her tone sharpened. "Perhaps it didn't reach you."

I knew my face reddened slightly, and I was very aware of my grubby clothes and the whirring camera. "It would be odd that neither my family lawyer nor I heard anything, yet someone in the prosecutor's office was talking to you."

She was definitely irritated, but probably not sure whether to be mad at me or some vague source. "So you did have a lawyer?"

"Most people *have* one, it's a question of whether you use them. Someone other than a local property owner tried to get me accused of trespassing because I hunted for Hal's car." I smiled. "Maybe the fact that no charges about that were filed made your source angry."

Now she had something to latch onto. "Why were you looking for his car?"

"Because it was missing, and I don't like loose ends any more than you do. It simply occurred to me to look in a wooded area not too far from here." As she took a breath to ask another question, I said, "I don't mind showing you where his body was found, but I would really appreciate it if you wouldn't show Mr. Seaton's house on the news. I'm by myself on the property a lot."

The camera operator spoke for the first time. "Already been on."

I nodded. "But not for the last couple of weeks and not with me on camera. There's no home close enough for anyone to hear me, if someone sees your story and decides to visit a woman on a lonely road."

News media hate lawsuits, so I knew that even if she didn't want to agree to keep the house off camera, Candi would tell her producers what I said and let them decide.

The cameraman grunted, "Where's the mulch pile?"

I turned and gestured they should follow me. "Pile's gone. It was removed immediately to look for evidence. You can take some video of the area near it. Flowers make it look peaceful now."

I had wanted something to take the focus off me, and it worked. Candi chatted as we walked. "Did you plant a lot of these flowers?"

"Some. A few were perennials that resurfaced. The property had been vacant for, oh, a year maybe."

We had reached the spot at the end of the driveway, and I pointed. "Not much to see now, but it gives you an idea of how isolated it is." I backed up a few steps.

Another mutter from the cameraman. "You wanna be in the shot?"

"I'm really, really tired of the attention."

"That's Bob, by the way," Candi said. She spent a full minute telling him where to point the camera, which explained Bob's gruff attitude.

When they were done and he had lowered the camera, Bob walked ahead of us toward the van.

"I'd like to ask you a couple more questions," Candi said.

I knew I was getting a version of reporter courtesy, since I'd taken them to the area where I'd found Hal. "I mind, but I know it's your job. Please don't sensationalize my role. From my point of view, I was in the wrong place at the wrong time, and I'm still hearing about it."

She nodded, and called to Bob. "Couple more questions."

He put the camera back on his shoulder and trudged toward us.

"Why don't you stand in front of the fence, near those, what are those flowers?"

"Irises. They're perennials, but they bloom later than daffodils and tulips." *Like she cares.*

As we walked, Candi asked, "Are you always here by yourself? Where does the owner, Seaton, isn't it, work?"

"He's working for a Des Moines firm. Sometimes he works at home."

She glanced toward the house. "He must do really well for himself. Do you know what he does?"

We had gotten to the fence, and I turned to face her. I didn't like talking about Syl's business. "Something to do with insurance, I think, but we've never talked about his job."

I stood where Candi directed. After more instructions on how he should aim the camera, Bob filmed as she spoke. "While there does not seem to be much evidence about who killed Mr. Morris, some have speculated that his successor Fred Simmons, who recently committed suicide, may have done so."

I had figured this was coming and had planned my answer with Fred's parents in mind. "You know, Fred would have to come back from the grave and give a positive answer to both of those things before I would believe them. I'm not sure who speculates to you, but I haven't heard anyone say that."

Candi interrupted before I could continue. "I understand that Hal Morris had not only fired Mr. Simmons but also worked to ensure he did not get unemployment compensation."

I spoke seriously. "If you've been talking to people around town, you know Hal fired a lot of people the last two or three years. Advertising revenue has gone down for most papers.

"I'm not suggesting you find out who else he fired besides Fred and me." I smiled. "It's just that Hal was not an easy person to get along with or to be around sometimes. I have to wonder if Hal was also in the wrong place at the wrong time. Maybe someone was trying to break into the house here, and Hal saw them."

"But why would he have even been out here?" she asked.

"That's the thing. Who knows if he was killed here? The autopsy report is public information. I read it. It doesn't say where he was killed."

Her tone was one of incredulity. "Killed somewhere else and brought here?"

"Who knows?" Then I remembered Hal's boat. "He would have to go by here sometimes to get to where he kept his fishing boat docked at Fairhaven. It would be an odd time to go there, but who's to say he wasn't going to the marina?"

She stared at me for a couple of seconds, and I looked at Bob. "I can't tell you what to film, but I can give you two some advice."

Candi and Bob looked at each other. She shrugged, and he nodded and took the camera off his shoulder. I noted he didn't turn it off. *Just like Ryan.*

I started walking toward their van. "The thing is, no one knows for sure Hal was killed here, hardly anyone liked the guy, and it's hard to imagine a motive for killing him. What was different in his life right then? If being a one hundred percent jerk was enough of a motive, he'd have been killed years ago."

This time Bob's grunt was half laugh. I noted his finger turned off the camera, and he began loading it into the van.

Candi stopped near the van, and I did, too.

"None of it makes sense," she said.

"Bingo. Hal's murder was the first major crime the *South County News* covered in I'm not sure how long. We've had serious assaults, always among people who knew each other, a couple arsons, always outbuildings. Sheriff Gallagher is good. But none of us have really looked into something like this. You've got an outsider's perspective, maybe you can come up with something. Be a good story."

If I was lucky, Candi would decide to chase at least one of my ludicrous suggestions and leave me alone.

"What was the last big murder?" Bob asked.

"Gee, I don't even know, and I grew up here. I've been through a lot of the paper's archives. Nothing sensational comes to mind." I shrugged. "It's probably been more than thirty years."

Candi frowned and looked at Bob. "Should be something somewhere that says when the last major murder was."

I swallowed. Fred could probably have told them.

I WENT HOME TO get Mister Tibbs, so she didn't sit in the apartment all day. She was now on a lead attached to Syl's back porch, and she barked as Stooper dug a huge hole for the maple tree I had picked out for the back of the house. I'd convinced Syl a tree would cut down on his summer air conditioning bills.

I got tired of the barking and thought it would be safe to have Mister Tibbs off her lead for a while, but she kept trying to get into the hole. When she wouldn't be deterred, I again attached her lead to a tree. She was worn out by then, so she didn't seem to mind. I began to think in terms of doggie obedience school.

In between shovels-full of dirt, which Stooper was throwing onto a piece of the degraded canvas tarp from the barn, I told him about the reporters and their questions.

When I finished, he stopped and wiped his forehead with the back of his arm. "Don't you think Syl will be mad you let 'em on the property?"

"Don't know. They were on it when they started talking, and I asked them not to show images of the house again. I think if I'd thrown them off the property, their visit here would have been the lead story."

"Prob'ly right." He went back to work, and more sweat poured down his face.

I took the small towel that I usually have on my belt loop, wet it with some water from my bottle, and handed it to him. "Try this."

"Thanks. Gettin' old."

I snorted it. "You're just a few years older than I am, right?"

"Yeah. Tryin' to cut back on the beer. I hear you sweat less."

I had noticed he seemed somewhat less round in front, but assumed it was from working for Syl. "It shows."

His grin was infectious, and I returned it. Stooper and I have developed a routine for working together. He says hello when he arrives, we agree about what he's going to do, and he often works on another part of the property than I do. He does the work that requires the most muscle, though I think I can do almost anything he can. It would take longer, sometimes, so I rationalize that while there are two of us at times, Syl will pay for fewer hours of work.

Sometime about six o'clock, Stooper is done for the day, says good-bye, and walks down the driveway. I have stopped offering him a ride. Sometimes we sit together on the porch to drink water, but most days not.

Just after six, Stooper was almost at the gate, when Syl pulled into the driveway. Syl put his window down, and they spoke for a moment, then Stooper started walking again. I put the rake I was using to loosen the ground for grass seed in the wheelbarrow and started toward where I knew Syl would park his truck. Since I don't usually walk over, he paused before going in the side door.

"I did my best to keep your house off TV."

"Damn. They were here again? Which ones?"

"This time from Quincy."

He sat his briefcase on the ground and leaned against his perpetually clean truck. "As long as it's not Des Moines. I actually know people in this state now, and they're mostly in Des Moines."

"We can blame the county attorney. I haven't seen the press release, but apparently he felt a need to issue something that said he isn't charging me with anything."

"Must be running again soon."

I laughed at Syl's cynicism and told him what I'd talked to the reporters about.

He frowned. "Sounds like a lot."

"Some with the camera off." *I hope.* "I asked them not to show the house or the full lot, since it would show I'm here alone. They'll be afraid of a lawsuit if I end up in your next mulch pile."

He shook his head. "I'm going to talk to that damn prosecutor. No one's been by for a couple of weeks. I don't need this."

"You could put up a no trespassing sign."

"I've thought about that. But I moved here because the Midwest is supposed to be friendly. I've seen them on some fences near livestock, but they don't seem to be commonly used."

"They aren't." *And they don't keep out murderers.*

THE PHONE IN MY apartment rang about seven o'clock that evening. Sheriff Gallagher's voice wasn't stern, but it didn't sound too friendly either. "I wouldn't go looking for the county attorney for a while if I was you. Smith is royally peeved at you."

"No plans. If I had a heads up about his damn press release, I'd have known how to handle the reporters who showed up at Syl's place." I'd picked up a copy of the press release at the paper, since I knew the courthouse would be closed by the time I finished at Syl's. It said nothing new and made it sound as if Myron Smith had investigated me personally.

"Now you know what to expect if you see him."

"I won't go looking for him. Syl Seaton wasn't keen on having reporters at his place again. Between you and me, his reaction was that good ol' Attorney Smith must be getting ready to run again."

The sheriff actually chuckled. "Not the first I've heard that." He grew serious again. "I wouldn't do anything else to encourage those Quincy TV folks. You hear anything concrete, you call me, right?"

"I have to. Ambrose will put an ankle bracelet on me and track my movements if I do anything else."

"Funny. He told me the same thing." He paused. "My wife is glad you stood up for Fred."

It registered that Gallagher had not said he was glad. "I just wish he were here to do it himself."

CHAPTER
TWENTY-THREE

AT THE DINER WEDNESDAY morning, consensus was that I'd done a 'smack down' on County Attorney Smith.

"Honest, Shirley, I didn't say one insulting thing about him. I think those reporters were ticked that they drove down here for nothing." I kept my voice moderately loud because a court reporter was in a booth toward the back. She could carry that message back to Smith for me.

I was at the counter, so Shirley put her elbows on it and leaned toward me. "There's no such color as that Candi girl wears her hair."

I grinned. It felt good to talk about something trivial.

I had paid and was about to leave when Sandi and Ryan came in. They both looked tired. Sandi had told me the interim editor was having them do a lot of stories about everyday activities. It makes sense. Life along the river in southeastern Iowa is all new to him.

Sandi pointed to a booth. "Park it."

Shirley called from the other end of the diner. "Regulars?"

"Yep," Ryan said, and Sandi nodded.

"I'm done," I called.

We sat. "What's up?"

"We're supposed to, officially, talk to you about what you said to Quincy," Sandi said, using reporter verbal shorthand.

"I didn't see the whole story, just the snippet on the ten o'clock news."

"Oh, it was more than a snippet at six," Ryan said.

Sandi started to describe the earlier newscast, but I held up a hand. "Whatever they said, it'll be what, sixty percent accurate? Let me just tell you what we talked about."

I finished, and Sandi's first question was, "Was Syl mad at you?"

"He knows I didn't invite them. I asked them not to show the full property. Did they?"

"Huh," Ryan said. "I wondered why it was just flowers and mud where the mulch was."

"Syl's tired of his house being on the news. I asked the Quincy guys not to show it again, because I'm there alone a lot."

Sandi leaned against the back of the booth. "Oh, good. They'll be afraid of getting sued. I think Susie or, what's her name?"

"Candi," Ryan and I said.

"She's on a quest to find a murderer. I saw Aaron Granger at the gas station this morning. He's more than irritated at you. Said it sounds like you said they didn't do their job."

"He told you that so you'd tell me, you know."

"Probably," Ryan said. "But Seaton won't like her angle on his job."

I groaned. "What did they say?"

Sandi answered. "They talked about the contract he got. They didn't say anything bad about him, but you could tell good ol' Candi wanted people to wonder why an outsider got such a big contract."

"Nuts. I didn't tell her that. Sheriff called me last night, but he didn't mention anything about Syl's work."

"Why'd he call you?" Ryan asked.

"Mostly to warn me to keep my nose clean. He knows it's the reporters doing the needling. He just wanted to make sure I wasn't doing any more looking."

"So you told him about Ambrose's threat?" Sandi asked.

"Ambrose had already told him." I looked at Ryan. "Heard you got a promotion."

"Yeah. Dollar an hour more, too. Mr. Iowa City was impressed I found the private security cameras. Wish he'd stay."

"What's his name again?" I asked.

Sandi and Ryan spoke together. "Scott Holmes."

Shirley walked by with an order. "You want another dollar, shug?"

"Not now," Ryan said. "He doesn't care how long my hair is. Said in Iowa City a guy my age'd look weird with hair this short."

BY TWO-FORTY FIVE I was back at Syl's place. He had decided I could spend two hundred dollars for plants, and I was having a blast. I was using the barn to lay out bedding plants and seeds and had been putting them on the floor. Yesterday Stooper had brought over a badly scarred table and nailed a piece of plywood to it, so I no longer had to sit on the dirt.

The diagram of locations for various plants needed some revision. I'd crossed hydrangeas off my list because, while I like the colorful snowball plants, they need too much water. The betting around town was on a dry summer.

Because I was buying a lot of plants and because Andy had been a jerk, Jody at Farm and More was giving me twenty-five percent off. I wasn't supposed to tell anyone although, if Andy knew, it was all over town.

I reached for a small hosta plant as a shadow crossed my hand. I jumped and turned. Syl's prior visitor stood there. He still had on city clothes, a collared shirt and sports jacket, and today he sported a straw hat. Not the kind a farmer would wear, a dressy one.

"I didn't hear you drive up."

"Saw your truck again, so thought I'd come back."

He was only about two feet from me, too close for normal conversation with someone you don't know. *And someone who shows up unannounced when I'm alone.* "Syl's not here."

"Noted. He never seems to be around. You tell him I come by, right?"

I turned fully to face him. I reached for a plant so it might not be as obvious that I was moving away. "I did, but you never leave your name."

"True. Syl and I, we aren't best friends."

My tone was sharp. "Why are you here? You have to know you're making me uncomfortable."

His demeanor changed to one of a friendly neighbor. "I'm sorry." He moved back and gestured toward the barn door. "You're working miracles with this place."

I relaxed a little, but not much. "Did you want me to tell Syl your name this time?"

His stare was impassive. "Just Bill."

"Okay, Just Bill. I do need to get back to work."

He walked to the barn door and stopped. "I saw you on TV last night."

"My agent is off today."

He laughed, loudly. "I knew I liked you."

I don't like you. Not one bit.

He studied me for a couple of seconds. "If that guy who committed suicide didn't kill your old boss, who do you think did?"

"I have no idea." I wanted to tell him not to talk about Fred, to yell at him not to. Instead, I simply asked, "Did you even know either of them?"

"No. Just seemed odd that two people close to you died recently. Not sure I'd want to be your friend."

Stooper's voice came from just outside the barn. He had walked to the far side of the building. "Not sure Mel is looking for new friends."

Just Bill started, but within a second he made himself appear casual. "Too bad. She seems to be losing some."

I'd never heard Stooper yell. "You get the hell off Syl's property!"

"Gee, I'm not sure Syl would appreciate…"

Stooper took three quick strides, stopping just a few feet from the interloper. "You listen here. Get in your fancy car, and get the hell outta here."

Just Bill looked at Stooper and at me before turning to leave. "And they say river towns are friendly."

I looked at Stooper, saying nothing.

In a low tone, he said, "Be right back."

Stooper followed Just Bill and stopped when he reached the driveway. I figured he could watch Just Bill leave from there. Stooper waited until about fifteen seconds after a car engine started and then turned to walk back to the barn.

I was at the front entrance of the barn, leaning against the door jamb.

"Know him?" Stooper asked.

"He's stopped by before, twice, looking for Syl. He's never done more than get out of his car."

"Did he park far down the driveway those times? He was halfway to the road."

"He stopped near where I was working, so I didn't give it any thought. He never even told me his name until today."

Stooper's frown deepened. "That guy wanted to block you in. Where's Syl?"

"Work, I guess. You know he's rarely here until five or so. Some days I don't see him at all."

"We need to talk to Syl tonight. You got your phone?"

I nodded.

"Keep it where you can reach it easy."

Stooper turned to walk toward a large pile of brush at the back of the property, and I got back to work with the bedding plants. It was hard to concentrate on which colors to put together when Just Bill's visit was fresh in my mind. Earlier he said he knew Syl's phone number. Why did he come by without being sure Syl was home?

Just Bill couldn't live near River's Edge. If he lived nearby he would have said the town he was from, same as any normal visitor. I decided to wait until Syl came home and insist that he talk about Just Bill, including what Syl would do to keep the creepy guy away from me.

My cell buzzed. I didn't recognize the number, but knew it was Illinois. I debated not answering, but if it was the Quincy people there would be no putting them off.

"Melanie?"

"Hello, Candi."

"Oh, good. You recognize me."

Good for whom?

"Can I ask you a couple questions?"

I kept my tone even. "I'll answer them if they seem reasonable."

"You're so funny."

You haven't seen funny from me, lady.

"Did you think Hal was either looking into something to do with Syl Seaton's business or with the insurance industry in Iowa?"

When in doubt, answer a question with a question. "Hmm. Why would you think that?"

She didn't even hesitate. "I heard word around town was that he was planning some exposé."

I laughed. "Hal never went far from southeast Iowa, very southeast Iowa. Last time he wrote something of substance about an insurance company he had to do a retraction."

"Yes, I read that when I was doing some research. That took me to Mr. Blackner, and he said he thought you were looking into stories Hal was writing."

Damn, she's good.

"Not exactly. I offered to go through the folders on his desk and credenza, to make sure there wasn't anything in there that Fred needed to use for a story."

"Even though you were a suspect?"

I said nothing for three full seconds. "It's Sheriff Gallagher's investigation. If he told you I was, he never told me. Listen, I'm working. Gotta go."

I didn't answer when she called back four times. Let her develop her own story.

STOOPER WAITED UNTIL about six-thirty, but I was determined to talk to Syl. He got home at seven, parked his truck, and went inside. He came onto the front porch from inside, holding two bottles of water. "You okay?"

"Mostly. That man who's been here twice before came today. I asked his name and he said to tell you just 'Bill.' Can you think who that would be?"

He sat in a canvas chair next to mine, and sighed. "I can guess. What did he look like?"

"Kind of tall, maybe six feet. Dressed like you, shirts with a collar all the time. Good tan." I thought for a moment. "The first time he was here he was driving an older Lincoln."

Syl sighed, but stared at the front yard without answering. Thinking, or so I thought.

"He also said you guys weren't pals."

His eyebrows went up and he looked at me before regarding the lawn again. "You asking as reporter or friend?"

"I'm not sure I'll ever report again. Friend." *I guess I'm your friend.* I watched Syl's profile as he spoke.

"He helps people write proposals, like the one I did to get the insurance industry contract. I paid him a fee. He never mentioned he expected five percent of the contract."

"How much was it?" I wondered if Syl would tell me the amount I'd seen in the Des Moines paper.

He studied me and looked away. "Between you and me, more than six figures."

"What makes you so smart?"

He laughed and turned his chair to face me. "You always get to the nub of things."

"My put-up-with-bull-o-meter is set pretty low. Can't you go to the sheriff?"

"That's two questions. First, I rented a very small office on the east side of Des Moines, near the fairgrounds. I have two people who work with me, each about ten hours a week, to develop the implementation plan. Never good to be the smartest person in a room. Second, what the heck would I tell him? There's no paper trail, as the auditors say. It'd be Bill's word against mine."

"I find him intimidating." I described Just Bill's behavior that afternoon.

He stood and paced the porch. "I'll call him." He stopped in front of me. "You willing to work only with Stooper here for a few days? If it's not enough hours, you can bill me now and do the work later."

"Sounds as if you think he's dangerous."

"More devious. He knows he worried you, and he hopes that'll make me call him."

I looked at Syl directly. "So you didn't call before?"

"I should have. Nothing he has to say will change my mind about giving him a cut. I didn't see how a call would make a difference."

"Did you know him long before he helped you?"

Syl shook his head. "Because of the size of the contract there was what's called a pre-bid meeting. A chance for people who are interested in the work to ask questions. Bill was there."

"So you beat him out for the project?"

"Ostensibly. I think he wanted to meet people who were interested to offer his services. Said he knew his way around Iowa government."

I thought about this. "Are you the only person he helped?"

Syl's laugh had a bitter quality. "For all I know he worked with several people. Could have made a lot of money."

I couldn't think of more questions, so I stood. "I'll talk to Stooper about being here when I am." As I got to the bottom of the porch steps I thought of one other thing. "I don't think I asked you. Did you ever meet Hal?"

The amused expression was there for a split second, and he sobered. "Briefly. He invited me to coffee at that run-down gas station at the north edge of town."

"That tacky place?"

"Their coffee seems to be the cheapest in town. He thought I sold computers. Wanted me to buy advertising."

I was halfway home before two things occurred to me. If I was on my toes, I'd have asked Syl about Just Bill's full name. And, in addition to not liking Just Bill, he was more than creepy enough to be Hal's murderer.

Buy why would Just Bill and Hal have been at Syl's the night Hal was killed? Was Syl hiding anything from me?

ON THE ONE HAND, suspicion about Just Bill was something I maybe should take to Sheriff Gallagher. On the other hand, suspicion was probably too strong a word, and I would have to say something about Syl's affairs that he definitely would not want the sheriff to know. I decided to keep my thoughts to myself. For now, anyway.

I turned into Mrs. Keyser's driveway about seven-thirty, ready for dinner, but needing to do one more thing. I said hush several times as I climbed the steps to my apartment. Mister Tibbs' only truly bad habit is barking incessantly when she hears me coming home. And whining when I leave.

"Come on, just a quick walk. Then I have to look for Stooper at the tavern." We walked halfway down the block and walked back, when I had a plastic bag of his business.

When we got to the bottom of the steps to go up to the apartment, he balked and sat.

"Come on, buddy, girl. I won't be gone long." Mister Tibbs sat on her haunches and gave me a gooey-eyed stare. "Okay, but you'll have to sit in the truck while I go into the tavern."

The plastic bag went into the outside garbage can, and I vowed I would wash my hands when I got to the tavern. Mister Tibbs settled on her blanket in the back seat and selected a chew toy.

I headed for Beer Rental Heaven. It was nearly dark and a cool sixty degrees. When I parked, I put each window down a few inches and locked the truck, promising a nervous Mister Tibbs that I would be back soon.

When I walked into the tavern, I went first to the rest room. I had planned to clean up a bit at home after walking Mister Tibbs, and I should have. I rubbed at a spot of dirt on my cheek, probably from rubbing my face with work gloves. *Syl should have told me that was there.*

I applied lipstick and walked out of the ladies room, almost directly into Stooper. "Whoa." I smiled, but he did not.

"I saw you come in. You okay?"

"Yep. And I want to stay that way." I started to the bar. "Syl had a request. Can I buy you a beer?"

He walked next to me and then behind me as we threaded through a few of the small tables. I saw no one I knew, not surprising because I only come in a few times a year.

Stooper sat in front of a half empty beer glass.

"What can I get you?"

"I only do two a night now. He glanced at a clock above the bar. And I don't do the second one until nine."

"Gee, that's…"

"Unexpected?" Gary said.

I frowned at the bartender. "I'll have an iced tea. The plain kind." Gary shook his head slightly as he walked away, and it irritated me. I tip well.

Stooper frowned. "I'm usually a lot of his business. If I'm sober, he takes a hit."

"You'll be his business longer if you keep cutting back."

"Yep." He met my gaze in the mirror. "What does Syl want?"

"That I be there only when you are for a while. He knew the guy and doesn't like him."

Stooper didn't say anything.

"You don't have to come more often. For one thing, I'm going to Dubuque to see Ambrose and Sharon for Memorial Day."

"I guess if my back hurts or something I can sit on the porch. You know, not charge him."

"Didn't know you had a sore back."

"Getting rid of this beer belly'll help that, too. If Syl's thinkin' the guy's no good, maybe we should wait until after Syl deals with him."

"We...could. He probably won't come two days in a row, and I need to get those plants in the ground before I go away. How about tomorrow and be done for a bit?"

Gary brought my iced tea. "Just tea." He nodded at a guy near the door and headed that way.

"Sure. I can check out mowers for Syl while you're away."

We agreed he would come at three instead of four the next day. After a couple of awkward minutes of small talk, which I have no idea how to make with Stooper, I downed the rest of my tea and headed home.

CHAPTER
TWENTY-FOUR

THE NEXT DAY WAS the Thursday before Memorial Day. I woke early, and by eight-thirty had done a load of laundry and spent an hour trying to teach Mister Tibbs to fetch.

I was also trying to get the little dog comfortable with the new crate I'd bought. Dr. Marshall needed his back, and I thought, if we had to travel outside of town, Mister Tibbs needed more space and, probably, protection if I had a fender bender. The crate cost as much as two weeks' groceries.

Mister Tibbs was apparently familiar with crates and not too fond of them. She would only go in one if I put a treat or ball in it. *So much for preparing her for a road trip.*

The day dragged. Since I couldn't go to Syl's until Stooper joined me, I of course wanted to get there much earlier. Instead I finished washing the sheets from the guest room and made Mrs. Keyser's day by siting on the front porch with her for twenty minutes.

I drove to Syl's about two-forty-five and parked at the far end of the driveway, thinking Stooper might drive his old car and need to park beside me. He had finally had his muffler repaired.

The watering can I'd brought from home filled quickly with the hose. Syl would have to get his own can, because I didn't feel like tugging a hose all over the yard to water small groupings of flowers and I needed my can at home.

I walked into the barn totally unprepared to see another person and just missed being grabbed by the right shoulder. I was off balance for a second, but managed to grab a potted geranium and hurl it at Just Bill.

He spit dirt. "You stupid broad. You need to learn to be quiet."

I ran to the other side of the plywood-topped table. *Why didn't I wait for Stooper?* "What do you want? I never did anything to you!"

He edged around the table toward me. I kept moving, meaning we were circling or, in this case, more like squaring off around the table. Thankfully, the plywood was too long for him to reach across.

I studied him more closely. Just Bill was slim and had muscular arms under his polo shirt. Just what I needed, someone chasing me who was stronger and could probably run faster.

"Stupid reporters and their questions. You need to keep your mouth shut. Have you got that?"

Maybe he doesn't want to kill me. Small favor. Big favor, really. "I'm not a reporter anymore."

"You're helping that phony woman at the TV station."

At least he knew how to tell which reporters had phony attitudes. "She called me. I'm not returning her calls now."

He stopped. "Why not?"

"Whatever she's working on, she wants me to do her legwork. I'm no sucker."

He almost growled. "Neither am I. You told her I helped Syl."

"Did not. You never even told me your last name."

That seemed to register with him.

How did sparkly Candi know to call him?

He started walking around the table again. "You're the only link between me and Syl."

Syl and me. "Syl said you gave him advice on applying for his contract or something like that. You mean to say no one else in Des Moines knows that?"

He stopped moving around the table and turned toward the door of the barn. "You mind your own business, girlie."

Girlie? It seemed he realized I didn't send Candi to him. I had nothing to lose. "Why did you kill Hal?"

He turned back, but his expression didn't change. "Thought it was your reporter friend. The guy who offed himself."

I felt hot all over. "Maybe you did it, and he saw you."

"From what I read, there's no proof of anything anybody did that night."

"Since you think that, you must have done it." My voice rose. "You killed Hal, and somehow you knew to frame me for it." *Are you insane? Why are you irritating this man?*

"I'm not saying I didn't stumble on your friend doing the deed. He shoulda stayed home."

He was there!

He must have seen something in my expression, because he blinked rapidly a couple of times and moved toward the table again.

My voice was calm. "You say you saw Fred do it. I bet he saw you."

He charged around the table at full run. He'd picked a good time to do it. I wasn't close to either the front or back barn entrance. I grabbed another geranium. I'd never get to the shovel that sat by the barn door, and even if I could get off a swing, he could deflect it. He'd grab the shovel, and my brain would turn into liquid plant fertilizer.

I ran out the barn's front door. My keys were in the truck. Could I make it that far? I got close to the house and could hear him breathing behind me. *I'm not going to make it!*

As I dashed by the side steps to the house, I took in something red. It moved.

Just Bill panted hard. "Gotcha you... little shi... argh!"

He went down hard, and Stooper sat on him before Just Bill could move.

Stooper was as red as his shirt. "Don't stand there. Use your phone thing."

AT LEAST I HAD asked Stooper to meet me. If I hadn't, my time alone at Syl's, no matter how brief, would have sent Ambrose into a hollering fit and an online website to buy an ankle bracelet.

"Ambrose, it was fifteen minutes. In a million years, I didn't think anything could happen in fifteen minutes.

"Tell that to Hal and Fred," he snapped.

"Oh, that's helpful. And mean."

He said nothing for several seconds. "Poor choice of words. You know what I'm saying."

If he says Mom and Dad were killed in an instant too, I'm hanging up. "I get the blink-of-an-eye concept. Even if this guy isn't the killer, I'm still going to work only if Stooper or Syl is there. For a while, anyway."

A woman's voice came from the doorway to Sheriff Gallagher's office, where I was sitting at the conference table. I turned to see his secretary, Sophie. "Sheriff would like you to talk to those two IDI agents. You know who I mean?"

"Wish I didn't," I muttered. "I'll finish with my brother and be right there." She left, and I spoke to Ambrose again. "Hear that?"

"Yeah. Is Brownberg there yet?"

"Did you call him? I didn't do anything. I don't need a lawyer."

"You didn't do anything three weeks ago either, and I'm damn glad we had him. He should be there soon."

I walked from where I'd been sitting in Sheriff Gallagher's office to the conference room down the hall, where I paused in the doorway. I had expected to see Stooper with the sheriff. Instead, it was just Gallagher and Agent Masters. "Where's Stooper?"

"Just answering a few questions," Masters said.

I stayed in the doorway and faced the sheriff. "Are you telling me you're questioning him like a suspect? He probably saved…"

Brownberg's voice was coming toward me. "Melanie."

I looked down the hall and nodded to him. "Sir, could you please go to where Stooper is? I think they're probably treating him the way they treated me for a while."

When Brownberg hesitated, I said, "I'll pay you. Lots of people would probably contribute."

Brownberg leaned into the conference room and looked at Gallagher. "I have been retained for Mr. Sanders. I believe I know the way."

I walked into the room, and Masters said, "Please close the door."

"Only if you have a tape recorder. You've been trying to railroad me since day one." When he said nothing, I sat without closing the door.

I looked first at Sheriff Gallagher. "Why are you letting them do this to people in your town? You said you called them in, that it was still your case."

Gallagher sat stiffly. "It is. I appreciate your help."

I took a breath. "Thanks, but I told you what I know. This guy," I jerked my head toward Masters, "is just looking for ways to get the egg off his face."

Masters sighed, apparently trying to appear plaintive. "I had thought we could…"

"Stuff it. Just ask me questions. I'll answer."

"Very well. What time did you get to Mr. Seaton's property?"

"As you know, about two-forty-five."

"And were you there alone?" Masters asked.

"As you know, I was by myself until the guy who seemed to want to shut me up showed himself."

"And what time was that?"

"As you know, he must have gotten there sometime before two-forty-five."

Masters was sitting very erect. "It's not necessary to say 'as you know.'"

"Ask me questions you don't know the answer to, and I won't say that."

"Melanie," Sheriff Gallagher said, "it doesn't have to take long. Mr. Masters needs to do his job."

"With respect, Sheriff, he's a criminal investigator. He thinks everything needs to be probed three times, even if what happened is as plain as a lightening bug on a July night." I faced Masters. "And he's seen the bug."

A door down the hall closed with force, and footsteps came rapidly toward the conference room. As I turned toward the door to the hallway, Ken Brownberg walked in.

He glared at the sheriff. "Mr. Sanders is leaving now. You've had his cooperation. You can send the browbeater home."

Quieter steps grew closer. Brownberg walked out of the room and nodded to someone down the hall. Stooper followed Brownberg toward the exit. He didn't even look in the conference room.

The three of us were quiet for several seconds. Sheriff Gallagher stood. "Agent Masters, how about you and I go visit with Agent Holcomb."

"I can stay here," Masters said.

"It wasn't a request." Sheriff Gallagher opened the door slightly wider, and Masters preceded him through it. The sheriff didn't look at me.

I stood and walked around the metal interview table twice, thinking it would be awhile before the men came back. However, Sheriff Gallagher and Agents Holcomb and Masters were back in less than two minutes.

Gallagher opened a small notebook. "Okay, we've established timing. Tell me when you first saw Bill Jefferson.

I told him about the prior times Just Bill, now known as Bill Jefferson, had come to Syl's property and then shared our brief conversations.

"Did you see a car today?" Holcomb asked.

Gallagher cleared his throat. "What about a car? Did you see one?"

"Wasn't in the driveway when I drove in. I think he was already in the barn. The earlier times weren't the same cars." I described the Lincoln and mentioned what I thought was a rental sticker on the second car.

A phone on the table near the sheriff buzzed, and he reached for it and pushed a button. "What is it, Granger?"

The deputy must have talked immediately because Gallagher concentrated as he listened.

I realized Jefferson must have left his car somewhere else, because he meant to hurt me and didn't want to be seen on the property. *Hurt me or kill me?*

"Okay, Granger. Ask him if he drove a rental car or the Lincoln this afternoon and where it might be. If he'd tell you and let you search, it'd save getting a warrant. If he won't, it tells us something else." The sheriff hung up without explaining himself.

Before he spoke, I figured it was my turn. "Does this Jefferson have a record?"

"I won't know out-of-state information for a bit." He glanced at the IDI agents. "Unless you two can speed that process."

Holcomb nodded at Masters, who stood and left the room.

Gallagher continued. "So this Jefferson made no overt threat toward you yesterday, but you and Stooper didn't, what, like his attitude?"

"He was trying to catch me off-guard, and he said he and Syl weren't friends or pals or something."

"And yet you were there alone today?" Holcomb asked.

"Just for ten minutes or so."

Gallagher gave a look of irritation toward Holcomb and then looked at me. "It can take far less than a minute to kill someone."

WHEN I LEFT THE sheriff, I drove first to the tavern and then to the north end of town where Stooper lived. I finally identified the house because there were several blank headstones in front of a lean-to. However, Stooper's car was nowhere to be found.

I felt as if I had dragged him into something unpleasant, something made worse when his somewhat sloppy demeanor probably meant the IDI agents treated him with less courtesy than they'd showed me.

As if they showed me any courtesy.

I SAT IN BED Thursday night, notepad and pen in hand, and thought about Just Bill. Between everything I'd told the sheriff and his own common sense, he would consider Jefferson Hal's murderer. That was good for me, but a good lawyer could say it was all circumstantial.

The only thing Jefferson's attack on me showed was that he was furious the Quincy television people contacted him and he blamed me for it. He could say he simply didn't want his demands to Syl made public.

Better an extortion charge than a murder rap, and since Jefferson's demands were likely to have been verbal, even Syl's testimony might not be enough to convict. After all, Syl hadn't gone to the sheriff to file a complaint.

The blank paper was taunting me. *You have to step outside the box you're thinking in.*

HALF AN HOUR LATER, I had what a journalism professor once said was the basis for most discoveries, whether delving deep for a big story or working to create a new medicine. My 'what if' list wasn't long, but if any item on it were true, it would change nearly all my thinking about the murder.

What if Hal had been in touch with Jefferson before that night, and he went to Syl's to meet Jefferson? Hal knew about Syl's large contract with the insurance organization. Had he connected Syl to Jefferson?

What if Syl had agreed to pay Jefferson a larger fee if he won the bid, and Syl backed out of the deal? What recourse would Jefferson have had other than to expose Syl as having unethical business practices? Or break into Syl's home to demand payment.

What if Hal had been at the house to harass Syl and running into Jefferson was a coincidence? An odd one, surely, but possible.

Unfortunately, I couldn't prove any of these things on my own. Phone records and email could show a connection between Hal and Jefferson, but it's not like I had access to them.

I looked up from my list. What would Hal's credit card and phone bills show? The sheriff must have them.

CHAPTER
TWENTY-FIVE

BEFORE I COULD START to delve into my list, a knock door woke me at eight o'clock Friday morning. I had meant to get up earlier so I could call Sandi and share my theories about Jefferson. She had left three messages on my phone last night.

I knotted my bathrobe and looked at Mister Tibbs, who viewed most noises as a call to eat. "You know who it is?"

She gave the kind of adoring stare dogs reserve for their best human buddies.

I peeked out the curtain on the door. Syl gave the peace sign.

"Give me two minutes."

This time I would get dressed before letting a man into the apartment.

Spit bath done and a clean navy blue top over beige slacks, I opened the door and gestured that he should come in. "Not as fancy as your place, but it'll do."

He glanced at the kitchen on the right and living room ahead, before walking toward the couch. "Sorry, thought you were up long before this."

"I've been up," I lied, "just taking it slower today."

He sat on the couch, and I moved to the recliner across from him.

"You think it's all done?" he asked.

"Since I'm not sure of all that's gone on, I don't know." I met his eyes. "I had to tell the sheriff what you said, about Just Bill wanting some kind of payoff from you."

"I believe the formal word is extortion."

"Whatever. Last I heard he hadn't confessed to killing Hal."

"The sheriff and your good friend Masters spent more than an hour with me last night. Now that they have Bill Jefferson's fingerprints, they could compare them to a couple of unidentified ones that turned up at my place."

"Really? Where?"

"A full hand print on the small banister on my back steps. He could easily say it's from another time he stopped by. But there was also a partial on an inside wall of the barn, near where that broom sat. When they dusted for prints after Hal's murder, the sheriff said it appeared that a lot of places on the property had been wiped down. Jefferson missed some spots."

I sat back in the recliner. *This is good, but it's not enough to convict Jefferson of killing Hal.*

Syl cleared his throat. "So, your buddy Fred could have seen Bill that night. Why wouldn't he speak up?"

I managed to shrug. "Maybe Fred saw him do it or got there immediately afterwards, and this Jefferson guy threatened him." My mind churned. *But why get my hoe?* How did Fred even know I had gotten the work with Syl? Sandi had only called me about the job that afternoon, and Hal didn't have his tantrum in Hy-Vee until late evening.

Since I had no answers about Fred, I pushed Syl about Jefferson. "What else does Jefferson do for a living besides help people write contract proposals?"

"He told me he used to be an investment advisor, and a hedge fund he was part owner of collapsed during the recession. I should have taken that as a sign that he might be desperate for money."

I looked at Syl directly and asked, "It never occurred to you that Jefferson could have been in your driveway the night Hal was killed?"

He shifted his position on the couch. "He's a wheeler-dealer, but until he came after you today, I figured he was only mad as hell at me." He paused. "Even now, it doesn't fit. Why come at night? If you'd asked me three days ago, I'd have said he was as likely to have been there the night Hal died as you or your friend Sandi."

"I guess I see your point." And I did. Why would anyone connect Jefferson with Hal? "Maybe he was going to break into your house."

Syl had a grim expression. "Probably the best explanation. It seems like, if he'd knocked hard at the door, I would have woken up. Maybe not."

I nodded and didn't say anything.

Syl stood. "I didn't come by to grill you. I, uh, thought I'd tell you again you're welcome to keep working, but you don't have to."

I stood. "I should have offered you coffee."

"No need. Stooper's going to put in those plants you wanted in before you go to your brother's for the weekend. He said if he doesn't do it right, you can always move them."

I followed Syl to the door. "That's a mouthful for Stooper. When did you see him?"

Syl grunted, and smiled. "He talks to me. Maybe he's just tongue-tied around you." He stopped smiling. "I took him to breakfast. Something the sheriff said made me think they were hard on Stooper."

"You knew where he lived?"

"No. He gave me his mobile number. I think he's been waiting for you to ask him for it." Syl took a folded piece of paper from his pocket and handed it to me.

I wasn't sure how to take that, so I simply said, "It'll probably be Tuesday before I'm back out to your place."

Syl went down my steps quickly. Jefferson's possible role in Hal's death stayed in my head as the coffee took forever to drip. Whatever altercation happened at Syl's place the night Hal was killed, it couldn't have been quiet. There had to have been conversation after Hal was dead, like Fred telling Jefferson how to frame me. But why? Why would Fred do that?

Syl was amiable and had been good to me, especially taking me to the sheriff's office the day Masters showed up with handcuffs. But I didn't know anything about him or his life in Los Angeles.

I had liked Syl, but maybe he wasn't to be trusted any more than his aggressive colleague. Okay, he didn't kill anyone, but he should have figured out it was Jefferson stopping by and told me about him.

I had my list to work on, but most of my questions would be hard to delve into on my own. I wasn't sure I wanted to inject myself into the sheriff's investigation again. I was off the hook, and I might put myself back in the bait bucket.

I probably had to accept that unless a murder weapon with his prints turned up, all Jefferson could be arrested for might be trespassing. And trying to tackle me, of course.

I COULD NOT LEAVE it alone. After coffee, I drove toward the diner for breakfast. I no longer needed to worry about innuendo in Hal's death, but even if the sheriff found a murder weapon, Hal's presence at Syl's didn't make sense. Why go there in the first place? Because he was mad Syl had hired me? Hal was impetuous. Maybe more so when he was drunk.

It didn't seem likely that Jefferson expected to find anyone there besides Syl. According to Fred there had been no vehicles other than Hal's and Syl's. That meant that the murderer had parked nearby and walked onto Syl's property. But he had to go back to remove Hal's car. Unless Fred had taken it. Fred never mentioned that he knew what happened to Hal's car. But could I trust anything Fred told me?

I decided to think one thing for sure. Hal's death couldn't have been planned. He was a jackass, but Jefferson wouldn't have had time to know that.

I walked into the diner, intending to sit by myself at the counter. Before I had closed the door, the place was quiet. I glanced around, finally locking eyes with Aaron Granger. He was standing beside a booth, apparently putting a tip on the table as he prepared to leave.

Talking resumed as I walked toward Granger.

"Any news?"

He didn't speak for several seconds, then said, "Nothing concrete. Your attacker's still in the county jail, but my bet is he'll be out on bail later today."

"Big bummer."

Granger walked to where I was and then moved past me toward the cash register.

"I don't even know where he lives. Is it near here?"

Shirley, walking by with an armload of dirty breakfast dishes, responded. "No, sugar. He lives in Ames."

I lowered my voice, still talking to Granger. "But he's not allowed to come talk to me, is he?"

He'd been pulling bills from his wallet, but stopped and met my gaze. "Judge would usually stipulate that. I hear he has a highfalutin lawyer. Probably tell him the same thing."

I sensed it was the first time Granger had thought of me as a victim. While I don't like to think of myself that way, I figured he should remember part of his job was to protect me, not just look for lawbreakers.

Instead of sitting at the counter, I walked out with Granger. "What about his car? Where did he park yesterday? Was there anything incriminating in his car?"

"Sheriff'll have to talk to you about most of that. His car was just down the road apiece. Near your walnut trees."

I stopped. "No kidding."

Granger kept walking. "I'd hang out with people for a few days, not work in yards alone, or whatever you do."

I called to his back. "I'm going to Ambrose's for a few days. Hope the SOB forgets all about me by the time I get home."

I thought Granger could have at least said he was sorry for giving me a hard time, but that was probably expecting too much.

Once seated at a booth, I ordered bacon and eggs and deflected Shirley's questions. She'd probably be mad at me for a month.

Jefferson's car was in the trees yesterday, so he might have used that spot before. Fred had not seen a third vehicle. Jefferson must have parked his car in the walnut trees that night. That's why he knew it could be a place to hide Hal's car.

So Jefferson walked to Syl's, probably to break in, maybe just to make Syl answer the door. If he wanted to break in, he might have brought tools to do that. *You're not in a B movie. Jefferson didn't have lock picks.* He didn't seem like the kind of guy to rely on an open window. So he had to bring something he already had, something easy to carry.

I went over everything Fred had told me. Did he mention where he saw Jefferson walk when he left? No, Fred thought he might have walked toward the barn. Fred had not mentioned a weapon. It seemed it might have been visible, since Jefferson had just killed Hal.

My mind churned. What could Jefferson have hit Hal with? Though I didn't like to think about the autopsy, the information on the size of the wound indicated that he was hit with something like a pipe. Certainly not a rock. Did Jefferson bring something with him? He likely did not expect to have to fight with someone, but breaking into Syl's house seemed like a good bet.

He must have discarded the pipe or whatever before Fred saw him. Surely Fred would have mentioned seeing a weapon.

I straightened up so fast I almost knocked over my coffee. *The crowbar from the bushes!* If Jefferson had pitched it as Fred walked up, it could have landed there. He didn't want to hang around more that night or let Fred see him with the crowbar. The night Jefferson hit me, he wasn't initially looking for the broom. He wanted the crowbar.

I racked my brain. I'd finally thrown out the small pieces of junk I'd been finding around the yard. There had been no crowbar in the pile, and I'd forgotten all about finding it. It could have even been what Jefferson hit me with. Thankfully, not as hard as he hit Hal.

I mopped up the coffee splashes I'd left on the table, left Shirley a bigger tip than usual, and walked outside. My hands were sweating. Could the crowbar be back in Jefferson's car? Who would keep a murder weapon? *Someone who thinks they'll never be caught.*

My phone almost slipped from my sweaty fingers. I was too excited to wait until I got home to call the sheriff.

"Melanie, unless you got something, we're kinda busy here."

"I have an idea."

"Go on."

"I saw Granger and he said where you found the car. Oh, maybe I shouldn't have said he told."

"Half the town knows. Keep going."

"If Jefferson was at Syl's to break in, he would have needed a way to do it. Was there anything in his car, um…"

"Melanie, we people in law enforcement tend to look over vehicles pretty well."

"Did he have a crowbar with his flat tire stuff?" I didn't want to say I'd found one in a bush and then hadn't thought to tell sheriff.

Gallagher's tone was sharp. "Why do you say that?"

"It's just reporter's instinct. I read the autopsy report. A crowbar could make that wound. Jefferson didn't expect to need a weapon, but he might have had something to use to break into Syl's house."

"If I find out you really know something and you're holding back, you'll spend more than a few hours in my jail."

I'd hung up before I realized my prints could be on the crowbar.

I wasn't content to wait, possibly for days, to see if the sheriff not only found a crowbar in Jefferson's trunk but linked it to the murder. Days? It could take weeks. I'd hear sooner if my prints were on it. Surely Jefferson would have cleaned it.

One of Hal's autopsy pictures came to mind, and I nearly vomited my breakfast.

Even before they knew about the crowbar, someone needed to develop a link between Hal and Jefferson, and it had to be through Syl's contract.

I called Sandi on her mobile. "You at the paper?"

"Nope. Just coming back into town from visiting cemeteries."

When I said nothing for several seconds, she laughed. "Oh, God. Not visiting people we know. It's Memorial Day coming up. Holmes wants photos of a bunch of cemeteries that have veterans, not just the big one in town."

"Gotcha. Can we meet for a cup of coffee? I have an idea about Hal."

"Uh, okay. Diner?"

"You know, we should meet at the paper. I'll bring in coffee and donuts."

I hung up before she could object.

WE HAD SPOKEN about the list of questions I'd developed for less than five minutes when Sandi said, "This is good. If we get the paper behind these questions, somebody'll have to look more at phone or Internet records. I'm going to get Scott."

I wanted to talk more first, maybe decide together, but I didn't work at the *South County News*. Besides, if Sandi had the lead, Ambrose wouldn't have to tell even more people that he'd threatened me with an ankle bracelet.

I hadn't formed an opinion about Scott Holmes when I met him so briefly at Fred's funeral. Today, I liked him before we had talked for ten minutes.

"These are good questions, and I think if Hal had had a different personality they might have come up as soon as this Jefferson fellow was found on Mr. Seaton's property. Maybe they have been discussed." He looked at me. "When we write a story about this, if we do, I want to identify you as the source of the idea. You can't write the article or come with Sandi and me when we approach the sheriff. I assume that's why you came here."

Sandi gets to go to the sheriff. She'll really like him now. "Pretty much. I might be able to help Syl Seaton get comfortable about talking to you."

Holmes stood. "Let's discuss it after we talk to the sheriff. I think it would be interesting to see if Syl Seaton tells Sandi and me the same things he told you."

SATURDAY MORNING, the back of my pickup was open and held Mister Tibbs' new doggie bed, bowls, and food. Play toys were on the passenger seat in her large crate. The crate also had a small step stool for her to sit on so she could see out the window. *I must be nuts.*

A high-end Toyota pulled into Mrs. Keyser's driveway, blocking my exit. I hoped they were just dropping off something for her.

Instead, Fred's parents got out. His mom held a stack of books, and his dad opened the back door and took out a very small pet crate. If anything, Harvey and Rose Simmons looked worse than they had at Fred's funeral.

"Mr. and Mrs. Simmons." I walked toward them, and when I got there, gave Fred's mom a kiss on the cheek.

She patted my hand as she pulled back. "You're sweet."

Scratching noises came from the crate. *Uh-oh.*

"Can you come up for coffee or tea?" I didn't know them well, and I was relieved when they said no.

"We just wanted to drop off a couple of things," Mrs. Simmons said.

Double uh-oh.

She handed me the stack of five books, and her voice caught as she said. "Fred left a note on these. He wanted you to have them, especially the one about habits for highly effective people. He said you often talked about that book."

We did? "Oh, gosh." I took the books, and my eyes filled. I brushed them with the back of one hand. "I'll treasure these."

Mr. Simmons sat the crate down. It held a cat that was not shy about hissing. "You and Sandi are the only ones he left anything for. Besides us."

I sniffed. "He said he wanted to call you that night, the night before he..." I had to stop.

Mr. Simmons sighed and reached for his wife's hand. "He did call, but he didn't tell us anything. He left us each a beautiful note, telling us how he had seen Hal after his death and really regretted not speaking up when people were questioning you. From what he said, he was terrified."

"It makes no difference. I'm not going to think about that again. I'm going to remember Fred," I so wanted to lighten the moment, "with his head in the bowels of the copy machine, cursing it because he burned his finger on the drum trying to get some paper unstuck."

They both laughed.

Yea!

"Seriously, he was really good to me, especially when I first started at the paper. That's what I think of."

They both looked relieved, and Mrs. Simmons spoke. "He talked about you now and then. That's why..." she looked at the crate, "We wondered if you could take Stowaway. We're driving Fred's car back to Florida, but I'm allergic and it's such a long drive..."

Oh, damn. Say no, Melanie. Say no.

I stooped down to peer at the cat. I'd met the grey, short-haired thing a few times. It snuck into his car one night when Fred was unloading groceries, and he could never find its owner. It hissed.

"I'll tell you what." I stood. "I'll do my best to keep it. But if it doesn't get along with my little dog, I promise I will find the best home in town for it. For her, right?"

"Oh, good." Fred's mom smiled broadly.

"We really appreciate it," his dad said.

After a couple of minutes of small talk, most of it dealing with their plans for selling Fred's house and how half the realtors in town had called about it, they left. Before they were out of the driveway, they drove back and retrieved a bag of litter, food, and a cat bed from the trunk.

Mrs. Keyser came onto the porch in time to wave goodbye to the Simmons. She walked down her front porch steps and looked at me with raised eyebrows.

It was so hard not to laugh. Her house dress was magenta dotted with white cats playing with balls of yarn.

"They couldn't take it to Florida." I lifted the small crate, and we both looked at the cat. It had stopped hissing and stuck its nose toward us, smelling.

She peered at it. "And you with a dog."

I sensed an opportunity. "Are you in the market for a cat?"

Perhaps detecting a need to be on good behavior, Stowaway meowed plaintively.

"Oh, I shouldn't really." She put a finger in the crate for the cat to smell. "I'm getting too old for pets, and I visit my daughter, you know."

"I could feed her and do litter and stuff, when you're away."

She cocked her head, and the cat did the same.

Mrs. Keyser looked at me. "Well, glory be. I must be meant to care for poor Fred's cat. With your help, of course."

Glory be is right.

"I'll carry her inside for you. When I get back from Ambrose and Sharon's, we can introduce her to Mister Tibbs."

FRED AND I HAD NEVER talked about *Seven Habits of Highly Effective People*. It had been on the shelf in his cubicle when we worked together, but I thought it was for show. Now I figured he meant for me to look for something in the book.

I sat at my kitchen table and took off the book jacket. No letter taped to it, and none slipped into a page. I started to thumb through it. Exactly in the middle were four words, near the binding. "Your garden tool bucket."

I was immediately chilled, and my stomach did a flip. I stood, started for the door, but stopped abruptly. "I can't do this." I sat back at the table and stared at the words.

A paw reached for my knee, and I looked at Mister Tibbs. I didn't realize I was crying until I saw him. I sat on the floor and buried my face in the back of his neck. I wasn't gulping sobs, but it took time to stop. After about fifteen seconds, he turned his head, tongue out, trying to reach some part of me to lick.

I pulled back and whispered, "You're such a good bo...girl. When am I going to stop thinking of you as a boy?"

Her tail thumped.

"You don't care, do you?" Another thump. "Okay, you'll just have to deal with the gender identity thing. I'm calling you a boy."

I stood and took a napkin from the holder on the counter and blew my nose. "Come on, we're going to the back yard." I snapped on the leash. It wasn't far, but the yard wasn't fenced.

Mister Tibbs wagged her tail and stood to lean on my knee. I gently put her paws on the ground. "No jumping, remember?"

It was a cool day for May, not supposed to get above seventy degrees the entire Memorial Day Weekend. The walk to the shed took a couple of minutes. There were several leaves that required inspection, and the corner of a row of peppers required Mister Tibbs' form of watering. Nearly all the marigold plants, meant to keep bugs away from the vegetables, had bright orange and yellow flowers. The rest would in a few days.

The weeder I used most evenings as I wandered the garden protruded from where I had last stuck it at the end of a row of beans. Weeds sprouted everywhere. I could never stay ahead of them.

I hadn't looked in the shed for more than a week. Most of my smaller tools were in a laundry basket in my truck, and the wheelbarrow and rakes stayed in Syl's barn for the time being. When I opened the door, nothing looked different, but it hadn't looked disturbed the day the sheriff had had me look for my hoe. I peered in.

I stared at the red bucket that held trowels, work gloves, and other small hand tools. Fred must have put a note in there. Or maybe he had started some stories he didn't want to leave lying around, and he wanted me to finish them. *Not.*

Mistererwas straining on his leash. There were lots of new smells here. I didn't want her sniffing around the bag of fertilizer. Even organic stuff isn't meant to be in a dog's nose.

"Okay, pal, here we go." Still holding the leash, I bent over to pick up the bucket by its handle. Once I had a firm grip I backed out of the shed and used my knee to shut the door.

A small bark came from near my ankle. Mister Tibbs' head was cocked, and if a dog can have a questioning expression, she was asking, "You dragged me out here for this?"

I smiled. "You can smell here." I let go of the leash. Instead of moving away he sat and leaned toward the bucket, sniffing without touching it.

"Nuts." There was no getting around it. I had to see what Fred had left. I knelt and took the green work gloves off the top of the contents and peered in. Leaning against the interior was a white, business-sized envelope. I took it out. Fred had written **Mel, Champion Reporter** on the outside.

I'm mad at him. I'm not going to cry about this.

My plan had been to take whatever Fred had left into the apartment to read, but instead I tore open the envelope and unfolded the single piece of copy paper. Fred's neat handwriting filled both sides.

Dear Mel,

If I wrote I'm sorry a hundred times it would never be enough. So, maybe you'll get an award if you write a story about your role in solving a murder.

What I told you about that night was mostly true, until the point of finding Hal's body. The only part that wasn't was that I was with a friend for a while before I went back to Hal's house. Anyway, I was seeing six different shades of red. I followed Hal and parked outside Seaton's driveway after Hal drove in.

I was just a few yards down the driveway, going toward Hal's car, when it got loud. One voice was Hal's. I didn't know Seaton, but figured the other was him. I'd already heard Hal knock on the door. Hal's speech was slurred, and he called someone a rat bastard. The other guy called Hal a stupid SOB.

It was funny to me that someone else was chewing out Hal. It got me calmed down, and I turned to go back to my car. Then Hal said something about a scheme, and the man said Hal didn't matter. Hal kind of shrieked, "No!" and it got quiet.

I wish to hell I'd kept going to my car, but I'd had a couple of beers and wasn't thinking too clearly. I ran toward Hal's car, and when I got to the other side of it, Hal was on the ground, between Syl's truck and the mulch. Some guy in a suit was standing near him. He was staring down at Hal. Then he came toward me.

I said I didn't see anything. That made the guy stop. He said I could be down there with Hal in a heartbeat if I didn't help the guy get rid of him. It was like a bad dream, but it wasn't.

I'm the one who thought of the mulch. It was right there, smelled wet. I still had a shovel in my trunk from winter. I kind of figured it wasn't Seaton. He wouldn't have wanted to bury Hal outside his door. Anyway, I kept waiting for Seaton to hear us, but he didn't.

We lifted Hal. Thank God I had his feet and didn't have to look at the gash in his head. Stupid to think about now. We sort of shoved him part way into the pile, and then I shoveled out a lot of mulch and pushed him in more and covered him up.

I cried the whole time. The guy kept calling me a pansy. He walked away for a minute and came back with that broom. He must have been back there to get it the night you got hit.

So, he swept a lot and then just walked away. He must've come back to move Hal's car. I didn't think of it for two days.

Getting something of yours, that was a wild thought. I was almost back to my house, covered in mulch same as my shovel. People knew I was furious Hal lied to keep me from getting unemployment. The sheriff would come to me ASAP. I thought if I put something of yours there, the sheriff would talk to you first, and I'd have more time to get rid of everything.

I had to toss my clothes somewhere, vacuum the hell out of my car. I got the hoe from the shed. The tangerine I had in my car. It was really gross putting it in Hal's mouth, but I thought it would lead the sheriff to you.

I honest to God never thought anyone would think you did it. Hell, I don't know what I thought. I was frantic, and I just wanted some time.

I'm so sorry. You're my good friend. I figured you knew I used to see Sandi, and you never told. I told her we had to break it off when I was her boss. It was really because I was afraid she'd figure it out if we were together all the time.

Help her, okay? She'll never understand.

Fred

OhmyGodohmyGodohmyGod.

I sat on the ground, cross-legged, shaking. Mister Tibbs put a paw on my thigh and tried to crawl into my lap. I leaned forward for a second and put my chin on the top of her head. "I'm so glad you're here, Mister Tibbs."

I sat up. The only other thing on the paper was Fred's name, first name only and typed rather than signed. "Poor Sandi."

If they didn't break up until after Fred was made acting editor, he could have been at Sandi's after the first time he looked for Hal. That's how he heard I got the work with Syl. Maybe he even heard my voice mail saying Hal was angry.

I could envision Fred frightened of the man who killed Hal, knowing he might never work for a paper again if he said he'd helped bury Hal. So he planted my hoe with Hal.

More important to Fred, high school class president, would have been the fear of public humiliation. Still, Fred had as analytical a mind as any reporter. Why not go to the sheriff after Just Bill left? Fred said he was buzzed, but that would have worn off by the time he finished burying Hal in the mulch.

Even if he thought he'd be in a lot of trouble, Fred had to know how much everyone liked him. We would have stuck up for him. If he'd gone to the sheriff immediately, I couldn't imagine Gallagher would even have asked the county attorney to charge Fred. Fred was in shock, under duress, when he buried Hal.

And Sandi? How could I let her know Fred wanted me to help her when she'd never told me about Fred? For sure I didn't want to share Fred's letter, not with her or anybody.

How could I prove what Fred had said without showing the letter to anyone?

CHAPTER TWENTY-SIX

I THOUGHT IN CIRCLES as I took Mister Tibbs for a walk and finished packing my truck for the visit to Ambrose and Sharon. There was nothing I could do immediately. If I told Ambrose I was sick, he and Sharon would probably be in River's Edge by tomorrow. If I told him I wanted to look into Hal's murder more, he'd show up with the ankle bracelet or, worse, leg irons.

My phone rang we walked. When I saw South County Sheriff on caller ID, I groaned. "Melanie here."

Gallagher sounded annoyed. "You talked to that editor instead of me."

"I promised Ambrose I wouldn't do anything. I didn't say Sandi and I wouldn't keep trading ideas. We think about Fred all the time."

"Humph. People in law enforcement have ideas, too. Your IDI buddies have already been helpful with phone and electronic records. Problem is, no phone records link to Hal."

"Nuts, he... Wait. I think one of the times he threw his mobile phone he got a second one, one of those you buy a monthly card for. It was his backup in case he broke his good phone again."

"Did he keep it?"

"I don't know. I just remember he was mad because he couldn't get a new Sprint phone for a couple of days after he threw his against the wall. He got one of those cheap things at the truck stop by the highway."

Gallagher sounded irritated. "You couldn't have told me this earlier? They might have a record of the purchase."

"Oh, yeah, because I had a clue what you were looking at." I hung up. I had a good idea and he was giving me grief about it.

I HAD TO BE careful that Ambrose didn't figure out Sandi and I were texting about a link between Jefferson and Hal. When he did notice me paying more attention to my phone than I usually would, I told him Sandi was going to put flowers on our parents' graves for Memorial Day.

This was even true. Ambrose, Sharon, and I have always done this together. This year, Ambrose simply wanted me away from River's Edge. He said he hoped I could reboot my curiosity chromosome.

Late Monday afternoon, Sandi texted, "Ryan's mom's cousin said they can link Hal's burner phone to Jefferson."

I handed Ambrose my phone. "What do you think about this?"

He studied it and passed the phone to Sharon. "Sis, I'm glad it might get figured out, but can't you forget about it for even two days?"

"I want Hal's murder solved so firmly that no one could ever again think I killed him." *And if it means I have to keep throwing ideas into the mix to get that done, I'm fine with that.*

All in all, it was great news, even better because Ambrose knew Sandi was the one digging. I certainly wasn't afraid of my brother's opinion. He cared about me. Also, he and Mister Tibbs hit it off. Sharon not so much, which meant she was Mister Tibbs' favorite person. It might have had something to do with the chicken scraps.

BY THE TIME Mister Tibbs and I were home Tuesday, Bill Jefferson had been arrested for the murder of Hal Morris. IDI arrested him in Ames and took him to Des Moines.

Jefferson's mobile phone had made many calls to Hal's disposable mobile phone. Hal likely thought he was crafty to use that phone. Sandi said that Jefferson's denial that he knew Hal was what really screwed him once the sheriff and IDI found the telephone connection between the two men.

A short stop at Hy-Vee let me know that the general view in town was puzzlement, but I was pretty sure how the two men connected.

Hal met Syl, and when he heard why Syl moved to Iowa he got some background information. Probably just basic curiosity. Maybe he had an idea for a story, and then something about the size of Syl's contract likely got Hal's dander up.

There was Hal, struggling to keep a small-town paper in the black, and in waltzes Syl with a seven-figure contract from a group in Des Moines. Certainly, Hal would have asked how Syl even knew about an Iowa bid or grant process.

If Jefferson hadn't yet started his extortion plan, Syl might have even mentioned him to Hal. Syl wouldn't have intended that Hal call Jefferson, but the chance to dig up dirt would have put Jefferson on Hal's speed dial.

When things calmed down, I'd ask Syl about that. I felt irritated with him now. Surely he could have made the link between Jefferson and Hal's murder. Or maybe not. As annoying as Hal was, he was someone I knew, and I wouldn't have suspected him of anyone's murder. Perhaps Syl couldn't think of Jefferson that way.

What seemed to have begun as Hal buying coffee for a new businessman, who Hal hoped would buy advertising, led Hal to dig. Hal learned more about the Iowa insurance industry by talking to Bruce Blackner. Knowing Hal, the eventual plan would have been a snide editorial about outsiders cheating Iowa businesses out of work.

I highly doubted that Hal and Jefferson planned to meet at Syl's the night Hal was murdered. It seemed more likely that a drunk Hal had driven out there to berate Syl for canceling his help-wanted ad.

Jefferson was there, car hidden, to break in and have it out with Syl. If Hal realized Jefferson was the person who helped Syl (anyone, really) get a big contract, Hal would have been irate. When Jefferson said Hal didn't matter, Hal would have blown a gasket and charged at him. Bad move.

And my thoughts were all speculation, unless the sheriff had been able to identify the crowbar as the murder weapon. If it wasn't in Jefferson's trunk, then it might never be found, and Jefferson might only be convicted as Hal's murderer if he confessed.

I supposed he could do a plea bargain, like on television. Still, as annoying as Hal was, I'd like his murderer in prison forever.

As I picked the last of my garden's strawberries, an unfamiliar blue Buick pulled into the driveway. I assumed it was a visitor for Mrs. Keyser until Sheriff Gallagher got out.

Damn. I'm in for it now. At least he wasn't in uniform. That probably lessened the likelihood of more trouble for me.

He stopped about ten feet from me, glanced at my tomato plants and then Mister Tibbs. "I need you to be straight with me, Melanie. Did Fred leave a letter I don't know about?"

I stood and wiped my hands on my cutoffs. "The thing about letters these days, if they're typed on a computer and there's no handwritten signature, how can you be sure where it came from?"

"True. That means even you could have typed a letter that identified the location of a murder weapon."

Uh-oh. "Except I didn't. If Fred had written me a letter, it might have had a lot of personal stuff not related to Hal's murder. Wouldn't you guys have searched Jefferson's car carefully anyway?"

Sheriff Gallagher sighed. "Yes, but we might not have sprayed the crowbar to see if blood had been washed off it and then checked to see if there was still enough DNA to show it was Hal's."

"That's a good thing, right?"

"I could get a search warrant."

I smiled for a second. "I'm hoping if you really planned to do that it would have been done."

"I don't like it when people withhold evidence, Melanie."

Ken Brownberg's face passed through my thoughts. "I'm not saying I did withhold anything, but if I had it would be because I thought it would embarrass Fred's parents."

His tone was sharp. "Do you have a letter from Fred or not?"

I shook my head. "If I had gotten one, I would have burned it." I nodded toward Mrs. Keyser's burn barrel.

He turned to walk to his car. Without looking at me, Gallagher said, "I'm not happy with you."

"Yes sir."

I listened to gravel crunch as his car backed out of the driveway. It was dusk, and Mister Tibbs explored a chipmunk hole near the shed. I whistled for him.

He ran toward me, barely stopping himself from running into my knees. I bent to scratch the top of his head. Her head. *Whatever.* "You're my good buddy."

If Fred had reached to his friends, he would still be alive. If Hal had known how to have friends, he might not have been angry all the time, might not have gone to Syl's that night, probably would not have been killed.

I still wouldn't miss Hal, but I was going to reach out to people who really needed their friends. I would start with Sandi.

THE END

Thank you for reading *From Newsprint to Footprints*. You may like the next book in the River's Edge Series, *Demise of a Devious Neighbor*, which was a finalist for the 2017 Chanticleer Mystery and Mayhem Awards.

Opening of *Demise of a Devious Neighbor*

THE REVERBERATING BANGS SHOOK my nerves more than my truck, and Mister Tibbs would have wet the back seat of the pickup if I hadn't left the door open. She rocketed out just as the second Roman candle fizzled and headed toward the cornfield.

Either someone was aiming at my vehicle, or they didn't know fireworks were supposed to go upward.

I ended up on my tailbone on the hard dirt, hands splayed behind me. I stood slowly, searching the twilight for the source of the two salvos. Whoever had shot them off had surely meant to scare me. It worked.

The cicadas, silent for several seconds, rejoined the cawing starlings as they regrouped on the telephone wires. I whistled for Mister Tibbs and watched her crawl out from under a juniper tree next to my late parents' farmhouse.

I looked at her meekly wagging tail and stooped so she could walk into my arms. "I'd call you a super wuss, but I didn't like it either."

Review of Demise of a Devious Neighbor

Ms Orr is such a delightful writer that I often slow down and just enjoy the way the words flow. She doesn't need on screen violence or colorful language to keep our attention. Good plot, great description, realistic characters, locale that's part of the story (not just backdrop) and pacing that keeps it all together.

Elisabeth on Amazon

Other Books by Elaine L. Orr

The Jolie Gentil Cozy Mystery Series.
Appraisal for Murder
Rekindling Motives
When the Carny Comes to Town
Any Port in a Storm
Trouble on the Doorstep
Behind the Walls
Vague Images
Ground to a Halt
Holidays in Ocean Alley
The Unexpected Resolution
Underground in Ocean Alley
Jolie and Scoobie High School Misadventures (prequel)

River's Edge Mystery Series
From Newsprint to Footprints
Demise of a Devious Neighbor
Demise of a Devious Suspect

Logland Mystery Series
Tip a Hat to Murder
Final Cycle
Final Operation

Many books are in large print and audio.
http://www.elaineorr.com
For articles on reading, writing, and publishing, check out http://elaineorr.blogspot.com.

Bio for Elaine L. Orr

Elaine L. Orr authors three mystery series, including the eleven-book Jolie Gentil cozy mystery series, set at the Jersey shore. *Behind the Walls* was a finalist for the 2014 Chanticleer Mystery and Mayhem Awards. The three-book River's Edge cozy mystery series is set in Iowa, and *Demise of a Devious Neighbor* was a 2017 Chanticleer finalist. The three-book Logland series takes place in small-town Illinois. Elaine also writes plays and novellas, including the one-act, *Common Ground*, and novellas *Falling Into Place* and *In the Shadow of Light*. A novella, *Biding Time*, was one of five finalists in the National Press Club's first fiction contest, in 1993. Nonfiction includes *Words to Write By: Getting Your Thoughts on Paper* and *Writing When Time is Scarce*.

Elaine conducts presentations on electronic publishing and other writing-related topics. She also blogs on writing and publishing and presents her musings at *Irish Roots Author* (found at htttp://elaineorr.blogspot.com). A member of Sisters in Crime, Elaine grew up in Maryland and moved to the Midwest in 1994.

Made in the USA
Middletown, DE
25 March 2020